Twisted but True

Darren Burch

PAGE PUBLISHING, INC.
New York, NY

First originally published by Page Publishing, Inc. 2017

ISBN 978-1-63568-081-2 (Paperback)
ISBN 978-1-64424-121-9 (Hardcover)
ISBN 978-1-63568-082-9 (Digital)

Printed in the United States of America

Contents

Every story is true, but some names were changed to
protect the innocent and embarrass the guilty!

Warning

Due to the graphic and explicit language, detailing homicides
and sex crime investigations, this book may not be suitable for
everyone.

CHAPTER 1

Twisted Metal

A DARK cloud hung over me as a cop tackling bizarre calls, generating 30 years of stories laced with twisted humor and madness. I've faced life and death situations on a regular basis, but my life-saving fixation started well before I became a police officer. My need to save lives started as a teenager when I stumbled upon the torn body of a young woman. I recall that night, feeling the wet blood on my hands and scorching heat on my face. It still haunts me today, and it's a story I seldom share.

Prior to this night in 1979, I focused primarily on just getting through high school and losing my virginity. Aside from thinking about girls, I spent my days hanging out with my three best friends, Ben, Rick and Keith.

We learned about a desert party from flyers passed around our high school. This was not just any desert beer party but featured 20 local rock bands, an unprecedented thirty kegs of beer, and most importantly, a lot of girls. We hoped tonight wouldn't be like other nights out; none of us even talking with a girl. We were typically self-defeating amateurs in this arena, and none more than me.

My low self-esteem was at odds with standing out as an undefeated high school wrestler, beaming with confidence on the mat, but too insecure to ask a girl out on a date. These same insecurities kept me from befriending the popular kids in school, but like an ending to a Hollywood film, I later realized popularity means nothing compared to lifelong friendships. I'm still friends today with Ben, Rick and Keith. These same friends tagged me with the nickname "Boo Boo" in high school, because I was a vertically-challenged, caring kid, who loved helping everybody.

Rick Ashe was nicknamed "Ostrich" due to his freakishly long neck. He had unabashed confidence talking with girls, yet his over-confidence often backfired. Once, we picked up three girls hitchhiking (again, this was the seventies), hoping to convince them to join us at a house party. The girls were in the car for mere seconds when Rick began a series of unsuccessful pickup lines. Upon the girls' lack of interest, Rick remarked innocently, "Come on, it's not like we are going to rape you." There was a collective gasp from everyone to the worst word Rick could have used in his failed attempt to gain the girls' trust. Impressively, the three frail looking girls commandeered my car shouting, "stop the car now," which I did, and they hastily exited the car in the middle of the street. We never let Rick live this down.

Keith Harbon was a misunderstood poet, and instead of typical flirtatious banter, or saying something normal to a girl, he recited the "Chaos Theory." We loved watching the bewilderment slowly unfold on the girls' faces, degrading from general confusion to blank stares. Keith not only conversed like an old soul, he also looked the part. The rest of us had sparse whiskers sporadically dispersed over our acne-inflamed chins. In contrast, Keith had a full beard and deep voice. His love for the film Blazing Saddles and resemblance to a lead character earned him the nickname, "Mongo."

The final member of our quartet was Ben Keibler. Ben had been dating Rick's sister, and was the only non-virgin of the group, to Rick's dismay. Ben's upbringing mirrored mine, raised by a single mother in a lower-middle class neighborhood. He, too, had that "good kid" moniker, like an "All-American" kid; even his sport of choice was baseball. He pitched his way all through elementary and high school. Excelling in "America's game" and his good-guy persona appropriately won him the nickname "Captain America." Ben drove an AMC Pacer, or as we called it, "The Cookie Mobile" (given his last name, Keibler, like the brand of cookies, and his bubble-shaped car even resembled a giant cookie).

We started our night in the Cookie Mobile, with Ben driving us to the desert party. I had never witnessed a larger desert party, more than a thousand teens amassed in the remote desert area. The collective sounds of laughter, cheering and music filled the dry night air. The bands were perched on a dirt berm, playing to the crowd down below gathered in an area the size of a football field. At the opposite end of the desert arena, another berm hosted a long line of seemingly countless beer kegs. Among the crowd, vast bonfires blazed under a sunset of pink and orange, lightly illuminating the scene. The desert party lived up to all the hype, as school yard talk about the wild party swirled for months leading up to the event. It was our own version of Woodstock with an overwhelming sense of freedom and immortality.

As with most parties, the guys outnumbered the girls, so my buddies and I sat around our own bonfire, listening to the music, and talking about the same stupid shit we always did, our enjoyable conversations littered with typical teenage angst.

Joy permeated my soul as we rejoiced in the rock-and-roll revelry. Then the party suddenly morphed into mindless mayhem. For whatever, and a surely unimportant, reason, a violent brawl had erupted, quickly escalating through the massive, testosterone-filled herd of horny, young men. We immediately decided to leave. As I joked about "discretion being the better part of valor," we all ran away, piling into Ben's Pacer and driving off.

On the ride back to Phoenix in the "Cookie Mobile," the four of us continued our inane conversations that were started earlier at the party, but now degraded by alcohol and fatigue, while listening to "KISS" in the under-dash mounted 8-track tape deck. I sat behind Ben in the back seat with Keith by my side. Rick sat in the front passenger seat, having shouted "Shotgun!" upon our departure from the brawl. We drove along in the darkness on a small two-lane road with gravel shoulders paralleling on either side through miles of desert.

The drive over the desolate road felt peaceful compared to the chaos we left behind at the desert party. We were blissfully unaware that this pleasant drive would be the calm before a firestorm that would change our lives. For now, the night sky draped silently around us, still and jet-black. The Cookie Mobile's headlights sliced into the darkness, revealing shadows of prickly shrubs and wispy mesquite trees on both sides. Spitting gravel launched from the tires, plinking in a hypnotic cadence as we drove back home.

Although traffic on the roadway was sparse, we eventually found ourselves stuck behind a large, white, slow-moving car driven by an elderly man. Next to him sat a woman, who we assumed was his wife, with a massive white bouffant pile of hair that almost touched the car's ceiling. We gave them the nicknames "Captain of the USS Boat-Car" and his first mate, "Q-Tip."

Ben followed patiently as we mused about how the elderly couple might have a secret, alternate identity as a swinging old couple, who, like superheroes, had special powers of late-night party capabilities. By day, upstanding citizens with a boring life of counting skin freckles, but by night, under the cloak of anonymity, they would be the life of any party—maybe even the same desert party that we had fled.

Keith suggested the elderly couple had to make a fast getaway from the desert party we just fled, since it was the "boat-car Captain" who put some major whoop ass on the unsuspecting teenagers, and the couple's ridiculously slow driving was a clever ruse. I quipped that "Q-tip" donned a beehive wig disguise, hiding her sexy Pat Benatar pixie-hairdo underneath.

While creeping slowly behind the elderly couple's car, Ben noticed in his rear-view mirror that our slow procession was joined by a Javelin. The sports car driver wasted no time demonstrating his frustration by slamming on his brakes and flashing his high beams in response to our slow speed. Blinded by the bright lights, Ben muttered several profanities under his breath (his All-American persona prevented him from saying such things loudly) while the Javelin kept riding the Cookie Mobile's ass.

Soon, the blinding light from the trailing car disappeared. The impatient Javelin passed Ben's Cookie Mobile off the right side of the roadway and onto the gravel shoulder, spewing a cloud of dirt into the air while quickly passing us, as well as the elderly couple. The Javelin drove through the gravel with little difficulty, but as the Javelin's wheels turned sharply back onto the road, only three of the four tires climbed onto the pavement, leaving the last tire spinning furiously in the gravel.

The Javelin fish-tailed, gliding completely sideways in the gravel, and careened into an electrical pole. The powerful impact into the passenger side of the car caused the transformer perched at the top to explode.

The brilliant burst lit up the dark sky, as a fiery rain of sparks showered down onto the Javelin. The elderly couple's sedan slowly crept past the scene, stopping for only a moment, then continued driving past the wrecked Javelin, as bursting sparks from the transformer sprayed wildly. The sparks popped like a flashbulb from a vintage camera capturing the grim picture.

Ben stopped near the crash site, but I had already jumped out the window of the moving car. An indescribable and uncontrollable urge propelled me out the window to help, fearing the twisted steel had become a coffin. I ran to the crash while Ben safely parked, with Rick and Keith still on board. They would all be joining me at the wreck a few minutes later.

Hastily, I ran to the Javelin's driver door, which wasn't damaged. Inside the car, I could see dark figures sitting motionless. Hearing no screams or moans of pain, fearing the worst, I grabbed the driver's side door handle but couldn't open it. I repeatedly failed trying to open the driver's door or break the window. I decided to run around to the passenger side, even though that side of the car appeared to be slammed tight against the power pole. My compulsion to remove everyone from the car may have been an unconscious awareness of the fire. An inconspicuous fire, unlike the car explosions in the movies, started as a small flame around the trunk.

Running along the front of the car, I tripped and fell to the ground. My open hands landed on a wet heap. I had fallen on the mangled body of a young woman; she had a deep, gaping wound that ran down from the top of her forehead to her chin, exposing facial bones, tendons, and muscle. I naively checked her neck and wrist, hoping for a pulse. The grisly realization that she was dead momentarily paralyzed me in disbelief. I got up off her body, still in shock, and trudged to the passenger side, trying not to think of the dead woman I had just fallen on.

To my surprise, the crushed passenger side rested several feet away from the wooden pole, providing some space to try to open the car door. Ben, Rick, and Keith had run directly to the passenger side, having seen my failed attempts to open the driver's side door. The passenger door was smashed in, resembling the empty beer cans we crushed at the desert party, which now seemed like a lifetime ago. With our combined strength, we were finally able to partially open the damaged passenger door, providing a narrow path to reach inside.

The foot-wide opening revealed the three remaining unresponsive silhouettes. A twenty-something white male lay still against the steering wheel. The front passenger seat sat empty, since the female passenger had fatally launched through the windshield. The two remaining bodies were in the back seats, and were unresponsive, or possibly dead.

Ben and Rick pulled the driver out of the car and all four of us carried his limp body to the side of the road. The flames consumed the Javelin's trunk as we returned to check on the rear seat passengers. Because of the massive damage to the side of the car, the front passenger seat only leaned forward a small amount. Through that small opening, we could see the rear seat passenger closest to us, a young, Hispanic man. He fell in and out of consciousness, muttering in Spanish, as Keith and I pulled him from the car. The four of us carried him to safety. Both men lay unconscious on the ground next to Ben's car on the side of the road.

The last occupant left to rescue was an unconscious girl, still in the burning car, sitting upright behind the driver's seat. She couldn't have been more than 20, dressed in a loose-fitting white blouse with blue jeans, her hands folded in her lap. The beautiful girl looked so peaceful and serene in stark contrast to her peril. Her long blond hair rested on the back dash, as her head tilted upward, as if gazing up at the heavens. I was determined to get her out, to save her from the burning car.

The narrow path behind the damaged front passenger seat would make reaching her difficult. As the smallest member of the quartet, I squeezed through the tight space. I forced myself against the back seat, and began my crawl to the other side to reach her. Thoughts of her happy parents filled my mind, as I would be the hero. I had no doubt I could save her before the approaching fire.

Then, the growing fire danced back and forth between the trunk and the rear passenger seats. My friends looked on in fear, as they watched the flames bounce sporadically into the rear compartment. The mounting fire forced my thin frame tightly against the back of the front seats to avoid being burned. My arduous crawl past the flames finally led me triumphantly to her, as I felt the scorching heat singeing my skin. Grabbing onto her arm gave me such an unimaginable sense of relief, as I would soon be able to pull her out of the burning car. Immense joy flooded my heart, knowing I was going to save her.

I pulled on her arm and shirt, but I couldn't move her. Then I discovered the problem: her lap seat belt kept her pinned in. I wedged her right hand up behind her head, giving me a better look at the stuck seat belt. It was a lift-up, clasp-style seat belt. However, the lifting of the clasp didn't disengage the lock. Panicked, I tried pulling her out of the belt, but the tight strap around her waist wouldn't release its tight grip. Repeatedly and desperately trying, I still could not unlock the seat belt. The heat intensified as the flames reached deeper toward us. My body betrayed me as I involuntarily reacted to the pain of the flames and kept flinching away from her side. With time running out, the fire repeatedly forced me away from her. On my last attempt, the flames had engulfed the backseat, and I barely escaped.

That euphoric feeling of saving her life had been cruelly extinguished by the fire. I stood outside the car with my friends looking helplessly in horror as the car fire grew. Later, Rick confided they had reached in to pull me out, as my friends believed the flames were going to engulf me as well. I don't recall their life-saving intervention, but I also didn't remember getting out of the burning car. As the immeasurable guilt and sadness of not being able to save her life became too overwhelming to endure, a deluge of tears streamed forth.

I stood watching in disbelief, feeling the heat on my face as the flames surrounded her. She moved slightly, almost in rhythm to the swirling flames as the car fire continued to grow. Her burning hands and arms began curling inward toward her torso, as if to wave good-bye, hopefully forgiving me for my failed rescue. Later in life, as a detective, I learned that the curling of the body's extremities is an automated response to the burning flesh, but in my distraught young mind, she had waved as she departed this earth.

My buddies walked me to Ben's car, where I sat crying next to the Javelin's driver. Both young men saved from the Javelin were still unconscious, but alive. I thought of the irony how the first person rescued was the driver responsible for the crash. My friends were standing around me while I sat distraught, with my head in my lap, crying uncontrollably for an unknown amount of time. Finally looking up as my tears subsided, I discovered my friends were no longer there.

Unsure where they had gone, I got up and noticed a large crowd had gathered not far from the crash site. The spectacle of the metal inferno enticed the approaching drivers to stop and park along the roadway, leaving their cars and flocking around the area. Our frantic life-saving efforts made us completely unaware of the gathering onlookers, standing and staring at the carnage. Their mesmerized faces gazed, aglow from the massive flames of the car fire, eerily reminiscent of the fire pits left behind at the desert party.

As the horde gawked at the roaring fire, the county deputies and fire trucks began arriving. Ben, Rick, and Keith had walked up to the deputies, leaving me behind. They were expecting a lengthy police interview, providing a detailed account of the crash. After all, that's what happens in every cop show we had ever seen; the arriving police want to talk to the eyewitnesses. Even as a teenager, I had no doubt the police and fire department personnel would certainly want to talk to us and learn the cause of the accident.

To Ben, Rick, and Keith's surprise, the deputies seemed uninterested in talking with them. Not only did they not ask for an account of the crash, the deputies neither requested their names and information, nor asked how the car crash occurred. They were simply dismissed. It was a ridiculous down-played ending to our horrid life-altering experience.

Now, as a police officer, and with the benefit of hindsight, I am appalled at the lack of attention my friends and I received from both the sheriff deputies and the medical team. Not a single question about the reckless driving that led to a car crash that killed two young women. The paramedics never asked if we were burned while saving people from the car fire.

My scorched arms now bear only small, faded scars from that living nightmare, but internally, the emotional scars are indelible. For many years, I couldn't even bring myself to wear a seatbelt, driving confined in the seat brought back vivid horrors of that night. And yet, not wearing a seatbelt made me think of the girl launched through the windshield to her death. There was no avoiding the painful memories.

Today, a popular shopping mall with movie theaters, stores, and restaurants covers every trace of a wreck that shattered so many lives. I know the crash altered my life, an obsession to save lives was born from the ashes of that night. And a lingering pain, wondering if a better outcome were possible had I done something differently.

Twist

I've agonized over the endless "what ifs" of that night. What if I remained longer at the driver's door and eventually got it open? Could I have pulled the girl out first and saved her from the burning car? What if I had not tripped over the girl lying dead on the ground? Could that have given me more time to figure out a way to cut the seat belt? What if my friends and I had moved quicker when pulling each of the other occupants from the wreckage? The never-ending list of "what ifs" isn't productive. The benefit of many life experiences in the military and police finally provided me with a positive perspective. My friends and I saved two people from that deadly car crash, and their subsequent existence may have saved or positively impacted countless more lives.

After that tragic night, I would finally graduate high school (and yes, I finally lost my virginity), and within a few years, my best friends and I would all answer the call of service to our country and join the Army.

At the time, I didn't know that I would eventually become a police officer and experience countless tragedies. My ability to survive the emotional pain of that horrific night of the car fire served me well. At seventeen, acting in the face of crippling fear, I gained an invaluable experience; an intrinsic edge dealing with duty-related tragedies. Because of that night, I acquired a unique confidence to act in harrowing situations as a police officer.

For instance, working the graveyard shift in 2005 as a newly-promoted patrol sergeant driving down a street, I observed an apartment fire. Immediately, I got on the radio, notifying the fire department of the flames coming from the third-floor apartment. Springing into action, I got out of my car and scaled up the backside of the apartment building, as I didn't want to waste valuable time driving to the front of the large apartment complex.

I got to the third-floor apartment and went inside through an unlocked back patio door. I walked through the apartment and discovered an occupant had already awakened to the danger. She was very surprised by my sudden and timely entry, as I helped get her three sleeping children out of the burning home. Some of my officers arrived, assisting to evacuate the remaining occupants out of the building. Watching me climb up the back-patio balconies, a patrol officer later commented that I looked like "Spiderman." I was both happy and relieved having helped save the lives of that family.

CHAPTER 2

A Family Affair

A FEW months after I graduated high school, my grandmother passed away after a long bout with cancer. Upon her death, my mother shared with me a family secret that would have a huge influence in my life. My mother told me about a horrible attack against my grandmother when she was a young girl, which both shocked and saddened me. The painful account of my grandmother's ordeal later influenced my decision and conviction to work as a sex crimes detective, bringing sexual predators to justice.

My mother told me that during the 1920's, a prolific sexual predator terrorized my grandmother's close-knit community in the small town in New Jersey, where she grew up. The serial rapist targeted young women and girls during his reign of terror.

The rapist attacked school girls and young women for the better part of a year, traumatizing the small community, as he abducted and attacked not only my grandmother, but her fellow classmates, including her best friend's older sister. Horrifically, the older teen became pregnant from the attack and her family arranged for an illegal abortion.

My mother told me about how my grandmother spent the night at her childhood friends' home, and seeing the older teenager returning from the procedure. My mother said, "Your grandmother saw her friend's sister screaming in pain as her father carried her into the house." My grandmother listened and watched in horror as the father carried the screaming girl to her bedroom. My mother sadly added, "She had a hard time sleeping that night, hearing her friend's sister screaming most of the night in pain, finally stopping in the early morning hours. Later that morning, your grandmother awakened to the wailing of the girls' mother, finding her oldest daughter lying dead in bed."

As the rapist continued preying upon young women, parents kept their daughters inside after dark. One day my grandmother's parents asked her to pick up some eggs from the neighborhood store after school. My grandmother walked to the store without any fear because it was still daylight and the rapist only struck at nighttime hours. She was walking on a well-traveled dirt path when an unknown man grabbed her from behind a bush. The predator dragged her off the walkway to a secluded area in the woods behind the homes. My grandmother never told my mother any details about the assault, only saying that she fought and got away from her attacker. I'd like to think she escaped before he consummated his crime; ignorance can be bliss.

My grandmother was only 10 years old when she was attacked by this serial rapist. She gave my mom many details of the horrific event, but didn't talk about the mechanics of the assault itself. My grandmother never explained if it was an attempted sexual assault or if she was raped. From my experience as a sex crimes detective, most victims understandably avoid describing the actual assault, providing painstaking detail leading up to the rape, or attempted rape, and what happened afterwards, skipping the specifics of the act itself. Also, young children have difficulty even comprehending the monstrous act, making describing the action too foreign to verbalize.

My grandmother immediately ran home and told her parents and siblings of the event. Her four older brothers stormed out of the house in search of the rapist. They later returned, but the predator vanished like so many times before. The rapist became even more brazen with several more daytime attacks. However, the daytime victims provided far better physical descriptions and with a more detailed suspect composite in hand, the local authorities arrested a suspect after police positively identified this monster. He was ultimately convicted and sentenced to a long prison term, but only a few years later he escaped from prison—never being recaptured.

The knowledge that this sexual predator could be back paralyzed the small town. Some of the victim's families moved to other cities, while my grandmother's family remained but lived in fear that the fiend might return and start attacking women and girls again. Although my grandmother eventually married and enjoyed her family, she stayed inside the house most of the time, never learning to drive a car, and made few friends.

My grandmother's ordeal solidified my deep admiration for her, and respect for all women for their inherent struggles. But the seed of that abiding respect was planted long before when I was a child, watching my mom's daily plight as a single mother. She worked long hours of manual labor at a plating plant, getting paid half of what men made for doing the same job. Watching her struggling as a single mother raising me and my older brother, affected all my female relationships—with teachers, neighbors, work colleagues, even my first girlfriend and future ex-wife.

During my last year of high school, I worked at a small newspaper company, starting in the circulation department, working my way up to manager. It is there where I met a work colleague named Bonnie. She worked as an "inserter," placing advertisements in the paper after they came off the printing press, working under my supervision as the circulation manager. I respected her immensely for her hard-working demeanor, and for living on her own at just 15 years old (as an emancipated minor). At my age of 17, I misinterpreted those feelings of respect for love, moving in with her before even graduating high school.

Upon graduation, I left the small tabloid printing business to work as a landscaper at an upscale apartment complex, which provided an apartment for me and Bonnie to live. We lived together for less than a year before getting married. I enlisted in the U.S. Army to provide a better way of life for me and my new bride, landing an opportunity to work in military intelligence after first completing basic training.

Unfortunately, my compassion and unconditional respect for women was not enough to pave the way for a successful marriage. Our union, unlike my military career, was doomed from the start. It was mere months before receiving a "Dear John" letter during my first week of basic training. I received the letter announcing she made a mistake getting married. The letter, not surprisingly, went on to explain she also wanted a divorce.

I still remember standing in the pouring rain talking on a pay phone, asking my mom to talk with my new bride, since I couldn't get back home to talk to her myself. The open-booth pay phone was attached to the outside corner of the commissary (military grocery store), so the departing shoppers all heard my story of domestic disharmony. I hated burdening my mother with such an uncomfortable subject matter, but after 18-hours of exhausting marching drills, weapons training, and physical exercise, I had little time on my own to resuscitate the marriage.

A month later, I received a second, more "*wifely*" letter reflecting her complete change of heart. I still wanted to salvage our two-month marriage and she promised never to stray again, wanting to move and come live with me. I agreed and arranged for her to come to a town near Fort Dix, New Jersey, joining her at the completion of my basic training. We got an apartment in the small town of Brown Mills, located on the outskirts of the military compound.

After completing basic training, I was honored with the selection to be a Drill Corporal, remaining at Fort Dix. Unfortunately, the new Drill Instructor position required me to stay for another training cycle of 20-hour days, leaving my easily-bored wife all alone. She garnered a lot of attention from the predominantly male-populated military training facility. Having a hard time withstanding the loneliness, she admitted to giving into temptation. Never telling me the details, she simply said she was getting too close to some male friends while I was away training for those four months. She, too, was happy when we were finally done with Fort Dix, and left for my Military Intelligence phase of training.

My next duty-station was at Fort Devens, Massachusetts for my advanced military intelligence training, or as the military refers to it as an MOS (military occupational specialty). It was an Electronic Warfare—Signals Intelligence; Emitter, Locator, and Identifier Course, which consisted of learning Morse Code, Russian, and other things I can't divulge even today. I could now dedicate time to a family, and soon we were the proud parents of a baby boy.

Darren Junior (DJ) was only a few months old when we had to relocate again, having graduated from the military intelligence school, traveling to Fort Campbell, Kentucky, the home of the 101st Airborne Division. Unfortunately, my wife again felt the pressures of being a military spouse with the lonely nights for weeks upon weeks, while I was away on maneuvers.

She emphatically apologized for her actions, but explained that she was always trying to suppress her yearning to be single. Her desire was so strong, making her not want to be a wife or a mother. Knowing that such a dating lifestyle wouldn't be compatible with marriage or motherhood, she asked that I take full custody of our son.

In all fairness, I should have listened to her from the very start, as early as our wedding night, when she stated, "I think it was a mistake getting married," believing she was not ready for marriage. Similarly, she had the same issue wanting to get pregnant, but not wanting to be a mother once it happened. She wasn't trying to be cruel, she just realized she had a problem with wanting something until she got it, then not wanting it.

I acknowledged her parental sacrifice and agreed to take full custody of our six-month-old son. Accepting my reality, I embraced my new life as a single father. I thought about the parallels of being a single father and having been raised by a single mother. I knew it would be difficult doing it alone, but I was also excited about raising my son, Darren Burch, Jr. (DJ).

Twist

I'm genuinely grateful to Bonnie for giving me the greatest gift, DJ. My pride and joy grew up to become my best friend! In time, I told him about my police and military stories, and he enjoyed them, including the tale about how I picked him over a career in the CIA.

CHAPTER 3

CIA Child Care

NEARING the end of my military commitment, and as a single father of a two-year-old, I knew I was running out of time and needed to find a job. My military intelligence background prompted me to apply for a position with the Central Intelligence Agency (CIA). A fellow Army sergeant, Mike, also applied and we were both invited to CIA Headquarters in Langley, Virginia, for interviews and testing. Mike's wife, Pam, agreed to babysit my toddler while I was gone. This would be my first break from single fatherhood, yet surprisingly, it depressed me for most of the trip. Fortunately, the elaborate, intensive testing forced me to focus on something other than missing my son.

Initially, there were more than 20 applicants in the same testing process, for an undisclosed number of positions. We would be escorted individually out of a central holding room for each test and then escorted back upon successful completion. The total number of applicants would dwindle rapidly from one day to the next, based on prospective agents failing a test.

Each day I noticed more and more of the group not returning after their respective testing. Their absence would spark conversations among the applicants to their missing colleague, wondering of their whereabouts. When asked, the staff would answer with a rehearsed sounding statement, "They are out to lunch." By the end of the week, only four of us remained.

On the first day, simple skills were tested, like typing and reading comprehension. On the second day, there were more difficult professional tests based on military-intelligence scenarios. I was evaluated on my successful use of direction finding equipment, locating the origin of communication signals around the world, and then identifying the emission source of those messages. The third day, there was a basic Russian language skills test, and other problem solving scenarios that I still can't divulge. On the last and final day of testing, I successfully passed an advanced Morse code test; sending and receiving Morse code at a rate of 20 words per minute. Since my military duties all related to the CIA tests, I passed them with ease and was offered a position with the Central Intelligence Agency. I was going to be a spy!

It was hard for me to not scream with excitement to a dream job coming true, upon hearing the CIA recruiter utter the words, "You passed everything, welcome to the CIA." I was escorted to an administrative office for my employment processing, filling out tax forms and the like. An older, male executive dressed in a three-piece suit briefed me on the various employment benefits. He explained there would be a transitional training phase from the types of apparatuses I used in the military for our Direction Finding (DF) mission to CIA's state-of-the-art DF equipment.

He informed me that my first year of employment would be at a CIA compound in Crete. The employment manager referred to this amazing, exotic destination as a "hardship tour," explaining that after the mandatory, one-year tour, I could apply to other assignment locations around the world. The idea of working in a vacation wonderland like Greece was exciting, but would there be daycare for DJ? As a concerned dad, I casually asked him what kind of schools would be available in Crete. He explained in detail all the postgraduate schools and college classes that were available on the CIA base, which were placed for American studies. I respectfully listened, though I realized during his extensive explanation that he misunderstood my question.

I then explained my need for day-care-type schools for my two-year-old son. His face went pale. The shock of hearing the word *daycare* turned his mouth from an upbeat smile into an open crater. He sat way back in his swivel chair, folded his arms, closed his mouth, and remained quiet for a moment. His simple, but pointed remark, "But you're single" broke the silence.

I explained my single father status and without saying a word, he frantically began looking through each sheet of my application packet. The CIA administrator rifled through my employment application paperwork for ten minutes, which seemed like an eternity, being completely caught off guard by a job application that had no screening mechanism to identify a single father. After reviewing the packet with intense scrutiny and no apparent resolve, he excused himself and left the office.

Sitting alone in silence, I desperately held back a strong bout of the giggles, thinking about the manager wrapping his head around the need for CIA Child Care. I knew by the employment manager's shock and awkward exit from the office, the job offer would be rescinded in some manner and understandably so. I felt honored to have been asked to join the agency, but with the manager's almost comical reaction came the reality that such a profession is completely out of line for the dedication required to be a single father.

I would never have the pleasure of talking with that fine manager again. A relatively short time later, an attractive female secretary entered the room and instructed me to follow her out of the office. As we walked down the large empty halls, passing the hallowed wall with the stars representing the heroes who died for their country, I felt humbled to have even been invited to such a magnificent place. We walked in silence, but she would look over at me several times without saying a word. She then stopped in the middle of the hall, turned to me and said, "They discovered one spelling error too many on your typing test." She looked at me with such genuine maternal nature and said, "If anything changes in your status, please contact us," and with that, I was both hired and fired by the CIA.

She started to walk me out of the secured building, when I recalled I left some personal papers in the holding room, where the last three remaining CIA recruits were waiting. Requesting to pick up the items, the secretary escorted me to the holding room, where she asked me to wait in the hall. She went inside to retrieve my property, and I heard a colleague ask about my status, she politely responded, "He's out to lunch."

After leaving the military, I applied to several police departments back home, landing a job with the Phoenix Police Department. Who says you can never go home?

Twist

(Now, the truly dark and twisted police tales begin…)

You will probably be both glued and repulsed at the dark humor contained in the following "Twisted but True Tales." Most of the ill-fated consequences are based on a suspect's own tragic, and sometimes, fatal mistakes. As police officers, we embrace this warped humor to help deal with the tragedy, allowing us to continue our work and not be compromised by sad emotions. It is not my intent to make light and belittle anyone's tragedy or death, but I do at times reflect with humorous overtones, their criminal or alcohol-induced missteps, which led to their own calamity.

Since we are all on that journey to the great unknown upon death, we might as well have a good laugh on the way. I equate this to the way we gather after a funeral to tell funny stories about the recently departed; it allows us to begin the healing process, so with that, let's begin the police-related Twisted but True tales.

Here is a taste of the stories I am about to share. I responded to an unusual domestic violence call that erupted after the elder father wanted to pass along the tradition of carving the Thanksgiving-Day turkey to his adult sons, but the siblings fought over the carving honors. I arrived to find the "losing brother" lying dead on the living room floor with the carving knife embedded in his heart. We then left looking for the "winning brother" and found him a block down the street, walking and eating a turkey leg. This is the kind of astonishing "Twisted but True Tale" that is sadly commonplace to cops, yet morbidly shocking to the average person.

CHAPTER 4

Accident from Hell

BY 1987, I had finished my on-the-job training period riding with a training officer, and was now riding solo on a rookie police squad, working weekend nights. One hectic Saturday night, I was riding alone and responded to a call of a serious injury traffic accident. The accident involved a four-car pileup at a busy intersection downtown. I immediately answered-up for the radio call; my drive to save lives kicking into high gear. Adrenaline rushed through my body as the radio dispatcher advised of a trapped motorist in one of the cars.

Because of the seriousness of the car crash, I switched on my emergency lights and sirens. But, I'll be honest, there is an incredible rush driving "Code 3" with the brilliant red and blues flashing, siren screaming and punching the gas pedal, taking full advantage of the emergency driving protocol to respond quickly to an accident scene.

Good police officers dream of saving lives; I myself was passionate about it, but this preoccupation could override my common sense sometimes, as the drive was manic. Racing in and out of traffic is dangerous regardless of a siren and flashing lights to alert other drivers. All I could think about was driving to the scene and saving a life, as if driving too fast could make up for a past life lost.

Arriving quickly, after a blur of sidewalks, streets, signs and strip malls, I realized that I was the lone officer responding to the serious-injury traffic accident. I parked my patrol car in the middle of the intersection, jumping out and slamming the door closed all in one move. A sick feeling sank into the pit of my stomach. As soon as the door shut, I knew my squad car door was locked, the blaring sirens concealing the sound of my running ignition. Yes, in my diligence and exuberance to save lives and the world, I locked myself out of my own police car.

At that time, the police department prohibited officers from keeping a spare set of keys with them during their shift. The only spare set of car keys were secured at the respective police substations. My police radio also remained housed inside a charging port mounted into the car's dash. Simply put, even if I wanted to call someone to drive over with a spare key, I had no police radio to do so.

I could survive my own embarrassment, but I was at an accident with possible life threatening injuries. There was no way to communicate my urgent need for paramedics, and no way to ask for help with all the other issues associated with a serious traffic accident blocking a major city intersection. At the time, cellular telephones weren't popular or affordable. I am dating the techno-availability at that time by the mere vernacular of the term *cellular telephone*. In the middle of a city, whose population was approximately a million people, I was utterly alone.

To make a bad situation worse, the sirens were blaring at the highest volume. The deafening wails made thinking impossible, and the patrol car could not have been in a worse position: parked smack-dab in the middle of one of the busiest intersections, blocking all lanes. The position of my patrol car made traffic flow impossible, plus the emergency lights and sirens justifiably kept all traffic at a complete standstill. And at some later point, I would need to reopen the intersection to resume the flow of traffic. Nothing moved, not even me, the stupid rookie cop standing in the middle of the intersection next to his locked patrol car.

All these problematic hurdles bombarded my thoughts within the first few seconds, only giving way to the urgency of checking everyone's welfare involved in the accident. I had no time to dwell on my major screw-up, quickly blocking the trail of my own mistakes out of my mind. I ran to the first wrecked car, a large dark sedan with a smashed front, and a reported trapped person inside. The only thing confined in the car was the loud snoring from the passed-out driver. He was responsible for the four-car pile-up, fast asleep blowing past the intersection's red signal light. I was too busy and focused with the totality of the situation to be angry at the drunk, but pleased that he would soon be dealing with his subsequent legal and financial woes for causing such an accident.

The inside of the car reeked like a brewery. I tried to wake the intoxicated gentleman in his business attire, but he would only respond by saying he "loved" me, so I stopped. Removing the ignition key from the steering column (the irony was not lost on me), I let this sleeping dog lie. After all, I had no patrol car to secure the drunk driver. I checked to see if there were any obvious signs of trauma, there wasn't, and slammed the door shut.

The next vehicle had a young couple, both sustaining minor injuries. They were talkative and in relatively "good spirits," considering they were in a major accident. I told them to remain in the car to ensure their safety, as I hoped paramedics had been dispatched upon the initial call, and proceeded to the third vehicle, only to find another drunk driver. Ok, now I was angry.

The third vehicle's intoxicated driver was alert and awake, but seemed surprised by my appearance. Only a drunk would be surprised by my approach, since it could not have been foretold any stronger with my blinding red and blue lights and deafening siren blaring. Everybody else within a square mile radius knew of my arrival. Only the sleeping drunk in the first car, and the alert drunk in the third car were oblivious to my arrival and the mayhem they caused.

Gently but firmly grabbing the intoxicated driver, I helped him out of his car. As I was cuffing him, I was thankful I didn't have to deal with the typical drunken passenger scenario. Many times, a drunken passenger is also present and invariably interferes in the arrest. Because they're so inebriated, they will usually object to the arrest of the driver and demand you read them their Miranda rights.

Ironically, and usually to their detriment, they never opt for their right to remain silent!

I walked the handcuffed alert drunk driver to the first car, where I sat him down so I could deal with drunk sleeping beauty. After jostling him a few times, I successfully awakened him, and thankfully he didn't tell me he loved me, or at least I couldn't hear him since my siren was still wailing. I secured the two drunks together, placing one cuff on each of their left wrists. This awkward cuffing placement makes walking, or fighting much more difficult. The two drunks were now sitting next to each other on the ground against the 1st car.

The paramedics arrived, transporting the mildly injured couple to the hospital. Prior to leaving, the paramedics also checked on the drunken duo's welfare, since they could have been too intoxicated to even know if they were injured. A second ambulance arrived and transported the occupants in the fourth car to a hospital for strictly precautionary measures. It was that second team of paramedics who looked baffled at my decision to leave the two handcuffed drunks sleeping on each other in the middle of the intersection.

That prompted me to relocate the drunks from the intersection onto a sidewalk at the corner. My earlier dilemma resurfaced: I had nowhere to secure them. My screaming and flashing patrol car was still locked. I instructed the two drunk drivers, handcuffed to each other, to sit on the street corner while I stood over them.

In my entire career in law enforcement, this was the only time I had thought about ripping off my badge and simply walking away. I had never thought about quitting, not even after having been shot at in three separate incidents later in my career or other near-death situations.

Now, the moment of truth; there was no other course of action but to break the window, a simple remedy that had far reaching implications. Thoughts filled my mind of how the discipline of "destruction of government property" could potentially jeopardize my career, which allowed me an opportunity to save lives and make a difference. What should have been an easy decision was gut wrenching, as it threatened the very reasons I found myself in this mess; my passion to save lives. As a rookie cop, any discipline is bad with the potential of a career ending termination. I had a good track record at this early stage of my career, so I doubted the discipline would merit such a consequence, but even a mild suspension with unpaid days off, or a slap on the wrist with a written reprimand would hurt my career. Any discipline would be a permanent entry in my department file, and adversely affect advancements (detective assignments), promotions (sergeant rank), and provide fodder for defense attorneys. At the very least, it would be a blight on an otherwise spotless record.

The fire department crew was leaving, and the ambulances already left for the hospitals. Soon, I would be alone with the drunken dynamic-duo, my loud blinking spectacle of a police car, and of course, the endless lines of cars and drivers waiting for me to reopen the intersection. There was no legitimate reason for me to keep the intersection closed. I needed to remove the damaged cars from the roadway, or get a tow truck to haul away the vehicles too damaged to move.

I also needed to transport the drunk drivers to the station and process them for their respective DUIs and complete the booking paperwork for their criminal charges. In addition, I had to conduct a traffic accident investigation; reconstructing the entire crash scene to file a state accident report. There were myriad tasks in need of doing, and no other recourse than breaking the window to get started.

Just as I resigned in the fact that I had to bust out the window of my patrol car, something magical happened. Another patrol car wove its way through the traffic, stopping next to me and the drunken duo sleeping on the sidewalk. The cop drove up next to me, rolling down his window, and I knew a wise-crack was coming. I mean, even a seasoned cop would sprain his neck doing a double take looking at the epic mess I made for myself.

He was a veteran swing-shift officer who worked another squad area, but instead of driving to the station to go home, he thankfully detoured to check on me. The officer had no reason to be this far out of his squad area, but heard something amiss on the radio that concerned him. It's procedure to advise the radio operator about the seriousness of a traffic accident, and when I failed to do so, he decided to check on my welfare.

My savior that night was Officer Ken Collins. I will always remember Ken as one of the best cops I ever had the honor to work with. Ken lowered his car window and in a very dry, sarcastic manner said, "You might want to turn off the siren." I explained my self-created blunder while still hovering over the secured drunken fools fast asleep at my feet. Once he finished laughing hysterically, he immediately sprang into action.

Ken took charge of the situation, breaking down our assignments stemming from the initial traffic accident. There were mainly two major investigations that needed attention; the DUI investigation, and the traffic accident investigation. The DUI investigation would consist of processing two intoxicated drivers and their related booking. The accident investigation consisted of reconstructing the traffic accident, drafting the report, and facilitating the towing of damaged vehicles.

I took on the reconstruction of the traffic accident and the towing of the cars. Ken took on the DUI investigation, handling the arrests of the two drunk drivers. He also picked up on my "Oh my God" gaze, as he explained in detail the many intricate steps involved with investigating a four-car traffic accident. He showed me the best method to document the numerous measurements relating to the length of the various skid marks and measuring the distances between each of the vehicles.

Ken secured the two DUI suspects in the backseat of his patrol car after contacting another patrol officer on the radio to assist. He arranged for the officer to pick up the spare set of car keys and had the officer bring it to my location. He also made a persuasive argument to the station chief to change the precinct's rule to allow officers to carry a spare set of keys during their shift. This new rule was jokingly referred to as the "Burch Rule."

I experienced firsthand the true meaning of the common police phrase "brotherhood." It's the way police officers look out for one another; not just on the street, responding to the obvious violent radio calls, but also in simple, even mundane tasks like helping with paperwork, or saving a rookie cop, who in his enthusiasm locked himself out of his patrol car at a traffic accident from hell.

Ken did not know me. We had never met or talked at the precinct, never worked together on any calls. He had no idea I was locked out of my patrol car. He didn't know how badly I needed his help. He was oblivious to all of this when checking on my welfare. He took on most of the responsibility of the investigation. I profusely thanked him, but he might not have known just how much I appreciated what he did for me. I think of Officer Ken Collins often and how he may have even saved my career.

Twist

A few months after the accident, Ken was involved in a shooting with two heavily-armed bank robbers. Ken worked off-duty at the bank and observed the robbery in progress. Staying out of sight to avoid a shooting situation among the bank customers and staff (and preventing a hostage situation), Ken immediately advised on his radio of the bank robbery.

Once the suspects left the bank, Ken followed, but the suspects spotted him and began shooting. Ken took cover behind a truck while returning fire. Tragically, one of the suspects' bullets went through the side panel of the truck. The bullet struck Ken in the head, killing him instantly.

Like those who talk about where they were when JFK was shot, I'll never forget where I was when I learned Ken had been killed. I was enjoying my day-off work, sitting on a lounge chair watching television at my mom's house. I still remember in vivid detail hearing the chilling words that Ken was dead. The news reports reflected the capture of one of the two suspects a short distance away from the shoot-out. It would be another ten years before Ken's killer, the second bank robber, would be arrested while hiding in Mexico.

Ken saved the lives of many customers in the bank that day by his actions. He is a hero. I think of Ken every time I think of how proud I am to be in this brotherhood.

Twenty years later, during a memorial marking the anniversary of Ken's murder, I met his father and sister and shared this story with them. I concluded that Ken saved my career that night so many years ago, and that he is my hero. They cried.

CHAPTER 5

He's Got My Gun

BILL Schemers and I met in the summer of 1986, as young, 20-something, earnest police recruits experiencing the academically and physically rigorous demands at the Phoenix Police Department's Training Academy. Little did I know as a recruit, many of the twisted stories in this book would have Bill by my side. He is still a life-long friend of mine.

The Academy tested our worthiness, and evaluated our judgment in becoming police officers. It also screened out those physically inadequate for the arduous, stressful job of a police officer. But grueling conditions are the perfect breeding ground for establishing strong bonds and friendships. Bill and I were both steadfast and focused with our training and academics, including challenging law tests, physical fitness mandates, obstacle courses, defense tactics, firearms qualification, and tons of homework.

My education at the police academy coincided with a different kind of difficult training that I was involved in; the potty-training of my son. As a father, I struggled through the trials and tribulations of this crappy job, truly in uncharted yellow waters. I didn't have time for the weekly get-togethers with other police recruits, as they would meet every weekend to review test materials and unwind with some beers. I spent almost every available hour sitting at home taking care of my son. Not to suggest that I had no available time, as I made time to date a beautiful woman. The last week of the academy, I married my girlfriend, Coleen, whom I had met a year earlier.

After graduating from the police academy, Bill and I were stationed at the same Cactus Park Precinct, which happened to be located directly across the street from where I went to high school. This was ironic due to my borderline criminal antics as a teenager with Ben, Rick and Keith. Though it was a bit surreal as a newly graduated police recruit going back to my old neighborhood, it was tremendously advantageous knowing every street, alleyway, business, and problem area like the back of my hand.

Bill and I also worked closely with another squad officer, Jerri Hubert. She was already on the squad two years before we graduated from the Academy. Our squad sergeant would typically allow us to choose our partners each night. Bill and I mainly worked together, but routinely Jerri would ask if she could ride partners with either Bill or me. The one advantage that Jerri had over Bill was she happened to be an incredibly attractive female officer, and Jerri's beauty unfortunately was very much known by my new bride as well…

There were many situations during those first ten years where Bill, Jerri and I helped each other out of many a jam. We even saved each other's lives on some occasions. One of the scariest of those life-threatening scenarios happened when Jerri and I were riding together. Bill heard our radio call and decided to assist as a third backup officer.

The emergency hot call described a particularly violent family fight. The radio dispatcher indicated the neighbor called the police upon hearing glass breaking and a woman screaming. The neighbor feared the woman's husband was trying to kill her. The screaming woman never called the police, which gave us cause for concern. She may have been injured or incapacitated in some manner and couldn't call 911.

The three of us arrived, and I went to watch the back door, while Jerri and Bill went to the front door to knock, hoping to contact someone inside. I positioned myself behind a tree in the backyard, providing an excellent view of the home. The inside of the home was visible through a closed sliding-glass door with a view of the kitchen.

I saw approximately twenty broken wine bottles scattered across the kitchen floor. Broken glass shards covered the entire wine-drenched floor. I informed Bill and Jerri of the broken wine bottles, proof of a disturbance inside the home—we had the right house!

Forcefully knocking at the front door, Bill and Jerri announced, "Police, open the door." At that moment, an adult white male with a stocky build ran into the kitchen. He attempted to make his escape through the rear sliding-glass door, but I was ready for him. He slid the glass door open, and I stepped out from behind the tree, making my presence known.

The fleeing husband stepped outside, but immediately turned back inside after seeing me. Stepping inside, he tried shutting the sliding-glass door, preventing me from entering. I grabbed the door handle and announced, "Police, I'm coming inside." I explained my sworn-duty to investigate the report of a woman screaming, and physically stopped him from closing the glass door.

"Mr. Stocky" yelled at me to leave his home, and I calmly replied, "No." Again, explaining my lawful obligation to enter the home to check on the woman's welfare, moving my grip to the door frame to get more control of the door. "Mr. Stocky" pushed my chest with both of his hands, trying to force me out of the doorway. I did not take this as a personal assault, though, such a push is absolutely an assault on a police officer. Not wanting to overreact to the push, I held my position and prevented him from pushing me out, while keeping control of the door. I reiterated my authority and obligation to check on the welfare of the woman, making clear my intent to enter his home.

Pushing him inside, I closed the door on my way into the home. I grabbed onto "Mr. Stocky" as I felt him again try to push me out, but this time through the closed glass door. The fight was on. I generally prefer to force anyone trying to fight me onto the ground; as a wrestler, I have a distinct advantage once on the ground. However, in this situation, I wasn't going to throw him on a floor to be seriously injured by the array of glass shards.

Locked in an angry embrace, grabbing each other's arms, our feet slid all over the wet floor. I tried steering him toward the living room, maneuvering him out of the dangerous kitchen. But getting him into the living room was made difficult with his repeated fist strikes to my face. Thankfully, he had difficulty landing a strong shot from such a close range, but I wanted to avoid the face strikes entirely.

I released my grip on one of his arms, and began swinging him wildly with the remaining arm. My "dance move" prevented him from hitting me, swinging him wildly from side to side, all the while trying to keep us both upright on the slippery tile. Our fighting-dance could have resembled a twisted version of the band, the Village People performing; a fully uniformed police officer twirling around a shirtless, construction worker-looking man.

Jerri and Bill were surprised to hear me yelling from inside the home, having knocked and waiting patiently for someone to open the front door. Jerri quickly raced to the backyard, leaving Bill to guard the front door. She ran into the home through the sliding-glass door, passing me and my dance partner, unlocking the front door to let Bill inside.

Bill joined the dance while Jerri looked around the home for the once screaming woman. We still didn't know what happened to the woman, never hearing a peep from her. We didn't know if she was his wife, girlfriend, or a prisoner he kept against her will. Jerri found "Mr. Stocky's" wife and teen son hiding upstairs, and walked them down to the middle of the stairs so she could also keep an eye on our struggles with "Mr. Stocky."

Bill grabbed onto his legs, wrapping them up, making it much easier for me to throw "Mr. Stocky" down to the carpet. The three of us fell with a mighty thud on the living room floor. I controlled "Mr. Stocky's" head in a headlock and placed his right arm in an arm-bar hold. "Mr. Stocky" was no longer punching me, so I assumed Bill had his other arm and legs tied up. Because of my position to his face, looking directly at his angry red "mug," Bill was out of my view.

Looking beyond the suspect, I could see the suspect's teen son and wife huddled in each other's arms, sitting midway up the living room stairs with Jerri. The stairs led to the upper bedrooms, which is where they were hiding upon our arrival. His wife looked scared and severely beaten, with numerous facial contusions and black eyes.

Suddenly, Bill screamed, "He's got my gun!" Bill's panic-stricken words still haunt me to this day. I instantly released my grip on the suspect's arm so I could place both of my hands around his neck. Squeezing with all my might, I placed massive pressure against his carotid arteries, hoping my actions would stop him from taking Bill's gun, or if too late, force him to drop the gun before he shot Bill.

I had to make a split-second decision, choosing not to go for my gun and instead applying a potentially fatal frontal carotid restraint. I would have been justified in shooting him, but I didn't want to take the seconds needed to get to my gun since my hands were already close to his neck.

This type of neck squeeze is not taught in the police academy, but the suspect's actions made the lethal choking improvisation necessary and permissible. Restricting his blood flow would render "Mr. Stocky" unconscious, but the massive pressure could also restrict his airway. The lack of air would eventually cause complete asphyxiation, resulting in his death. As I continued to apply pressure, I saw his facial coloring go grey. Realizing that he could die soon, I yelled, "Bill, did you get your gun back?" I was mortified when I heard Bill's voice from across the room say, "Oh, yes. I am fine now, thanks."

Stunned that Bill was no longer in mortal peril, I stopped choking "Mr. Stocky." After several seconds, he regained consciousness and began gasping for breath. I placed him in handcuffs and looked across the room at an exhausted Bill, sitting on a small, antique-looking, wooden chair, returning his gun back into the holster.

I learned that due to Bill's position on "Mr. Stocky's" lower torso, controlling his legs, he was unable to see my actions relating to my frontal carotid restraint (choke). Bill and I couldn't see each other during our respective struggles with the combative "Mr. Stocky," and to our detriment, we both thought the other could. I didn't realize Bill couldn't see me strangling the gun-grabbing suspect, and he didn't know that I never saw him recover his gun. Bill assumed I used a less lethal pain-compliant hold, forcing "Mr. Stocky" to quickly release his grip on Bill's gun. It was upon the instant release of his gun that prompted Bill to move away from "Mr. Stocky" to safely return his gun back into the holster.

"Mr. Stocky" only remained unconscious for a few seconds, unlike in television shows where they remain unconscious for hours. A side-effect of the carotid restraint, or my lethal choking modification, is the combatant's involuntarily loss of control to their bowels and bladder; "Mr. Stocky" pissed himself. Pissing his pants seems like a mild consequence for taking my partner's gun, repeatedly hitting me, and beating his wife senseless, and all in the presence of his teenage son.

Bill and I carried "Mr. Stocky" to our police car, while Jerri talked with his battered wife, learning his wife had been abused for many years. "Mr. Stocky's" anger on this occasion stemmed from not being greeted with a glass of wine upon returning home from work. He punished his wife's oversight by throwing bottles of wine at her in the kitchen, joking about the various vintage years of each bottle thrown. Once out of wine bottles, he proceeded to hit her repeatedly with a closed fist. Her injuries were not life threatening, but her emotional pain went well beyond the physical attack.

Bill and I placed "Mr. Stocky" in my police car, and Jerri gave his wife a Victim Right's Pamphlet. Handing her the information, she wanted Jerri to thank me for not killing her husband in front of his son, stating, "I thought for sure he was going to get shot for taking that officer's gun." Jerri strongly suggested she consider moving in with a relative or friends and seek counseling for the years of domestic abuse. She nodded politely, but Jerri could see in her eyes that her words fell on deaf ears, probably due to the long cycle of abuse the wife experienced.

"Mr. Stocky" was ultimately charged with two misdemeanor crimes; an assault against his wife and resisting arrest for his actions against me. The prosecutor refused to file any felony charges for aggravated assault against a police officer or for threatening Bill's life by grabbing his gun.

Twist

Day-shift officers transported "Mr. Stocky" to the county jail while we started on the various police reports. I wrote the report in which he threatened Bill's life by taking the gun, Bill wrote a report about how he was assaulting me, and Jerri wrote the report regarding the assault against his wife. We were far from finished when another domestic violence call came from "Mr. Stocky's" home. We had no idea that once at the jail, "Mr. Stocky" paid a predetermined bail and never saw a judge, or the inside of a jail cell. We didn't even have time to finish the police reports before he was released from jail, returning home to beat his wife for a second time.

A few years later, much-needed Arizona domestic violence laws were enacted. One of the new provisions made it mandatory that all domestic violence arrestees be incarcerated and held in jail until such time they are presented before a judge for bail consideration.

CHAPTER 6

A Bad Place for a Cramp

POLICE work is arguably one of the most dangerous professions. In our country, 135 police officers were killed in the line of duty in 2016 alone. I have been shot at three times in my career, and I had many other close calls involving weapons other than a gun, but somehow, I always made it out of those situations alive. Someone must be watching over me, saving me from what otherwise would be life-threatening or career-ending events. One such incident where divine guidance, or just dumb luck, played a hand at saving my career was the night I happened upon an armed robber. And the weapon that almost ended my career wasn't the robber's gun, it was my own actions.

While driving to a burglary report, a man running out of a convenience store caught the corner of my eye. He was a black man in his early 20's, and running surprisingly fast for having such a large, muscular build. He had what appeared to be a handgun in his right hand, and a small paper bag in his left hand. Even to the untrained eye this looked very suspicious, I believed he had just committed an armed robbery.

I immediately drove into the large strip mall parking lot where I saw the robber, and relayed my observations to the radio dispatcher, requesting additional police officers and the police helicopter to assist. I drove behind parked cars in the parking lot, trying to remain out of his sight, fearing if spotted, he could easily jump over a wall into an alley and get away. It was 9:00 on a busy Saturday night, so there were plenty of parked cars to navigate behind in the parking lot.

The suspect stopped running and walked in between several cars while looking behind to see if the store employee or security were in chase. After breathing a sigh of relief with apparently no one in his line of sight, he then spotted me over his right shoulder, almost breaking his neck with a whiplash-worthy double take. I drove quickly across the street to intercept, knowing he could outrun me in a foot chase. My strategy was to chase him in my car as long as possible before initiating a foot chase, as my chances of catching this cheetah were much better if he was exhausted.

After a minute or two, I finally bailed-out of my patrol car, running after him. I parked as close to his location as possible, and the chase was on. I heard another police officer, Brett Draughn answer up to assist with my foot chase. Brett's bear-like size made him a great backup officer to help deal with a cheetah on steroids in case he decides to fight. My plan was working, getting closer and closer, as the tired robber began slowing down.

The suspect ran across the street toward a large car dealership. The car dealership had rows of cars, which made it the perfect place to hide. I needed to catch him before he could disappear in the dark, shadowy rows of cars. He threw his gun and bag to the side as I got close. I made a mental note to the location of the gun, as I would need to retrieve the evidence after his arrest. Criminals routinely throw away evidence of their crime, hoping a bystander might take the item or that a cop will stop chasing to recover the evidence.

I discovered after working just a few years, most criminals willing to run are equally willing to fight to avoid arrest. Perhaps it's just because of my small size, but I seemed to have to fight a lot of suspects, and fighting this large-framed man would be difficult. A fresh sprint brought me within the suspect's reach. A diving tackle would both end the chase and the subsequent fall might knock any fight out of him. There was still no sign of Brett.

I dove toward his slowing body, taking him down to the ground. We both hit the parking lot pavement with a hard thud. Various bystanders, car dealership employees, and patrons gathered as the robber immediately resisted arrest. The struggle was based on his noncompliance rather than aggressively trying to hit me. The robber used his strength to pull away from my grasp trying to get back up to his feet, but he was exhausted, having little strength to resist. I subdued him with an arm bar technique, holding him down without inflicting any actual injury. I quickly secured him in handcuffs, while the crowd watched only yards away in the parking lot.

Few officers are fortunate enough to witness an armed robbery in progress, and fewer turn that good luck into an arrest. Making a diving tackle was the "cherry on top," as that is what kids daydream when thinking about being a cop when they grow up. I had caught the armed robbery suspect without anyone getting hurt, then all hell broke loose.

The robber began screaming, appearing to be in genuine and horrific pain. Having no idea what the nature of his injury was, I thought he may have broken his leg during the tackle. Asking him to tell me where he was hurt, he stopped screaming long enough to say that he had a powerful muscle spasm in his right thigh, *a bad place for a cramp*. His pleas for help led me to quickly respond with a treatment I learned during my high school wrestling days.

My high school wrestling coach taught us to administer a repeated single-knuckle punch to the opposite limb from the spasming muscle. This technique would force the distressed wrestler to involuntarily focus his attention to the knuckle-punched muscle, automatically reducing the severity of the other limb's muscle spasm. This ridiculous-sounding technique really does work. But what the hell was I thinking!

So, I began applying this bizarre-looking first aid technique on him without even thinking how it might look to the gathering crowd. Yes, a white police officer striking a noncombatant, handcuffed black man repeatedly in the leg while he screams for help looks exactly as bad as you can imagine. As good citizens watched in absolute horror and disgust, they had no idea the robber's screams of pain were from an unbearable muscle spasm in his right leg, and not from the white cop's repeated knuckle-punch to his other leg.

It is important to note, my knuckle-punching incident occurred a short time after the release of the infamous video of Los Angeles police officers beating Rodney King. Again, what was I thinking! But the incident got worse. The police helicopter finally arrived, illuminating my "police brutality" with an incredibly bright spotlight. Now, citizens outside of those already gathered could also witness my beating of an unarmed black man with vivid clarity.

My salvation of this incredibly stupid, albeit kind act was the robber himself. He finally stopped yelling in pain as I successfully reduced the muscle spasm in his right leg, saying in a loud voice "Thank you!" He rested his head against my body, as if to hug me for relieving his pain. Tears in his eyes waned as he repeatedly thanked me for all to hear.

After helping him to his feet, I realized how badly this must have looked to the crowd. The thirty or more onlookers gasped and muttered to each other, even as the robber profusely thanked me for relieving his torment. He even told the shocked crowd that I had stopped his painful muscle spasm. A less moral minded criminal could have easily convinced the most hardened police supporter that he was brutalized, instead he surprised even me by making a complete confession to the store robbery.

Twist

During the foot chase and capture of the "cheetah on steroids," I assumed Brett would be close at hand to help, but for some unknown reason he never showed up, which was completely out of character for him. I escorted the suspect to my patrol car and observed Brett standing on the outskirts of the car dealership. He looked upset, standing next to a tow truck and his patrol car, parked along the freeway access road. That was when I learned Brett was having a bad day too.

When Brett first drove into the area, he heard on the radio that I was chasing the armed robbery suspect toward the car dealership. He believed the freeway access road would be the perfect strategic location to park and assist in the foot chase. Brett drove up the access road, pulling into the car dealership's adjacent drive. He bolted out of his patrol car and inadvertently put the patrol car's transmission in "Neutral" instead of "Park." After running past the front of his patrol car, to help me in the chase, his car began rolling backward toward the freeway. Brett tried turning around to stop his car, but the patrol car already gained too much speed to stop as it rolled down the access road's slope. A vehicle driving up the off-ramp collided into the back of Brett's runaway patrol car. Brett watched in stomach-churning disbelief as his patrol car butt-rammed the unluckiest of motorists. Brett ran down the access road and got inside his car, driving off the road to deal with his driverless traffic accident. The only good news, he didn't lock himself out, like some other cop we know.

CHAPTER 7

The Whore of Rose Lane

H AVING a runaway child is a frightening ordeal for a parent, but having your child kidnapped is a nightmare with no equal. Police officers responding to a runaway child call must establish if the child left voluntarily, opposed to missing under suspicious circumstances. Jerri Hubert and I responded to a runaway child call with a concerning twist, suspicious for completely different reasons.

Jimmy's parents called 911 to report their son ran away from home, providing little information about their son, only that he was last seen wearing a *Star Wars* shirt and jeans. The parents did advise they may have information regarding their son's present location. The father broke down when the 911 operator asked where and when was the last time he'd seen his little boy. The 911 operator was unable to get any more information from the distraught caller.

We responded to the parent's home in an established neighborhood on Rose Lane. My partner Jerri and I knocked on the front door and were greeted by a tall, elderly man, in his late seventies. He was polite and welcomed us into his modest home. Sitting on a worn-out red couch was a much more frail-looking, elderly woman. Jerri and I were invited to sit on the couch opposite of the woman in their front family room.

After escorting us into his home, the man sat next to his wife and out of nowhere began excitedly talking to us about their lives growing up during the depression in a small, New England Coast town. Jerri and I instantly glanced at each other, wondering when their adult daughter or son would enter, assuming the grandparents even made them aware of our presence. Waiting for Jimmy's parents, we listened as the older-couple took a stroll down memory lane, and I noticed there weren't any pictures of kids, grandchildren or any extended family mounted on the walls or sitting in frames on tables.

The elderly couple seemed content to just talk to us about their youth in their Norman Rockwell–painted memories, not pausing long enough for us to ask them about their missing grandchild, Jimmy. Feeling compelled to interrupt, I asked the very nice grandparents about Jimmy, hoping to assess the urgency of Jimmy's welfare and his current location. The grandfather never stopped telling the story of his youth, continuing to talk over me as I asked about Jimmy.

I finally stopped the elderly man in midsentence, insisting to speak with Jimmy's parents, telling the grandparents that I needed to talk with their son or daughter about Jimmy running away from home. The elderly gentleman began to tell me that his son was having trouble finding a job, even asking about potential job openings with the police department.

Politely, trying to redirect the elderly man's attention to his grandchild, I implored him to tell Jimmy's parents we needed to talk with them, using the employment question as a ruse to contact the parents. I said it was best for me to explain the police hiring process directly to his son. When I asked how I could contact their son, the elderly woman stuttered something about her anger toward her son, wanting my assistance in correcting his behavior.

Getting nowhere, I had to be blunt, telling the couple we demanded to talk with their son or daughter about Jimmy's disappearance. The elderly gentleman replied that Jimmy wasn't really missing, but staying across the street. Jerri and I both let out a sigh of relief. We only needed to verify this new information with Jimmy's parents.

When I began asking questions about the welfare of Jimmy, the elderly couple became very animated, angrily expressing their strong dislike that their son had moved into a house across the street. The elderly woman added that her son is living in sin with the "whore" there. When we asked if Jimmy was living with his father and the lady (whore) across the street, their response came as a complete surprise to Jerri and me: Jimmy *was* their son!

The elderly man called 911 to report that his 50-year old son ran away to live with the "whore" across the street on Rose Lane. Considering this new information, Jerri and I didn't want to waste any more time. Saying our goodbyes and walking toward the door, we passed the elderly couple still seated.

The elderly woman began muttering in a soft voice, too faint to make out. Not being able to hear her, I walked close to her on the love seat. She then began rocking back and forth, as if in a rocking chair, while continuing to speak in the soft voice. Due to the incoherence of her mumbling, I leaned down close to understand what she was saying. She quickened the pace of her rocking, as I was bending down to her.

With my ear close to her mouth, I became concerned, hearing her rapidly repeat a single word, "be, be, be, be" in a soft voice. The elderly women's string of "be, be, be, be" were genuinely creepy, which prompted my partner to quickly open the door, giving me a look, as if to say, "Let's get the hell out of here." I looked over at the elderly man to assist his wife, but he just sat with a huge smile, oblivious to his wife's strange behavior.

Jerri held the front door open and earnestly said, "We really need to go, Darren." Suddenly, the elderly woman clutched my right wrist with both her hands. She startled me, prompting me to lean away speechless, as the elderly women held tight. Jerri looked-on with puzzlement, trying to stifle her laughter. As the woman's shaking, wrinkled-hands squeezed my arm, she shouted, "be, be, be, be my son!" She repeated the bizarre request over and over, "Be my son! Be my son!" The elderly man with his strange smile, nodded in agreement adding an eeriness to the surreal scene.

Jerri, now laughing hysterically, stepped out of the house to regain her composure. The elderly woman continued her odd maternal request as I gently and cautiously pried her delicate hands with paper-thin skin from around my wrist. Jerri peeked her head back through the open door, announcing to the elder couple that we needed to leave, while still stifling a laugh.

As my wrist regained circulation, I looked around the home to ensure the elderly couple could take care of themselves, I checked the various rooms, including the kitchen and refrigerator to ensure they had food. It appeared they were either doing a good job caring for themselves or their son was still taking care of them while living across the street with the "whore."

Jerri and I said good-bye, as the couple proceeded to converse with each other in idle conversation. We walked across the street to talk with Jimmy, making sure his parents' welfare was in his capable hands. Talking with both Jimmy and his new love interest, we confirmed he was still caring for his parents and that he was indeed the runaway adult child.

Twist

Surprisingly, we found the "whore" of Rose Lane to be an attractive and intelligent woman. There is no telling for taste, because Jimmy was indeed wearing a *Star Wars* shirt (during a time when it wasn't cool for an adult to wear such a shirt) and looking every bit the part of a 50-year old man living in his parents' basement.

CHAPTER 8

Chasing Mad Cow

ONE of my most memorable police calls involved a wild cow loose on the streets of Phoenix. Riding solo during a night shift, I decided to forgo a backup officer to a radio call of "a wild cow running around downtown." It seemed too silly to be true, an anonymous caller reporting a cow running loose, interfering with traffic at a major intersection. Someone must have called in a prank, since there were no farms or other livestock facilities in the area.

The notion that a wild cow could be strolling around downtown in a busy city seemed ridiculous. I didn't want to play into this prankster's hands, providing them with the spectacle of multiple police cars racing to the area looking around for a mad cow. The radio dispatcher even heard someone laughing in the background during the 911 call.

But I drove into the supposed cow-ridden area, just to make sure, and had difficulty getting to the actual intersection. The traffic flow slowed to almost a standstill; unusual for ten o' clock on a weekend night.

Refusing to believe the possibility that the intersection was cow-jacked, I finally reached the intersection, and the proof was in the pasteurized pudding. An angry-looking cow was indeed running wild in the street. Snorting a flow of red ooze from her nostrils and mouth, the cow angrily bucked, jumped and stumbled in and out of the halted traffic. The only thing moving in the intersection was the cow, with complete, wild abandonment.

She wasn't acting like any cow I had ever seen. Having grown up in a major city, I knew next-to-nothing about bovine behavior. The full extent of my cow knowledge was what I had observed from the highway—as I watch seemingly bored, lazy cows chewing their cud or grazing in the wide-open, green fields. My ignorance would become quickly (and painfully) clear in short order.

I drove my patrol car close to the cow to maneuver the beast away from the intersection, as her behavior posed a real threat to motorists and pedestrians alike. Surprisingly, using the patrol car to herd the cow worked, steering her down a side street away from the traffic jam. Taking advantage of a small, dry canal that ran parallel along the street, I herded and contained the cow down into the shallow, dirt and grass-filled canal.

Strategically parking my patrol car, I blocked her from getting out of the canal. The cow appeared to be content and out of harm's way from the honking metal monsters. Within a few minutes, the red foam from her nose subsided, and the spooked animal appeared more passive, and she even grazed on the grass lining the canal walls. I informed the radio dispatcher of the wild cow's existence, asking for assistance from an agency that handles livestock situations.

The dispatcher made several urgent messages to County Livestock, receiving a call-back 30 minutes later from a representative. The awakened on-call representative relayed instructions directing me to keep the animal detained, re-assuring me they dispatched a cattle transportation vehicle. The estimated arrival time could take as much as an hour. Translation: I would need to babysit the cow for up to two hours.—Did I mention they don't teach bovine-babysitting at the Academy?

Stepping out of my patrol car, I started talking to the cow in a calm, cow-sounding voice. Think Kermit the Frog talking like Tarzan; I became a cow whisperer. The traffic was moving slowly, with drivers trying to catch a glimpse of a cop talking sweetly to a cow in a canal.

The calm lasted less than 30 minutes. Two state troopers with blaring sirens and emergency lights flashing, drove into the area and spooked the animal. She sprang out of the canal, and climbed onto the hood of my patrol car with an impressive show of acrobatic speed and power. I only saw a blur trampling over my car on her way back onto the pavement.

I was right back where I started, chasing a mad cow. But after a long rest, the cow regained her strength and with renewed energy she was stronger and harder to control. I jumped back into my patrol car, took off after the cow, and advised on my radio, "The mad cow is back on the loose," sounding like I was chasing a murderous hit-and-run driver. She sprinted back onto the main road, but I diverted her onto a side street and away from heavy traffic.

The cow ran into a small apartment complex parking lot. Knowing the apartment complex layout, I knew the gated community only had one way in and out. The cow would soon be trapped… or so I thought.

Once the cow ran deep enough into the complex parking lot, I put my cow-catching plan into action. After parking strategically to block the only way in or out, I got out on foot to execute phase two of my plan. I would follow her to the dead end and then, with my high school wrestling training, grapple her to the ground. I never said it was a good plan.

I didn't think through the part about wrestling two tons of beef. Keep in mind, I came up with this terrible cow-catching plan after witnessing the cow demolish the front of my patrol car upon jumping out of the canal bank. Any plan hatched from anger is inherently flawed.

Walking after the cow, I followed her at a distance as she neared the dead end. She trotted to the very end of the complex, pausing to contemplate her dilemma. Okay, maybe she wasn't contemplating anything, but simply turned around upon hitting the dead end. In my adrenaline-fueled state, I visualized that after the cow turned around, we would begin our slow walk toward each other, never expecting her to charge full steam ahead like a bull rushing a matador. Impulsively, I reciprocated and charged at her. My plan degraded into a game of chicken, but with a cow. The odds of a victorious outcome were a million to none.

Running full speed toward the cow, I threw my body into her like a hockey player throwing a body block. Instead of knocking her to the ground as hoped, I was catapulted into the air, landing with a thud more than twenty yards toward my patrol car. The pain and aches of that fall were eclipsed by my mounting anger for the cow.

Between the trampling of my patrol car, chasing the cow down crowded streets, being hurled like a rag-doll, and being covered in bloody nostril foam, I was beyond angry—I was filled with white-hot rage. I no longer had a plan, not even a bad one. The cow had clearly won our dim-witted chess game, my only move now was hoping she would get tired and simply stop.

Storming out of the apartment complex, the cow stampeded toward a freeway access road. I gave chase, needing to reach her before she made it to the freeway, but I didn't have a clue how to stop her. The fear of her getting onto the freeway ran so deep in my brain that multiple slaps to the back of my head went unnoticed. It wasn't until a half dozen hits before I realized someone was striking the back of my head. I turned and found myself staring at an honest-to-goodness cowboy with a lasso rope.

This real life, chaps-wearing cowboy yelled for me to get out of his way, using repeated lasso strikes to the back of my head. I gladly complied. My cavalry had arrived, so I got out of the cowboy's way, allowing him to lasso the beast with the greatest of ease. The noose dropped around the cow's neck and we both held onto the rope, bringing the creature to a stop. We ran up to the cow, and the cowboy tied her back legs, allowing us to take her to the ground. I assisted the cowboy by holding the cow down while he continued to tie all her legs together, immobilizing her.

Of course, after chasing a cow over hill and dale, it was a real cowboy that saved the day.

The cowboy's takedown was exactly how I envisioned my plan working in the apartment complex, flawed execution withstanding. Not long afterward, the County Livestock representative arrived and the three of us untied the cow, leading her into the cattle truck without a hitch.

While the cowboy and I were waiting for the cattle truck to arrive, he provided me with the backstory to my cow nightmare. The cowboy was driving to Tucson to deliver cattle to a rodeo, but in Phoenix he got in a traffic accident on the freeway. His semi-truck jackknifed, breaking the cargo doors that secured his cattle. Two cows got loose on the freeway, but he quickly got one back inside the cattle truck. He lost sight of the second cow, until the State Troopers' lights and sirens directed his attention to me.

Twist

It is standard protocol to inform the radio dispatcher when the emergency is "Code 4," which means the situation is under control. The "Code 4" should succinctly explain how the situation is resolved, such as, "Code 4, the suspect is under arrest." At the end of my ordeal, I advised, "Code 4, cow in custody." Upon returning to the precinct, I got into far more trouble for making a silly joke over the radio about the cow's arrest than I did for my damaged police car.

CHAPTER 9

Cheek-Filet

A SKIRMISH at an outlaw biker bar can be a cop's worst nightmare, cramming a bunch of opposing gang members in a small room with an unlimited supply of alcohol–what could possibly go wrong? Thankfully, there are only a few troublesome biker bars in the city of Phoenix, and none were in my beat. That's not to say, I never dealt with them outside my beat, I did. One night, I found myself in the middle of a violent barroom brawl at one such outlaw biker bar.

The Library Bar was a notorious biker bar, with a name more befitting to beer-sipping bookworms. It just goes to show, "you can't judge a book by its cover." The bar catered to a wide variety of different outlaw biker gangs. At that time, in 1987, the two major biker gangs in Phoenix were the Hells Angels and the Dirty Dozen. A truce between gang leaders kept the peace for the most part, but the treaty was broken on a regular basis with drunken fights at this biker-friendly bar.

Inevitably, the moment someone loses the fight, that same person incorrectly believes they are now a victim of an assault. Since most of these fights are mutually agreed upon, the police refer to both fighters as "mutual combatants." This status counters either fighter from trying to claim they were a victim of an assault upon their loss, as both were the aggressors and mutually to blame for the fight. The only victim of a mutual fight is the business establishment and patrons, whose peace may have been disturbed while in a bar with a well-earned reputation for such fights.

Its location along a minor side road in a residential area allowed it to operate cop-free for many years. We knew about the bar's existence, but were typically too busy going to one radio call after another to pay it much attention. Any free time to patrol, most cops drove on the major streets, where most of the problems occur. Therefore the bar's secluded location kept it unnoticed by the understaffed, overworked police. The only time we really rode to the bar was when a citizen in the neighborhood called about drunken patrons passed out in their lawns, broken car windows on the residential streets, and other disorderly conduct by the criminal clientele.

On a busy Saturday night, my partner and I, whose large, grizzly appearance earned him the nickname "Wookie" answered up for one such disturbance call at the bar. An anonymous caller described two disruptive bikers fighting in the parking lot. By law, the bar's management is required to call the police upon any disturbance, but not surprisingly, calls for police assistance rarely came from the bar's employees. This call probably came from one of the neighbors walking by and seeing the fight.

Rolling slowly into the bar's parking area to ensure we weren't driving into an ambush, we saw two guys standing next to the bar's front door, drunkenly yelling at each other until they saw us. They were dressed in typical biker apparel; black leather vests with their respective gang patch, black t-shirts underneath with anti-society slogans printed on the front. Looking disheveled, drunk, and screaming at each other just outside the front door, they were likely the fighters from the call.

The winner of the fight immediately went back into the bar, leaving us with the loser walking toward us. In most cases, the winners of these mutual fights are happy and in no need of the police. It's the loser who is sad, usually injured or bleeding, wanting to tell police their story of woe. However, this loser walked toward us sporting a bizarre half-grin on his bloody face.

"Mr. Happy," obviously inebriated, stumbled toward our patrol car, frantically waving his arms thinking he needed to wave us down even though he was the only person outside the bar and we were driving right toward him. His odd grin began looking more amiss the closer he got to our car.

Parking a few yards from "Mr. Happy," we got out of our patrol car to hear his pain-filled screams through a Cheshire cat smile. His creepy clown-like grin was so unsettling, my partner mused, "What the hell is he smiling about?"

At that instant, I realized "Mr. Happy" wasn't sporting a smile, but rather he was missing a chunk of his cheek. His wound resembled a cheek filet, a dangling flap of skin exposing his upper and lower teeth, creating the wicked, grim grin. We could see inside the entire left portion of his closed mouth, his teeth exposed through the gaping flap of cheek, which dangled loosely below his chin. The painfully surreal sight was reminiscent of the medical model in a doctor's office, which displays facial muscles and teeth.

While talking with "Mr. Happy," the other half of the fight happened to come back outside, and seemed surprised by our presence in the middle of the parking lot. "Wookie" went to detain him and learn more about the fight, as I got stuck with "Mr. Happy," as he angrily and excitedly told me about the fight, with his dangling cheek flap dancing wildly with each spoken syllable. As he gave his account of the fight, I became mesmerized by the otherwise concealed movements of his tongue working in concert with his teeth. Even in his intoxicated state, he busted me several times for my inattention, as I gazed in horrified awe at the inner-mechanics of his mouth.

After breaking my trance and focusing on his words, I learned the fight erupted over whose turn it was at the pool table. The argument quickly escalated into a fistfight, leading the bouncers to kick them both out of the bar. As "Mr. Happy" was walking to his car, he heard the other fighter yell something. As he turned something struck him in the mouth. I learned from Wookie's" interview that the other fighter threw a beer bottle as he yelled, and that's what struck "Mr. Happy" in the face, slicing his cheek open and shattering his jaw.

Because he was so drunk, he didn't realize his cheek had been sliced wide open until I brought it to his attention. He screamed after placing his finger inside the open wound of his closed mouth, touching his tongue. I'm not sure which was more impressive: watching him touch his tongue through the gaping hole, or seeing his tongue venture out the same wound while he was screaming.

An ambulance had arrived for "Mr. Happy" and we stood watching two paramedics working to patch the outside of his cheek with gauze and tape, as they instructed their patient to stop talking with his now medically diagnosed broken jaw. "Mr. Happy" kept talking excitedly about the other fighter against medical advice, and would probably have continued the trash-talking until his jaw was wired shut.

The paramedics eventually got "Mr. Happy" lying face up on the gurney, as they wrapped cold compress bags around his jaw. The non-stop chatter of the patient suddenly became gurgling sounds, as he started swallowing the loose cheek flap inside his mouth as he talked. To remedy this, the paramedics laid him on his injured side, and got the cheek flap to rest downward against the covered gauze. They then loaded him onto the ambulance and one paramedic drove, and the other stayed in the back with "Mr. Happy" pleading with him to stop talking while transporting him to the hospital.

I was no longer stuck baby-sitting our potentially violent victim around the paramedics and could join "Wookie" with the other fighter. The suspect admitted to throwing a bottle at "Mr. Happy," unaware that his throw was right on target. Upon seeing the police, he went back inside the bar and was stopped by a bouncer, who let the suspect remain after learning police were outside. The suspect sat back down at his table of biker friends, and later word got around that "Mr. Happy" had been decked by a thrown beer bottle. After learning that he threw the perfect "pitch," he bragged about his baseball-throwing prowess, boasting that he was as good as "Nolan Ryan." The news of his jaw-slicing pitch landed him applause from his biker friends, and condemnation from "Mr. Happy's" biker friends.

We arrested the suspect, "Nolan Ryan," for turning the initial mutual combat into a felony aggravated assault when he struck "Mr.

Happy" with the beer bottle. The fight was well over after bouncers threw both subjects out of the bar (the same bar employees that were letting them both drive away drunk), when "Nolan Ryan" became an aggressor, severely injuring "Mr. Happy" with a beer bottle as a weapon.

"Nolan Ryan" was placed in the backseat of our patrol car, while still laughing about his perfect throw. "Wookie" went inside the bar to obtain a few quick witness interviews from the respective biased friends. I remained in the patrol car with "Nolan Ryan" and prepared the booking paperwork.

I completed most of the paperwork, as "Nolan Ryan" passed out in the back seat. "Wookie" had been in the bar for about twenty minutes when I heard him yelling for help on the police radio. A large fight had erupted in the bar, and my partner was in distress. Dropping everything, I tried running into the bar but initially couldn't get inside, due to the mass exodus of patrons fleeing from the ugly barroom brawl—which is saying a lot considering it was hardened criminal bikers running away.

Unknown to "Wookie" and me, the biker patronage inside the bar had split down gang lines, each choosing the side of their respective biker friend. Both gangs were enraged over their perceived "unfair" outcome; half the crowd became angry at "Nolan Ryan's" arrest, the other half at "Mr. Happy's" facial disfigurement.

"Wookie" never saw how it started, but suddenly everyone in the bar was hitting each other. My partner was finishing his last interview when the barroom brawl broke out, and they weren't just hitting each other with their fists. Every pool stick was quickly commandeered as weapons, glass mugs were thrown with abandonment, and broken chair parts were used as make-shift clubs.

As I forced myself past the wave of bodies, "sucker punches" landed all over my upper body and face from the departing biker patrons. I weaved through the crowd like a trout swimming upstream in a rowdy river of bikers, finally making it past the long hallway into the bar, only to find "Wookie" fighting to hand-cuff a combative subject.

I made my way to Wookie, grabbing the combative subject's left arm. Placing an arm-bar hold on the unruly biker, I wanted to force him to the floor. With my high school wrestling skills, it was easier for me to control someone if I got them on the ground. But the pain compliant technique, a staple in my take-down arsenal, wasn't working on this biker. In fact, he withstood the pain and remained standing as I continued to pull on the arm bar to bring him to the floor. But to no avail, as much as I manipulated his arm into an unnatural and painful manner, he wouldn't comply, maintaining his stance in what I assumed was defiance.

What I didn't know was that as I pulled the biker's arm downward to the floor, "Wookie" was pulling him upward against the wall. Pulling in opposite directions with extreme pressure, we were working against each other. Realizing our tug-of-war on the man, we immediately released our grips and the pretzel biker dropped to the floor with a loud thud.

Thankfully, the biker didn't sustain any major injuries and was surprisingly very cooperative after that. Prior to my arrival, the biker sucker punched "Wookie" as he tried to break up one of the many other fights. "Wookie" arrested the biker for aggravated assault to a police officer and other disorderly conduct charges.

Eventually, additional police officers arrived answering "Wookie's" radio call for help. In all, there were more than a dozen arrests ranging from fighting to damaging the bar. Thirty or more patrons were involved in the fracas and twice that amount struck me upon their quick departure. I had more bruises than the battered "Wookie."

The damage would amount to tens of thousands of dollars: broken tables, splintered chairs and pool sticks, shattered glass windows, felt ripped from pool tables, and medical bills for the security staff and employees. As I was looking around at all that damage caused by the melee, a sudden gut-wrenching feeling overcame me. I left "Nolan Ryan" unattended in our patrol car.

Racing outside to check on my prisoner, my worst fear was realized. "Nolan Ryan" was not in the patrol car. Upon hearing "Wookie's" radio broadcast requesting help, I had jumped out of the car and without thinking, I left it unlocked, and the prisoner unattended. That sinking feeling in my gut became more excruciating with the realization I would need to alert my entire chain of command of the escaped prisoner.

I would be responsible for any crime the escaped prisoner committed while "on the lam." As I stood next to my empty patrol car, watching my career flash before my eyes, "Nolan Ryan" walked up to me from a dark area behind the car. He simply said, "Thanks" and opened the car's back door, and set himself inside, promptly shutting the door behind him. It was like watching Otis (the friendly town drunk from the *Andy Griffith Show)* letting himself back into his jail cell after using the restroom, and that is exactly what "Nolan Ryan" did as well.

To my surprise, "Nolan Ryan" explained that after waking up, he had a strong urge to urinate. He repeatedly asked my permission to "take a piss," having no idea that I had already left him alone in the patrol car. The back door finally opened and he left to take a piss. I suspect one of his biker friends fleeing the fight opened the door, but "Nolan Ryan" assumed I let him out to urinate. The timing could not have been better for one of the bikers to let him out at the same time "Nolan Ryan" was asking me for a restroom break. My reputation and career remained intact.

"Nolan Ryan" only spent a few days in jail, as a sober "Mr. Happy" refused to prosecute, citing a biker's code of getting revenge as a gang, and not by police. "Mr. Happy's" notable scar probably gave him fodder to fabricate a better tale by which to impress the biker-ladies. And for the two rival biker gangs; a few years later the truce was lifted, sparking many violent altercations. The Hells Angels gang ultimately won out, appropriating those Dirty Dozen members willing to wear a new gang patch on their leather vests.

Twist

The next day, Wookie, myself and various officers worked in conjunction sorting out the numerous violations of liquor laws, zoning laws, and fire codes at the Library Bar. We returned with a thick stack of citations based on the collective observations by all the police officers present during the previous night's barroom brawl and clean-up. Several neighborhood activists were trying for years to close the Library Bar due to the many problems with outlaw biker gangs and their criminal activity in the area. As a result of our post brawl liquor violation enforcement, the bar remained closed due to management's inability to pay on a litany of serious and expensive criminal citations. Ultimately, the bar burned to the ground after being left abandoned for several years. I received lots of punches at the Library Bar's last brawl, but the police and community ended up landing the last knock-out punch.

CHAPTER 10

Old Man and Batboy

MOST of the twisted tales involve my experience working in law enforcement as a patrol officer or detective in Phoenix, Arizona. However, this tale happened when I was off-duty and in the daytime performing a weekly, mundane task—grocery shopping. In 1989, I lived in the city of Peoria, a small community outside Phoenix, and had just paid for my groceries, wheeling my cart out of the store. As I made my way over to the parking lot, with my pop bottles rattling as the wheels of my cart dropped off the concrete walkway and down onto the pavement, I suddenly heard the squeal of tires.

Looking up from my cart, I saw two cars speeding into the grocery store parking lot. Even on days off, police officers go into "cop mode," regardless if they are unarmed or have no means to radio for help. I immediately began to assess the situation because, in some cases, just being a good witness is all you can do.

I watched intently as the two cars zigzagged into the store's parking lot. A newer light colored Cadillac sedan was chasing a red, older, beat-up sports car at wildly fast speeds for a parking lot. Had I not stopped where I did, the cars would have run me over, missing me by a few feet, while driving quickly past the front of the store and turning into the main parking area.

Two teenage boys in the sports car being chased, abruptly parked in a space in the center of the lot. The pursuing Cadillac immediately stopped in the same area, and to my surprise, was driven by an elderly man with an elderly woman in the passenger seat.

The elderly man sprang aggressively from the Cadillac, yelling angrily toward the teenagers' car. I was too far away to hear the elderly man's words, but his loud, harsh tone made his intent clear, while he briskly hustled toward the sports car. Though he looked 70-plus, he had a large, fit frame, and moved faster than a man half his age. His long intense strides toward the teens implied genuine conviction; he intended to do the teenagers harm.

I propped my shopping cart against one of the store's front pillars, and began running toward the older man, hoping to intervene before he reached the teenagers' car. The teen driver stepped out of his car in a defiant stance aimed at the elderly man. The teen may have had the advantage of youth over the elderly man, but his small frame and slender build made him the definite underdog on any fight card. Even though the teen stared the old man down, I could tell he was seconds away from shitting his pants as he clung close to his open car door watching the fast-approaching elderly man.

The old man's face was creased with anger as he quickened his pace toward the defiant teen, who then reached behind the driver's seat, pulling out a large wooden baseball bat. This emotionally-charged conflict just escalated to lethal proportions. One strike of the wooden bat to the old man's skull could be fatal. I ran full-out-sprint toward the cars.

Since I was off-duty, I had no protective vest, chemical spray, baton, handcuffs, handgun, or even a police radio to help me (this was the era when no one had a cell phone). I only had a badge, but nothing to protect me from an armed combatant. Police never want citizens to place themselves in harm's way, but I had to intervene to prevent a serious tragedy—lives were at risk.

The teenager squeezed the bottom of the bat handle with a two-handed death grip, looking ready to "hit the long ball." With the top of the bat hoisted well above his head, focusing on the oncoming old man, moving the bat back and forth, he looked like a home run king waiting eagerly for that perfect pitch, ready to unload at just the right second. But then the teen started walking backwards away from his car, still looking at the old man. His back-pedaling stride became faster as the elderly man kept his direct war-path toward the scared teen.

The bat-wielding teen never looked behind him in the direction that he was going, but rather, he kept his gaze at the aggressively approaching elderly man. My focus that started on the aggressive elderly man, then changed to the teen after he introduced a wooden bat to the fistfight, and then was diverted back again to the old man when I saw a large hunting knife in a leather sheath on his belt; their feud quickly escalating into a potential bat-knife fight.

I made my presence known by yelling forcefully, "Police!", hoping to take control and successfully stop the two from inflicting serious injury on each other. I really should have given more thought to my lack of protection from either the bat or the knife. Regardless, I placed myself in the middle of a potentially deadly conflict between "Old Man and Batboy."

"Batboy" initially ignored my commands, continuing his backward retreat, swinging the bat in a circular motion over his head. "Old Man" stopped spewing unintelligible venom at his nemesis, surprised at my appearance, but kept walking toward the teen. Holding my police badge high in the air, again I yelled "Police, stop!" This second official identification worked, if only momentarily, as both halted their movements. Shocked by the presence of a plain clothes police officer, they stood still in the parking lot, about 50-yards from the store's entrance. The three of us looked back and forth at one another, like the gunslingers in the classic gunfight scene in *The Good, the Bad, and the Ugly*, but more appropriately "*The Old Man, the Batboy, and the Unarmed Cop.*"

"Old Man" looked at my badge, revealing an expression that I could only describe as shame. His irate demeanor melted into sadness, and he told me, "Yes, sir." "Batboy" on the other hand, showed no signs of repentance, only momentarily stopping and lowering the bat to his side. I walked up to the elderly man, taking possession of his knife without any resistance. He lowered his head, nodding, relaying an apology for his conduct, after placing the knife in my back pocket, I turned my attention to the bat-wielding teen.

"Batboy" watched, standing ten-feet away from me, but once my attention focused on him, he returned to his bat-swinging ways. I slowly walked toward the teen, matching him step for step, as he resumed his backward walk toward the store. I repeatedly told the teen to drop the bat. Ignoring my commands, he continued swinging the bat aggressively in the air. Using a calm voice, not to escalate the situation, I again told him to drop the bat. I didn't want to be aggressive, since he was the one being chased, nor did I want him to charge at me and connect with a swing of his bat. Yet, I needed the teen to drop the bat as he continued marching backward toward the store.

Surprisingly, "Batboy" persisted in ignoring my insistent, albeit calm, commands. He kept the bat swinging and now directed it at me. With my police badge in hand, as if it were a magical protective oracle, and identifying myself as a police officer, I repeatedly ordered "Batboy" to drop the bat. Still refusing to obey my increasingly tense commands, he continued his backward walk, getting closer to the store with every step.

I matched him step for step, my mind racing because, I couldn't allow him to enter the store while armed with a bat. His behavior was now diametrically opposed from the start of the confrontation with the old man. Instead of behaving defensively and being pursued, he was now no longer being threatened, but still swinging the bat aggressively, making him a possible threat to the patrons inside the store. And, I still didn't know what started the chase. "Batboy" may have been the catalyst for this entire event, having committed some horrible act, prompting "Old Man's" rage, especially considering his compliant and remorseful demeanor when I identified myself as a cop.

As all these possibilities swirled in my head, I knew two things: first, "Batboy" refused to obey my lawful commands, and secondly, his closeness to the store reached "Rubicon," prompting me to yell, "Drop the fucking bat, before I take it, and turn you into a popsicle!" I apparently conveyed genuine intent, "Batboy" dropped the bat to his feet, looking more scared than when he was dealing with the "Old Man."

While taking possession of the bat, I told Batboy to sit down on the sidewalk next to store, and asked for the "*Reader's Digest*" version of the story. "Batboy" simply replied, "Reader's what?" After rephrasing my question, I learned he and his teen friend were driving on the freeway when they encountered the elderly couple's car in the next lane. He began making stupid facial gestures at the elderly woman, for what he said were "unknown" reasons, causing the ensuing feud.

I asked the teen to reenact the gesture, prompting the teen to mimic an act of oral sex. The teen's closed hand moving briskly back and forth toward his open mouth, while pressing his tongue hard against the inside of his cheek, and directing this simulation of giving a blow-job at the elderly woman. This insult enraged the elderly driver, who then initiated the subsequent car chase. The elderly man chased the teen on the interstate for several miles before exiting onto a major road in Phoenix, making their way to the city of Peoria, where he and the teen entered in this shopping center.

After obtaining "Batboy's" account, I returned to the elderly man, still standing in the location where I left him. He, again, apologized for his actions against the teen and asked forgiveness for acting violently in front of a police officer. I asked why he became so angry over a stupid juvenile act. Tears started streaming down his face as he explained to me that his wife was dying of cancer. They were driving home after one of many chemotherapy sessions when the teen made the demeaning gesture. He admitted to overreacting due to his heartache and frustration with a disease killing his wife of 50 years.

I could see that the "Old Man" was a respectful gentleman, who acted out, admittedly inappropriately, because of this insulting gesture toward his loving wife, who was battling an insidious disease. This is something "Batboy" couldn't understand or appreciate, at least not in his youth. Having lost my own grandmother to cancer, and later watching helplessly as several other family members would also suffer and succumb to this ravaging disease, I had a lot of empathy for him and his wife.

I expressed my sorrow to the gentleman for his wife's condition and I explained that though his actions were aggressive, it didn't become physical, and no one got hurt. I decided to chalk-up the incident as an important life lesson for both "Old Man" and "Batboy." After escorting the elderly gentleman back to his car, placing his knife in the trunk, I asked him to consider how the confrontation might have ended if I hadn't showed up. Painting him a picture, I described him seriously hurting the teen, thus getting arrested, or getting hurt himself. Either scenario would have left his wife without a much-needed care provider. Both he and his lovely wife thanked me, crying as they drove away.

I returned to "Batboy," who was angry seeing "Old Man" driving away. The teen wanted to prosecute the older man, so I explained that there were two separate criminal acts committed in my presence. The less serious misdemeanor crime when the "Old Man" chased him, and the other far more serious felony crime when he repeatedly swung a baseball bat at a police officer. My displaying a police badge and identifying myself as a cop made such a charge permissible even though I was off-duty. Further, the "Old Man's" crime at the most would earn him probation and a fine, but "Batboy's" felony crime could net him a lengthy prison sentence. "Batboy" changed his position and now appreciated my discretion, embracing the life lesson.

Twist

"Old Man" and "Batboy" were long gone, and an hour had passed while I talked with the grocery store manager. Upon returning to my grocery cart (with melted ice cream), I heard more squealing tires. This time six police cars rushed into the parking lot, responding to a call of a subject threatening with a baseball bat. Who says there is never a cop around when you need one?

CHAPTER 11

Devil Driver and the Abortion Cop

S OME twisted tales start out as mundane radio calls that morph into mayhem. Others are ugly from the start, due to someone's depraved actions. Many of the dilemmas are the result of self-inflicted stupidity, or the result of people unable to reconcile with their own moronic decisions, blaming others rather than taking responsibility. Too often these "blame someone else" types use police officers as "scapegoats," claiming the cops mishandled the situation.

But the culpability of this tale's stupidity rests solely upon me. The toxic ingredients for this twisted concoction; an intoxicated woman, her insane boyfriend, and a poorly-spoken police officer. It doesn't matter how long you've been on the beat, how much crime tape you've strung up, or how many arrests you've made. Sometimes the words just don't come out right, and I was about to have one of those nights.

My partner Bill and I were riding together for the entire month, alternating the driving duties, with Bill at the wheel for tonight's shift. Bill and I loved riding as partners, as we had completely different police styles, which complimented each other.

When I was at the helm, we primarily answered up for radio calls all night long, responding to family fight calls, burglaries, alarms, or just checking out the home of a woman living alone who feared

71

someone was prowling around her back yard. My passion to help citizens drove our workload, and we took one radio call after another.

Bill on the other hand, had a real knack for locating bad guys with traffic stops. He preferred finding suspicious vehicles, observing traffic violations, enjoying the action and arrests that came from finding drivers with criminal warrants, hauling drugs, or driving intoxicated. Tonight, Bill observed a little-known Arizona traffic law: vehicle weaving in one lane of traffic.

Most states have weaving laws, but those drivers must weave in and out of their lane. Our one-lane weaving law violation happens when distracted drivers weave slightly while changing a radio station, or talking on the phone. With the current saturation of cell phones, these single-lane weaving violations happen constantly.

Early in our shift, Bill spotted a suspicious-looking vehicle weaving constantly in its own lane. We profiled the car as being suspicious based on the poor condition of the automobile; multiple dents, amateurish half-done paint job and red duct tape covering the broken tail lights. The car's "Rent-a-Dent" appearance is consistent with the type of cars owned by criminals. It's been my experience, and most cops if you ask them, that many criminals are, at their core, lazy. Not motivated to get a job, they would rather steal to make a living. This same laziness also translates into how they maintain and care for their cars. They don't. The car Bill was following would soon prove our suspicious-car theory correct.

Bill observed the initial weaving, but looked for additional traffic code violations before deciding to flip on our lights and stop the car. We wanted another traffic violation, because most drivers have perfectly reasonable excuses for weaving. Though the driver clearly knew of our presence, the driver continued using turn signals to change lanes to avoid us.

The driver increased his speed after we mirrored all his lane changes, then abruptly turned off the main road into a housing development, trying to avoid us. We had enough to make the traffic stop, so Bill finally turned on his overhead red-and-blue lights before pulling off the main road into the dark neighborhood. The driver in the suspicious car refused to stop, maneuvering erratically.

Trying to evade us, the driver made unsafe turns, speeding around street corners. The driver then turned off the headlights, making following him difficult, but not impossible. We followed the sporadic red flashes of his brake lights, tracking the car through numerous winding, dark streets. The car continued without headlights, increasing its speed, risking injury to people and damage to property in the dark neighborhood.

Because the police are responsible for the public's safety, increasing our speed to keep up with the evading car was contrary to that public trust. We couldn't match the speed of the evading car, so we eventually lost sight of his flashing brake lights and, ultimately, lost sight of the car. Driving out of the neighborhood onto the Main Street, we hoped the suspicious car might double back once the driver thought he lost us in the neighborhood. Bill drove slowly on the main road, as we watched all the side streets in hopes of seeing the car.

The streets were empty at this late hour of the night, so it was easy to catch a movement out the corner of my eye, spotting a dark car coasting to a stop in a city park. It was only the motion of the car that drew my attention, having no headlights or taillights, and we watched until it finally came to a full stop. Excelling in police-evading tactics, the driver must have used the hand break to achieve such a stop. It quickly became clear to Bill and I, this was not this driver's first rodeo with law enforcement, having honed their cop-avoidance driving skills to an elevated art form.

Bill quickly drove into the city park parking lot, and behind the suspicious car, blocking them into their parking space. The vehicle matched our suspicious car, as we could see it after lighting it up with our powerful spotlight and overhead high beam "take-down" lights. Like vampires convulsing to the deadly sunlight, the two people inside the car reacted franticly to the direct, saturating beams of light.

Not knowing what they may have done to prompt such reckless driving, we cautiously got out of our patrol car, as Bill walked toward the driver's side, instructing the male driver to stop moving. I approached the passenger side, keeping an eye on the female passenger, ensuring she did not pose a threat by reaching for a weapon in the glove compartment. The ignition key had already been removed prior to our approach, more than likely an attempt by the driver to make it seem he had not been driving.

The plan was to instruct the driver to get out of the car, and walk him back to the front of our car to talk with him. Leaving the passenger behind, the bright lights would continue blinding her, giving us the upper hand in case she had a gun or other threat while we were distracted dealing with the driver. But none of that was going to happen, the plan was about to fall apart.

Bill instructed the driver to get out of the car, while my focus remained on the female, telling her not to move. The female passenger sat quietly, intensely watching the driver, as if waiting for something, maybe a cue from him. She seemed oblivious to my presence standing outside her car door, as I kept an eye on both her and the drunk-acting driver. The driver's head was in constant motion, like a bobble-head with long, ratty hair, appearing to have gone months without a combing, let alone a shampoo. His scraggly goatee added a perfect fashion statement, if the intent was to look like Satan.

"Satan" spoke to Bill in a language all his own, like speaking in tongues, spewing gibberish in response to Bill's instructions to exit the car. The female passenger remained quiet. She looked similarly grungy, from what I could see, as her head was always turned away maintaining her sole focus on "Satan," never looking back at me.

Bill's repeated instructions for the driver to step out of the car went ignored. "Satan" neither reacted or acknowledged Bill's repeated orders to get out of the car. Bill let me know his intent was to physically pull "Satan" out of the car, as it became apparent "Satan" had no intention in complying to any order. I went to the driver side and helped Bill arrest the driver, extracting "Satan" out of the car, prying his death grip loose from around the steering wheel.

Once we got him out of the car, the female passenger began screaming, as if in pain, at the top of her lungs. Her loud diversion an obvious attempt to aid Satan in some manner. Bill and I stayed on task, placing Satan in handcuffs after a brief scuffle. "Satan" fought hard against his arrest, spitting, kicking and scratching through the entire extraction process.

We walked the handcuffed "Satan" to our patrol car, as the woman's scream intensified to a blood-curdling level. Once we got the combative "Satan" into our back seat, I returned to check on the screaming banshee. To my surprise, I discovered she was not only intoxicated but also very pregnant. Initially, I assumed her scream was a simple, diversionary tactic, but now she held her protruding belly, screaming, "the baby is coming!" I tried calming her, still not sure the veracity of her alleged pain, telling her I would call for medics to help her.

"Satan" continued causing problems, kicking and spitting at Bill through the metal screen cage in the rear seat compartment of our patrol car. His hands cuffed behind his back, but his feet and mouth still wreaking havoc on a none-too-happy Bill. I left the screaming woman, returned to our patrol car, and helped pull "Satan's" shirt over his head, negating the effectiveness of his prolific spitting, but couldn't help my partner from stopping "Satan's" pounding kicks to the interior door and window.

My nerves were also on edge, dealing with the woman's ear-piercing screams, and hearing Bill's futile attempts stopping "Satan's" violent and loud antics. Adding to my frustration, was trying to find a lull in her wailing so I could be heard on the police radio to request paramedics and verify or denounce a health problem with her pregnancy.

Her screeching reached a new high, as she screamed that she was "losing" her baby. The loud screams no longer shrieking sounds, but relaying intelligible words, repeatedly announcing that she was losing her baby. She never said the word *miscarriage*, but "Satan's Bride" was clearly conveying an imminent loss of her unborn child. I still hadn't requested paramedics or got an additional officer to help Bill with the kicking "Satan." She paused to take a long breath, I had a silent moment. Jumping at the chance, I grabbed the radio to make my request.

I first advised the radio operator we needed another patrol officer to assist with a combative prisoner. When I said the word "*prisoner,*" "Satan's Baby-Momma" began bellowing at the loudest level yet. Her ear-piercing shriek struck simultaneously with my request for medical assistance. The combination of my tension, anger, frustration, and eardrum-deafening pain confused my brain. Instead of saying the appropriate word, "miscarriage," I said, "I need paramedics to assist me with an *abortion.*" As soon as I said the word, the dispatcher's quick and confused reply was, "Are we allowed to do that?" The dispatcher had no difficulty obtaining an additional officer to assist, as many officers wanted to see the "Devil Driver and the Abortion-Cop."

More than ten officers responded to have some fun at my expense. Miraculously, the screaming passenger recovered instantly from her painful miscarriage upon the officers' arrival. Her screams went silent, getting out of the car and walking away. We had no legal power to restrain her, and frankly, I was glad to see her leave. Without saying a word, she calmly walked away in a painless manner, confirming the obvious; her screams of agonizing pain were nothing more than a simple diversion.

She was still in the park, walking away, when the paramedics arrived. Running behind her, the paramedics advised they wanted to check on her medical condition, she said nothing, until the well-meaning medics placed hands on her to check her welfare. She screamed a barrage of expletives, making the life-savers release their hold and allow the not-so-nice-lady to leave.

"Satan's Bride" knew any continued faking of a problem pregnancy would end up with her transportation to the hospital. Even in her intoxicated state, she knew that her subterfuge had failed, and she wanted to leave. In fairness, her screaming frenzy failed only in her mission to provide "Satan's" release, but was effective enough in rattling a cop into verbal-palsy.

Bill and I began the short drive to the police station, which felt like forever, due to "Satan's" antics of urinating, repeated kicking, and loud rants from the back seat. His gift for gargoyle-babble rose exponentially along the way, taunting us with an unending series of plague-inflicting incantations. His animated actions and uncanny likeness to the Lord of Darkness aroused a crowd of curious cop onlookers when we arrived to process "Satan" for DUI.

"Satan" registered such a high blood alcohol content, BAC .35, (over four times the legal limit in Arizona) it should have killed the devil himself. Based on his blood alcohol content, we were forced to take "Satan" to the hospital for a medical release before the jail would accept him.

What usually takes several hours to receive a medical release went unprecedently fast. The hospital staff gladly expedited our departure, based on "Satan's" continuing spitting, expletive filled curses and casting of evil spells, letting us skip to the front of the triage line. In a matter of minutes, we were out of the hospital with a medical release in hand, taking "Satan" to jail.

Twist

The DUI trial initially went badly for us, looking as if "Satan" would be found "not guilty." The legal issue was Bill and I couldn't positively identify the intoxicated "Satan" as the same driver we initially observed weaving, speeding, and driving erratically without headlights. The defense attorney did a brilliant job showing we could only place the drunk "Satan" in a parked car in the city park, not with the evasive and erratic driving seen earlier. This would establish reasonable doubt for a jury, giving cause to acquit "Satan", since it is not against the law to be intoxicated in a parked car with no key in the ignition.

The jury deliberated for a mere thirty minutes, returning a unanimous "guilty" verdict. "Satan" had not bathed, looking and smelling even worse than the night we dealt with him. He also slept at the defense table during most of the trial, only awakening from his snore fest to yell, "fuck off" at me during my testimony. His multitude of angry sneers and vile mumbling was not lost on the jurists. The jury panel's "guilty" verdict was largely due to "Satan" presenting his true nature at trial. All-in-all, justice was served.

CHAPTER 12

Sheer Sheep Slaughter

I CAME to realize I had a self-destructive tendency as a cop: I responded way too often to calls by myself, and more importantly, I clearly didn't give barnyard animals their due respect.

A farmer called 911, informing the radio operator he needed the police due to his "sheep looking funny," causing a bewildered radio operator to reluctantly dispatch police to his small residential farm. Hearing the limited details of the call, I advised the radio dispatcher there wouldn't be a need for a backup officer. It took all my self-control to not jokingly tell the radio operator that I didn't want a back-up officer, as I was looking forward to some alone time with the sheep.

The caller's farm was in the residential heart of the city, and allowed for animal-zoned property. Not on a large parcel of land, like a dairy farm, but a small plot "grandfathered" from pre-existing zoning laws, having been originally purchased in the 1950s. At that time, the property was well outside the city limits; one-acre lots zoned for farming made sense. But the area had degraded into a low-income neighborhood, consisting of residential homes and numerous apartment complexes around the one acre farms. The neighborhood's decline was met with an increase in criminal activity, not sure if sheep-rustling was among them, but cops referred to the area as "Crack Alley."

When I met with the farmer at his barn, I quickly realized that there was more than just a funny-looking-sheep problem. The 911 telephone operator translated the message, incorrectly passing along the "funny-looking sheep" call to the police. When in fact, the farmer told the 911 operator that he heard "funny" noises in the barn, alerting him that a wild animal was attacking his sheep. He thought a coyote or other predator may have been in the barn stirring them up, but by the time he got dressed and checked, it was too late.

The scene in the red barn was like something out of a horror novel. My first observation was a dead sheep's head sticking out through a broken panel in the front of the wooden barn. I assumed the rest of her body was dangling down on the inside of the barn. The sheepish-looking head looked straight down at me from a height of over six feet, her eyes were bulging outward from the orbital sockets, like plastic doll eyes. Her mouth was wide open, as if screaming at the time of her death, with a protruding swollen tongue sticking six inches outward from her open, oddly crooked jaw.

Inside the barn, her back hooves swung several feet above the ground, having jumped head first through the barn's wall, trying to escape the massacre. All four of her limbs were in intact, dangling downward toward the ground. A massive chunk of flesh had been eaten away from her hindquarters, her stomach chewed opened with the entrails ripped out, unraveling as she hung suspended. Pieces of her flesh were strewn about on the ground below her body.

The walls of the barn were constructed with two-inch thick wood slats. For the sheep to hit the inside of the barn with such incredible force to break through the wood panel, the tremendous trauma to her skull impacting the wood could have killed her, if not breaking her neck dangling from her wooden noose. She could have also died from strangulation, as her airway could have been forced shut from her full weight pressed on her neck stuck through the broken wood slat. If none of these contributed to her death, she could have died from being eaten or disemboweled. No matter the exact cause of her death, it was truly a horrific and sad sight.

The barn door was left wide open, apparently, murderers never close the barn doors behind them. Throughout the floor lay massive amounts of blood and sheep body parts, evidence of the carnage that occurred. All the sheep had missing patches of skin and wool, having been torn apart by a predator, or a pack of them. The barns once faded red interior walls were now partially stained dark red in blood. The mess made the head count difficult, but all ten sheep were eventually accounted for, and all dead.

This would be a hard crime scene to reconstruct. The most seasoned homicide investigator would have a tough time figuring out exactly which sheep died first and where, and more importantly how they were killed. I feared that whatever had done this could also devour a child or even an adult. The brutality of the barn massacre was so overwhelming, I had to collect my thoughts and start with the basics, like looking for clues to the direction of the fleeing murderous beast(s).

I observed what looked like two separate sets of bloody paw-prints leading out of the barn. The tracks went past the farmer's home, continuing down the block along the sidewalk to a newer residential neighborhood about a mile away. I followed the bloody trail into a housing development. The trail led directly to the side fence of a modest, brown, one-story home. The size of the considerable paw print seemed larger than that of a common family dog. Such a dog would have to be enormous to have such a large paw print.

I knocked on the door and a young lady opened the door, surprised by my visit. She asked the typical questions often asked during an unexpected police officer visit. I explained the reason for my visit, omitting the graphic details and simply providing a headcount of the slaughter. She eagerly wanted to cooperate, inviting me inside to prove the innocent nature of her two dogs, which she said. "wouldn't hurt a fly." She walked me out the rear arcadia glass door to the backyard. As I walked out past the back patio, I saw the two largest Rottweiler dogs I've ever seen.

The two giant Rotties were excitedly playing with each other, oblivious to my unannounced appearance. Both the woman and myself could clearly see the two pets' muzzles were soaked with blood. The shock had shown on the nice lady's face as she discovered her cuddly friends had blood not only on their faces, but crimson wet streaks on their bodies, too. Then the dogs noticed me, and ran at a full-gallop in my direction, I didn't even have time to turn back toward the house. The dogs were both on top of me in seconds.

But instead of being their next victim, I was delighted (and disgusted) that these two killers only wanted to lick me to death, with sheep-meat still wedged in their teeth. Within seconds, I was covered in bloody dog drool. It took some mighty effort for their lady owner to pull back the two fun-loving family pets.

After inspecting the yard and gates, we discovered the two carnivorous canines had somehow unlatched the side gate, returning the same way after their rampage. In fact, as I was helping the woman secure the gate with thick-gauge wire, she remarked how the family never got a pad lock, thinking who would be stupid enough to go into a backyard with such huge dogs. They never thought the dogs themselves would figure out how to lift the latch, coming and going at will.

If not for the large volume of bloody evidence, one would have a hard time believing these sweet dogs were capable of such carnage. I notified County Animal Control of the dog attack, advising the two culprits no longer posed a threat to the community. After the Animal Control officer arrived and documented the incident, he cited the owner, allowing both pets to remain with the owner after completing an inspection of the home. But the owner had to promise to purchase a padlock.

On my way out, the Animal Control officer educated me to the unique tools he uses to catch various dogs based on their specific breeds. For example; When catching a pit bull dog, he uses a long handle device with an attached noose for snaring at a distance. For Rottweilers, it's a squeaky toy.

I returned to the farmer, informing him that I'd found the friendly beasts responsible for the sheer sheep slaughter. Tonight, the farmer would be able to sleep soundly, knowing the sheep-eating dogs would not be back. Sadly, he would not be able to count his sheep to help him sleep.

Twist

Interestingly, the entire herd of sheep were only a few days away from a scheduled trip to the slaughterhouse; but their end would have been more humane than the one they encountered with the massive sheep-eating Rottweilers.

CHAPTER 13

Painful Bite

B OWLING is a fun way to spend the evening with friends, which is what my bride and I did with Jerri Hubert and her husband one night. Jerri's husband, Paul, was also a police officer at the same precinct, but on a more senior squad. As a great police officer, Paul was well aware of the strong bond between police partners and very supportive of my friendship with Jerri.

During our double-date outing, Jerri and I spent most the evening talking amongst ourselves about different radio calls that we had worked. Jerri and I never intended to leave our spouses out of the conversations, we just found ourselves talking like we did when we're riding together. By the end of the night, I was still oblivious to my wife's understandably unhappy feelings about the lack of attention.

I haven't a clue who got the best bowling score, or made the most strikes, but I recall with vivid clarity how Paul scored a great joke upon leaving. The four of us walked out of the bowling alley together, Jerri and I still talking non-stop with Paul and Coleen following closely in silence. Paul picked-up on Coleen's disapproval of my night-long banter with Jerri, and used it as perfect fodder for a prank.

Most cops have a dark sense of humor, and Paul was no exception. While walking next to Coleen, he leaned in real close and whispered, "You know they're having an affair?" Coleen impulsively screeched. Startled by the outburst, Jerri and I stopped in our tracks, turning back to look at Coleen, who immediately realized the joke when Paul began laughing hysterically.

The earsplitting sound drew attention from inside the bowling alley, it stopped most of the bowlers in mid-stride, many peering out into the parking lot to look for the cause of the loud, weird, squawking sound. Paul finally stopped laughing long enough to fill Jerri and I in on the joke. Coleen turned beat red from embarrassment, prompting even more laughs all around. Maybe related, Coleen and I never went bowling with them again.

The next twisted tale also starts out after a night of bowling. Jerri and I answered-up for a radio call of a "domestic violence" fight, which started after the couple returned from a night bowling. A male called police after his girlfriend attacked him in the home. While speaking to the 911 operator the male remained calm, explaining his female roommate assaulted him. He didn't sound upset or frantic, simply stating he needed the police to come to his home.

I've found that calm sounding 911 calls don't necessarily mean the cops will experience a calm scene, as you never know what to expect at a domestic violence incident. Family fights can initially appear to be nothing more than a verbal disagreement over a silly, trivial matter and then suddenly escalate into a life-and-death situation.

The male told the 911 operator that his platonic female roommate bit him during oral sex. While driving to the caller's home, we mused about the obvious contradiction of platonic roommates having sex. Or, perhaps they believed that oral sex wasn't actual sex. This occurred in 1989, well before the "oral sex is not sex" precedent set during the President Bill Clinton and Monica Lewinsky scandal, but maybe they were ahead of their time.

On the ride to the caller's home, Jerri and I discussed how we never heard the female's version of the fight. The 911 dispatcher never heard the female's voice in the background, as sometimes couples are still yelling at each other during the call to police. Many times, police will receive separate 911 calls from both sides of a dispute, each wanting to tell their opposing versions of the fight.

The male never made a request for paramedics and didn't answer the dispatcher's questions regarding his injury. He didn't describe the severity of the bite or its location, only that it occurred during "oral sex." We had many questions in need of answering, and soon we would arrive and learn the full nature of this disturbing and violent crime.

Arriving at the male caller's home, we were greeted at the front door by a 50-year old, balding, portly male. His calm and polite demeanor mirrored the manner he displayed during his 911 call. He thanked us for our quick response and escorted me and Jerri into the living room. The house was clean and orderly, not in a disarray like most knock-down violent domestic fights.

The portly man wasn't avoiding my questions, and appeared candid as he replied to each one. He explained how his female roommate lived with him for more than a year, but prior to tonight they hadn't engaged in any kind of sexual activity. She pays rent, and they have separate bedrooms, pointing in the direction of her bedroom.

I asked if she was currently in her bedroom, since she wasn't in the living room. Jerri and I hadn't seen her since arriving at the home, and she never called out, or made her presence known. The portly man said he last saw her walking into her bedroom, and to his knowledge hasn't left. I remained in the living room to question him further about the "biting incident," while Jerri went into the female's bedroom to do the same.

My partner and I were out of listening range from each other, so I didn't know what Jerri learned from the female roommate. In most domestic disputes, police officers try to separate the couple, or in this case the roommates. Cops like to interview the couple separately for several reasons; 1) if left together, the subjects will react angrily upon hearing the other's account, which are usually contradictory "he said-she said" statements. 2) if not separated, the couple continue to argue with each other, increasing the potential for more violence even in the cop's presence.

The down side to separating the couple is that conversely the police are also separated, which can create safety concerns for the police. Sometimes, a third police officer is requested to act as a kind of floater between the separated officers during their interviews.

The third officer acts as a backup, monitoring both sets of officers to ensure they have help in case a violent situation erupts. In our case, the portly male was extremely cooperative, he wasn't posing an immediate threat, so we felt no need to make a request for another officer.

"Mr. Portly" continued talking to me in a mild manner, but almost too relaxed, as if talking to a friend about the weather. He informed me that earlier tonight a mutual friend had asked him and his roommate to join a group of friends at a neighborhood bowling alley. They accepted the invite and "Mr. Portly" drove them to the local bowling alley. In a cool and composed manner, he described how they had fun bowling for several hours, admitting they both drank far too many beers before leaving.

At no time during the entire evening did they talk or act in a sexual manner. But once home, they walked into the house and began kissing each other. He couldn't adequately explain how the sexual activity started, and it seemed odd that their non-sexual relationship would suddenly turn sexual without at least some dialogue to initiate it. I pressed him on details to their actions that lead to the sexual activity, but he couldn't provide any, other than to say, "we ended up making out" in the kitchen.

They were standing next to the kitchen sink kissing when she kneeled on the floor to perform oral sex on him. During the "blowjob," and for reasons unknown to him, she bit down on his penis. He instinctively struck her in the face with a closed fist, which made her release her death-grip from around the shaft of his penis. Again, he couldn't give me any details as to why she would suddenly do this.

After failing to provide me with adequate details to explain what lead up to the oral sex, I began concentrating my questions about their physical positions during the sex act. It seemed unlikely to me that he could be standing over her, while she is kneeling with her face in his crotch, and could punch her in the front of her face. If bitten, such an instinctive punch more than likely would have landed on the top of her head. Pressing him on the mechanics of their oral sex act, I kept getting a picture that just didn't add up.

His story also appeared rehearsed, each time I asked for clarification he would simply repeat word for word what he had just said. I patiently listened, acting as if I believed everything he was saying, as I didn't want him to realize his story was starting to fall apart.

I asked him to show me exactly where her head was in relationship to his body during the "blow-job." He remained calm and spoke in a monotone voice, providing the same prepared verbiage, while physically staging out the sex act. He stood upright against the sink and used his hand to show that the top of her head was at his waist while she knelt at his feet. Her head was nestled in his crotch, and within seconds and without warning, she bit down on his penis.

"Mr. Portly" then simulated a closed fist strike to her face, but slipped saying he "hit her in the mouth." This was the first time he went off script saying his punch struck her in the mouth, opposed to striking her in the face. It would be impossible for him to hit her in the mouth if his penis was in her mouth. Any supposed instinctive strike couldn't have hit her in the mouth, unless it was an additional strike after she released her bite.

The adage, "The devil is in the details" is a good guide for suspect interrogations, and this was quickly turning into a calculated suspect interview. I learned early in my career, and later honed it while working detective details, always let them think you believe their story, so they feel comfortable continuing to make up lies that you can add up to discredit them. Even rehearsed lies like "Mr. Portly's" fall apart when comparing or reconstructing the story with the physical evidence. In this case, the injuries to her face would prove he didn't strike her just once.

Jerri returned to the living room with a look of dire concern on her face. She discreetly informed me that she requested paramedics, but couldn't provide any more information for fear of alerting "Mr. Portly." I later learned that when Jerri first walked into the female roommate's bedroom, she found the woman unresponsive and lying face-up on the floor. She had severe trauma to the front of her face, which resulted in massive head swelling. Her swollen face was distorted, and her head was almost the size of a watermelon; she would die without immediate medical attention.

The woman's clothes were torn in a manner consistent with a violent sexual assault. Due to her unresponsive state, Jerri couldn't learn if she consented to the sex or if she was raped. The only statements we were going to get was from "Mr. Portly", so it was more important than ever to keep him talking, hanging him with his own words.

Jerri returned to the female still lying unresponsive in the bedroom, trying her best to treat the woman's life-threatening injuries, while I continued my interview with "Mr. Portly." I downplayed my concern for his roommate's medical condition, and we left the kitchen to sit and talk in the living room. He continued talking, digging his own grave, tripping up his story with contradictions and falsehoods.

I asked if he might have struck her more than just the one time, and he stuck to his story that he only hit her one time when she bit down on his penis. I explained that her injury looked more consistent with having been hit several times, asking if it were plausible he struck her a second time after she released her bite. He then admitted to striking her "only a few times" until she released her bite.

I pondered about how his penis didn't get partially severed or completely chopped off if his "few" punches only occurred when his penis was in her mouth. Dropping the questions for a moment, my inquisitive tone changed to a serious terse explanation. I told "Mr. Portly" that based on the severe trauma to her face, she had to be hit more than just the few times. Waiting for a response, I allowed a deafening silence to build for what seemed like an eternity, putting the burden on him to explain. He finally broke the awkward silence with befuddled stammering, sounds really, not words.

After shooting holes in his story, like a deflating balloon losing air, his chest collapsed with a sigh, confirming that he hit her repeatedly, more than a few times, but unsure to exactly how many times. He owned-up to repeated punches, but still resolute that all his strikes were instinctive; in his mind, this eliminated any criminal culpability. I continued to play along that I believed they were engaged in consensual oral sex, and the punch was the result of an instinctive reaction to the bite. I wanted his continued cooperation for another idea that I hoped would get to the truth, an unusual medical exam.

The paramedics arrived, saving the young woman's life. A team of five paramedics and firemen arrived, stabilizing her for transport to the hospital. I asked one of the paramedics to assist with assessing "Mr. Portly's" penis bite. The paramedic gave me a perplexed look, but I explained that it could help prove or disprove "Mr. Portly's" story, a medical examination of his penis might provide some evidence of the truth.

I politely informed "Mr. Portly" that I wanted a paramedic to perform a medical examination on his penis to document any possible injuries. He agreed and the three of us went into the bathroom, where "Mr. Portly" lowered his pants to reveal his injured penis. He did have a bite-looking injury to his penis, but the injury wasn't consistent with him hitting her multiple times with her unclenching jaws. The injury was minuscule compared to the massive injuries he inflicted on his roommate. The paramedic totally dismantled "Mr. Portly's" pathetic story, saying, "The bite looks defensive in nature."

I asked him to clarify his "defensive-bite wound diagnosis," The paramedic explained, "In my professional opinion, the injury appears consistent with someone biting to prevent the penis from entering their mouth." I had everything I needed to arrest "Mr. Portly," hoping that the woman would make a full recovery and give a full story about her horrible ordeal.

I placed "Mr. Portly" under arrest for aggravated assault, and transported him to the station to process the booking. When word reached the precinct officers that I had arrested some poor man for defending himself from a woman who tried to chew off his penis, I was chastised. Apparently, they couldn't get past the idea of a woman biting a man's penis.

The victim's medically-induced coma saved her life. It would be several weeks before she regained consciousness. Ultimately, she did tell a sex crimes detective that her male roommate sexually assaulted her. I learned from the sex crimes detective that "Mr. Portly" became fixated with her, wanting a sexual relationship. She met him through mutual friends and learned he had a bedroom for rent. They only knew each other for less than a year before becoming roommates, but she was only in the home for a few months before he began asking for sex. She had no sexual interest in him, rejecting his repeated sexual advances.

That night after returning home from bowling, he forced his way into her bedroom and sexually assaulted her. She ran out, trying to leave the house through the kitchen. He caught up to her, and threw her to the floor. While kneeling over her, he shoved his penis into her mouth. She tried closing her mouth, but he forced her jaw open with his hands. She bit down on his penis and he immediately removed it from her mouth. He then began repeatedly punching her in the face. She had no memory of anything after that, as she lost consciousness and awoke in the hospital weeks later.

The suspect pled not guilty, and a year later, a jury trial began. Jerri and I were called to testify about our initial investigation. My testimony revealed his repeated lies and how if not for Jerri's immediate call for paramedics, the female roommate would have died in her bedroom. Jerri painted a detailed picture of the torn-up bedroom, visualizing a sexual assault crime scene for the jury.

By the end of the trial, I had been threatened—not by the suspect, not by the brutal cross examination of the defense attorney, but from the testifying paramedic forced to explain his expert penis-injury determination of a "defensive" bite wound.

The defense attorney had brutally cross-examined the paramedic for days. The trial should have lasted only a few days, but the defense attorney clearly wanted to spend extra time badgering the paramedic about his penis-bite training. The beleaguered paramedic was instructed to draw a huge penis, dozens of times over scale, for the jury. The paramedic had a *hard* time supporting his medical expertise on penis bites.

During breaks in the trial, the paramedic would return to a common break room looking completely drained of his energy from the humiliation of drawing penis after penis in open court. The only emotion displayed on the paramedic's face were death-daggers directed at me. I assumed the paramedic had to be overreacting, until I witnessed the defense lawyer's barrage for myself. Once court resumed, I peeked into the courtroom, observing a large penis drawing on the court's whiteboard next to the witness stand. The awkwardly large phallic was as big as a wall poster having various comments written in a legend on the side, remarking to the nature of the defensive bite. I listened to the paramedic's ramblings as he explained the difference between a non-defensive penis-bite and a defensive penis-bite. He appeared to have a terrible time explaining the difference to the mortified jurors, but truth and justice prevailed.

The suspect's guilty rape verdict earned him 99-years in prison. However, another crime had been completely overlooked; the threat against me by the paramedic. After the last day of trial, the 6'5" mountain of a paramedic leaned down to my small frame and said with deadly sincerity, "If you ever write another report about my penis-biting statements, I will kick your ass." The disgruntled paramedic became even more upset when I started laughing. How can you not?

Twist

After the guilty verdict was announced the Judge excused the jury, and they returned to the Jury Room. The defense attorney, prosecuting attorney and the sex crimes detective were permitted to debrief the jurors. This standard post-verdict practice allows both defense and prosecution teams to learn the strengths and weakness of their respective presentations. The lawyers learned the obvious, the jury believed "Mr. Portly" was guilty beyond a shred of a doubt. To the contrary, the sex crimes detective learned something surprising. After hours upon hours of deliberation, viewing disturbing pictures of a large penis, hearing the perilous account of a brutal rape and testimonies from all the police officers; they simply informed the detective they thought Jerri and I looked like a cute couple, wanting to know if we were romantically involved.

CHAPTER 14

Transvestite Tongue

MOST nights, I'm going to one radio call after the next, sometimes as many as twenty-five radio calls in a single night. Police refer to these busy shifts taking call after call as "chasing the radio." But this night was unusually quiet, allowing me free time to find a place to park and write some burglary reports, which I was holding from earlier in the shift.

My favorite place to write reports was a three-story parking garage, located away from the busy street between two large business complexes, which only operated during daylight hours, leaving the secluded parking garage to just me and the elderly security guard. The guard kept trespassers and homeless subjects away, providing me with a safe environment to write my reports without the worry of someone walking up to talk, or worse, sneaking up while I'm distracted to do me harm.

I parked at the top of the parking garage, looking over the city lights and listening to the police radio, while getting down to the business of writing two burglary reports. My squad area was uncharacteristically slow, but the other two squads that comprise the precinct boundaries were flowing with the typical volume of radio calls.

While writing, I heard some patrol officers chattering away about a red Mustang. The officers were working an affluent part of the city, ten miles away from my crime ridden beat. I discerned three things from what I could make out from their frantic and constant talking over each other–1. They were chasing a red Mustang, but failed to explain why they initiated the high-speed chase. 2. The way the officers were talking over each other, and monopolizing the entire radio frequency, which is dedicated to the entire precinct, quickly surmised they were rookies, and 3. Because of this realization, I feared the car chase would not end well.

I didn't know the rookie officers, as we briefed at different times and their area was located completely on the other end of the precinct. Their loud panicky voices covered each other, as five officers excitedly broadcasted each street they passed chasing the Mustang. The officers described the Mustang, which eluded them at every turn, but provided no information about the driver or the infraction. It became glaringly obvious that no one officer had taken control of the situation. One of the officers finally asked the radio dispatcher to ensure a supervisor was monitoring their car chase, which is protocol.

Anyone in law enforcement will tell you that the over-arching, primary rule in every vehicle pursuit is the concern and welfare for public safety. The police constantly weigh the cost of catching the suspect driver with the potential risk of pursuing a fast car through a highly-populated city. Police try to avoid such car chases unless a driver's intent is to commit a deadly act, which would then warrant the risk of the high-speed car chase.

Patrol officers are required to give a brief explanation, making it clear to inform the other officers who are risking their own lives, why the chase is happening and strategically how to intercept the vehicle being chased. When all the officers are on the same page, the public's safety is better ensured and there's a greater likelihood of a safe apprehension. But not this time.

The chase went on for several minutes and the rookie police officers had yet to explain why they were chasing the Mustang. On a few occasions, their supervisor got on the radio and asked that very question, but no explanation was provided. Instead, the young officers just continued to list off the quickly passing streets, keeping the radio dispatcher updated to the route of the vehicle chase. The rapid succession of passing streets made it clear they were chasing the Mustang at high speed, making the prospect of the chase ending in a crash or a fatality likely, and for possibly nothing more than a speeding ticket.

I only had four years of experience at the time, but it may have been more than their collective years put together. We refer to these squads of rookie officers as "Baby Squads," because you need to spoon-feed them the right course of action. And a car chase even undertaken by an experienced officer is a scary thing, but life-threatening in the hands of rookie officers.

A "Baby Squad" officer finally advised of the reason for the chase, advising the male driver refused to stop for a speeding infraction alone. Shortly after the "nothing but a speeding ticket" affirmation, another officer declared it an official "pursuit," placing onus on their sergeant. Once a car chase is officially labeled a "pursuit," it is the sergeant's responsibility to either terminate it for insufficient cause for placing the public at risk, or allow it to continue, taking the responsibility for the outcome, good or bad.

The speeding infraction being the only reason to chase the Mustang should have prompted their patrol sergeant to terminate the vehicle pursuit, but he didn't. I was surprised as many times the patrol officers themselves will terminated the car chase for anything less than a violent felony crime.

Many police departments, including the Phoenix Police, utilize police helicopters to surreptitiously monitor the criminal's course of driving in lieu of a car chase. The helicopter pilot relays the suspect's directions to the ground, so officers can drive undetected along parallel streets. Once the unsuspecting driver stops on his own accord, the paralleling officers swoop in to make the arrest, not risking the lives of citizens with a vehicle chase.

I knew little about the "Baby Squad" sergeant, or his experience level, as he was recently promoted from another precinct. Listening to his failure to stop the chase, it seemed possible that he was promoted only after working a few years as a cop, and never handled a car chase. This prompted me to drive to the "Baby Squad" to lend a hand, fearing it would go from bad to worse without some experience to help direct a safe apprehension. The baby squad and their inexperienced sergeant would be in major trouble if the pursuit ended tragically for such a silly reason as a traffic ticket.

During the ten minutes it took me to travel to the area of the chase, the rookies' radio chatter suddenly went silent. With no information coming from the radio, I drove to the last street updated by an officer. I pulled up behind six parked patrol cars in the street, immediately seeing the mangled Mustang crashed head-on into a brick wall of a fancy home. Ten yards down the street I saw five young police officers, all standing in stunned silence around the driver's body lying in the middle of the street.

The Mustang driver, though sustaining a head injury from hitting the windshield, ran away from his car after the crash for ten yards. The rookie officers ran after him in a short foot chase. With adrenaline still pumping, the officers quickly caught up to the driver, but he collapsed to the ground without warning, where he still lay motionless upon my arrival.

I ran to the officer's semi-circle around the driver, seeing a lot of problems that could have caused the driver's collapse; The suspect's massive size, approximately 300-pounds, making running problematic for his heart; His inebriated and drug-induced state also ill-advised for a late-night run; or a serious head wound from striking the windshield could have finally been his downfall. But it wasn't his obesity, or inebriated and drug induced state, nor the head injury that caused him to collapse–it may have been his tightly fitted dress.

The driver looked like the main character in "The Rocky Horror Picture Show," but with a heavy build. And "Rocky's" running difficulties were a result of his female fashion violations; a tightly fitted, red dress squeezed over his large body-frame, while running in red stilettos. I observed the six bewildered police officers huddled over the suspect's body. Their shock appeared equal parts surprise at the sight of a big man in a little dress and "Rocky's" apparent fatal collapse.

Puzzlement turned to panic, when these rookies realized their suspect died. This type of police-initiated death appropriately creates a media nightmare. The media loves to sensationalize these horrific police mistakes, month-long headlines keeping the cop's blunder in the community consciousness. Newspapers printing headlines like, "LGBT-Hating Police Kill Transvestite Motorist with Dragnet."

I instructed the tongue-tied officers to request paramedics for an unresponsive crash victim, which they had not done yet. Next, I kneeled down over the transvestite's body, checking for a heartbeat and felt none. In preparation to perform CPR, I tilted his head back, and opened his mouth, sweeping my fingers inside to remove any foreign matter before initiating mouth-to-mouth resuscitation. This was definitely not what I envisioned doing when I woke up that morning.

Pushing my fingers in his mouth to clear his airway, I felt his tongue, hard and rigid. "Rocky's" tongue, protruding partially out of his open mouth, was unusually stiff and a dark shade of red. Even a rookie cop would know rigor mortis couldn't occur in a matter of minutes. Upon further inspection, I found the tongue was not a tongue at all.

Using my ballpoint pen, I tore into the object wedged in his mouth. After a half-dozen attempts, I pulled out a baseball-sized canvas pouch lodged in his throat, completely sealing off his airway. The pouch was filled with an off-white powder substance later identified as methamphetamines.

"Rocky" began gasping involuntarily, convulsing and thrashing, making bizarre suction noises, regaining consciousness, and opening his eyes. His air deprived gray skin-tone transformed to a livelier color, better suited with his heavy cream makeup and painted rosy cheeks.

Everyone was relieved. Jubilant rookie cops with their salvaged careers, my bliss at saving a person, the transvestite speeder happy to be alive, but rather than giving us hugs and kisses, the suspect recovered sufficiently to bestow a gauntlet of angry and threatening insults, littered with profanities directed at all the police officers.

Even I, his savior, wasn't spared as he accused me of various depraved sexual acts.

To my astonishment, all but one of the "Baby Squad" officers left before determining assignments relating to the car chase, crash and any criminal investigations. The lone rookie thanked me for saving the driver and helping figure out the mess. Soon, the "Baby Squad" sergeant arrived, and didn't call his paperwork-fleeing cops back to the scene. I figured he would have those rookie officers return once he learned about the vast amount of police work resulting from the incident. The lone rookie and I briefed the sergeant of the situation and required paperwork, after taking some time to figure out what we had, no less than seven separate police investigations and related police reports.

Here's how the police reports broke down: 1. A stolen vehicle report; upon calling the registered owner of the Mustang, I learned the female owner had no idea her car was even missing, and now demolished. 2. The traffic accident report; reflecting the suspect's flight from police officers and how he collided into the brick wall after failing to make a turn while evading police for fear they would find his drugs. 3. A possession of dangerous drugs report; based on the methamphetamines pulled out of the suspect's throat and in his pockets after the police chase. 4. A felony pursuit report; detailing the police chase stemming from the drug-induced speeding violation. 5. Driving under the influence of drugs and alcohol report; to include processing the suspect's blood alcohol content. 6. A vehicle impound report; needed to generate an invoice number allowing for the heap of red metal to be towed to the police impound lot. 7. And finally, arrest paperwork; necessary to book "Rocky" for all his crimes.

Once the sergeant learned of the mountain of work, he still did not recall the other rookie officers back to the scene. He tasked all the work to just the lone rookie officer and me, and I didn't even work in that squad area. I was only too happy to help, but amazed that he thought just two cops could do a job best suited for three-times the number of officers to work.

To make matters worse, he assigned the bulk of the investigations and reports to me. He instructed his rookie officer to take credit for the arrest, after transporting "Rocky" to the hospital for his head injury, where he would also process him for the DUI. He tasked me with everything else, conducting the traffic accident investigation, which occurred before I even arrived at the scene. Tasking me with the stolen vehicle investigation, and the related towing of the demolished vehicle to the police impound lot. I was assigned to conduct the vehicle chase investigation and related police report, even though I was not a witness to the car chase, which also ended before my arrival.

The sergeant never even said, "Thanks" for responding to his area to help, or for taking on the bulk of the work, and didn't even acknowledge that I saved "Rocky's" life. Later in the week, the rookie sergeant talked to my supervisor about me, and I was thinking he told my sergeant about all my hard work and how I saved a person's life, but no. He told my sergeant that I took too long writing a report, failing to mention I took an appropriate amount of time investigating and writing five separate criminal reports. My supervisor laughed when I told him the full story, and I learned that the rookie sergeant had earned a reputation for making his superiors think he was a tough, hard-nosed disciplinarian.

Twist

I always try to look at the bright side of things, as the cup is half-full. I didn't need or want the rookie sergeant's accolades or a lifesaving medal. I was just thankful that the rookie sergeant wasn't my supervisor. A month later, the rookie sergeant transferred and became my squad sergeant—it sucked.

CHAPTER 15

Unknown "Spanich" Language

I N 1989, I signed up for a "Spanish for Law Enforcement" language course, which was designed to assist patrol officers interacting with the Hispanic community in Phoenix. The program focused on words and phrases that were most common when interacting with Spanish-speaking citizens, such as routine traffic stops, but also emergency-related calls.

The course consisted of an 80-hour block of classroom instructions, followed by a two-week Spanish language-immersion component. The immersion component entailed the students traveling to a small town in Mexico, where they resided with a Mexican family. The student officers socialized, traveled, and dined with local Mexican families while only communicating in Spanish.

Unfortunately, I couldn't participate in the immersion portion of the course due to my many digestive issues. The medical profession has clinically referred to my diminished digestive disability as a mix of ailments, syndromes, and conditions. I have been treated and diagnosed with identical conditions, but with different names: Irritable Bowel Syndrome, Enzyme Depletion Disorder, Digestive Disorder, and Extreme Lactose Intolerance. I more descriptively like to refer my condition as; Bowel Acid Disease (with) Stomach Hating Internal Testiness; it's the perfect acronym.

For me, eating in Mexico would be tantamount to committing intestinal suicide. Digesting American crackers and water was rough for me. I couldn't even imagine how my stomach and intestines would react to the spicy food.

The course was like a Russian language-training course I took in military intelligence. Both courses were similar in their accelerated focus on memory skills instead of grammar-based techniques. By the end of the Spanish language course, I was engaging in simple conversations, providing precise Spanish instructions for traffic and subject stops. The final examination consisted of communicating instructions in Spanish during a high-risk traffic stop. The commands consisted of the following phrases in Spanish: "Turn off the engine, throw the ignition key out the driver's window, place both hands out the window, get out of the car, raise your hands in the air, turn completely around slowly, and walk backward toward my voice." I passed the course with flying colors, but any memorization is lost if it's not practiced.

Upon completion, I used my new Spanish-speaking skills at every opportunity. However, most of the Hispanic citizens in my beat spoke better English than I spoke Spanish, making them want to change the conversation quickly to English. I tried immersing myself in our Spanish-speaking communities by greeting business owners with "Buenos dias!" I would chase people down just to tell a Spanish-speaking citizen "Good morning." Upon reflection, I was probably traumatizing these folks, seeing a fully uniformed cop with a holstered gun running at them from across the street just to say, "Good day!" in Spanish.

My Spanish-speaking interactions became increasingly sparse over the years. Lack of practice and chances to use my language skills made my Spanish become progressively unintelligible. I didn't speak Spanish for well over a year, until a violent situation required it, leading to the next twisted tale.

In 1996, I responded to an emergency radio call of a shooting. A Hispanic man shot his pregnant girlfriend with a handgun in their apartment, fleeing in a dark pickup truck. Another patrol officer arrived before me at the apartment, advising the shooter left southbound less than ten minutes ago, and I just happen to be ten-minutes away and south of the crime scene.

Immediately parking strategically on the corner of a major intersection, I was in the perfect position to see the shooter's truck if he continued driving southbound from his apartment. In a matter of seconds, I spotted a dark-colored, pickup truck speeding toward the intersection. The suspect drove erratically around other vehicles, circumventing stopped cars by driving on the sidewalk, continuing until the truck turned right at the intersection. The truck's erratic and excessive speeds led me to believe the driver could be the suspect leaving the crime scene.

Matching the description of the truck, the suspect looked consistent with the shooting suspects' description. Driving behind the truck, I turned on my overhead emergency red-and-blue lights. The likelihood of a shooting suspect complying and stopping for police emergency lights was doubtful, and I used emergency lights to simply alert other drivers to the hazard.

To my complete surprise, the suspect stopped abruptly in a parking lot next to the road while I was still on the police radio requesting backup officers. I didn't have enough time to get additional officers to help, as standard practice dictates there should be at least three additional patrol officers assisting in a high-risk felony traffic stop. The driver's unforeseen obedience made the traffic stop premature, so I was forced to deal with the high-risk traffic stop alone.

To make matters worse, the Hispanic driver quickly got out of his truck, yelling "No problem" in Spanish. The driver walked hurriedly toward my patrol car. I immediately yelled "stop" in Spanish, "Alto!" The driver complied, stopping were he stood. I wasn't sure my Spanish was the only reason he complied—I was also pointing my gun at him. Regardless, I still felt confident that he understood the Spanish spilling out of my mouth.

Even though the driver was cooperating, I still needed backup officers to assist, as any high-risk traffic stop with a possible shooting suspect is too dangerous to do alone. The driver remained frozen, trying to calm me in his broken English, repeating over and over,

"No problem." I yelled for him to put his hands in the air in Spanish, and again, the driver responded appropriately, eagerly reaching for the sky. Standing approximately twenty yards away, staring down the barrel of my gun, he waited nervously for my next command. My next order in Spanish should have been, "turn around slowly and keep your hands in the air," but he didn't move, and the confused look on his face made me think I screwed up the Spanish words.

The reason for commanding the driver to "turn around slowly with his hands in the air" is to provide a complete view of the driver's waistline. Many times, criminals try to conceal handguns in their front or back beltline. This movement will typically raise their shirttails, revealing a weapon. I repeated just that part of the command for him to "turn around," hoping it would remedy the problem, since his arms were already in the air, but to my chagrin, he just stood looking confused when I said the Spanish words, "Desay Welta."

The driver stood still, looking confused, and as the volume of my Spanish gibberish raised, so did the confusion on his face. My restored confidence in speaking Spanish vanished, as I repeatedly screamed the same apparently wrong words, or as my police friends would tease; speaking some unknown "Spanich" language.

A smart suspect might pretend not to understand, as complying would reveal his weapon. However, if so, the look of fear on his face should have earned him an Oscar nomination. As I kept screaming obviously butchered Spanish words, I second guessed the driver's involvement in the shooting, as all the suspicious elements could be explained away with perfectly acceptable reasons other than being a shooting suspect.

His erratic driving may be for myriad reasons, not because he was fleeing after shooting someone. The vehicle matched the shooting suspect's vehicle, but it was a common-looking, common-colored, black truck. The suspect did match the shooter's description, but again, it was a very general description. I had to weigh legitimate officer safety concerns against the possibility that the driver was not the same suspect involved in the shooting. This Spanish-speaking driver could have only been guilty of looking like a shooting suspect, as well as committing several driving infractions.

Keeping in mind he could be innocent, I still had to see his waistband, ensuring he didn't have a handgun. In training, we learned that violent criminals will act calm while fully intending to shoot an officer prior to the arrival of additional police officers.

Unfortunately, I could not think of anything else to say other than to repeat the words "Desay Welta," yelling it louder, but none too surprising it just resulted in the same confused look. The driver was now shaking uncontrollably while standing with his hands in the air, no longer calm, no longer saying, "No problem." We definitely had a problem.

Could I have been mixing my waning Spanish with Russian that I learned during my years in Military Intelligence? Maybe a Russian speaking person standing in the area was turning around slowly this whole time. Thankfully, another police officer arrived, witnessing my translation difficulties, he yelled the only Spanish word he knew, "Sientate," and the driver dropped to the ground with a mighty thud. The officer yelled for him to "sit," and the driver hit the ground hard.

I still needed to determine the driver's involvement in the shooting, requesting an actual Spanish-speaking officer to help me out since my Spanish was as effective as screaming gibberish. Detectives arrived, taking over the investigation. I never spoke Spanish again as a cop.

Twist

A neighbor from the original shooting scene arrived and positively identified the driver as the boyfriend who was seen shooting his pregnant girlfriend. She survived the shooting, but their unborn child did not. I discovered the blood-stained handgun tucked in the waistband of his pants when we picked him up off the ground. The suspect talked candidly with the Spanish-speaking detectives, admitting to shooting his girlfriend in their apartment during an argument over rent. He also said he meant to shoot me, but became intimidated by the way I pointed my gun and screamed gibberish.

CHAPTER 16

Good News, Bad News, and the Dog Bite Ruse

I T was hardly easy raising DJ as a teen, but a day never passed without me telling him, "I love you." My headstrong kid, testing me every minute of the day, required a metaphoric short leash, but DJ always knew he was loved. To me, this was the key element responsible for him growing up as a good and loving person.

Dealing with children is difficult, but dealing with difficult children is downright daunting, if not impossible. And there is a whole other category of kids that police officers must deal with; delinquent children. Often, cops interact with these troubled kids who are seemingly well past a point of no return. Whatever led them down the path of antisocial behavior for years, cops can't fix it in a single encounter.

After almost thirty years of interactions with troubled children, and having dealt with so many, I've noticed a common thread. These so-called "bad kids" either received no discipline from their absent or uncaring parents, or on the other end of the bad-parenting spectrum, they were overdisciplined, victims of physical or emotional abuse. Children need to understand consequences, but they absolutely must feel loved. It is the lack of these two important parenting factors, love and consequences, that can create delinquent children, growing-up to become violent criminals plaguing our community. It is just those types of loveless and violent criminal youths that this next twisted tale is based.

Bill and I were riding patrol together one night in the late 1980s. It was my turn to take the helm, with Bill riding shotgun. A call came on the radio of a stolen car and we were only a few miles away. The owner saw two male teens drive off with his car after hot-wiring it in the carport. I immediately pulled off the road into a parking lot and turned off all our lights, wanting to see them before they saw us.

I advised our precinct radio operator that we were already in the area of the stolen vehicle call, and would switch to the different "crime in progress" 911 radio frequency. Bill then turned the car radio's channel to the designated emergency frequency working the stolen vehicle call. The same car radio ejects from its port, becoming my portable police radio. Bill, as the passenger, had his own portable radio, but he forgot to switch it over to the frequency working the stolen vehicle call.

We soon observed a car matching the description of the stolen vehicle approaching our intersection. The stolen car rolled suspiciously slow toward us, noticing our dark car since we were the only two cars in the area. The slow speed of the vehicle allowed Bill and me to see two teenage car thieves. Both of us saw their "I'm guilty as hell look" on their faces, as they stared back at us. They knew we had spotted them, but they didn't get spooked and continued to drive slowly through the intersection.

I announced on the car radio (emergency 911 frequency) that we were behind the possible stolen car. We requested a helicopter to assist in monitoring the vehicle. It is standard practice to ask for an "eye in the sky" prior to even initiating a felony traffic stop. We knew such a helicopter request would be in vain, as we had not heard them all night and they were probably back in the hangar, but we had to try, hoping to get lucky–no such luck.

As we pulled out onto the street, the teen driver took off. Now it was a car chase. I radioed the 911 dispatcher, advising that we were behind the stolen car, and got confirmation on the license plate.

Unfortunately, for reasons unknown, our fellow squad officers didn't switch over to the radio frequency working the stolen vehicle call. With Bill forgetting to switch his radio to the 911 frequency, I would soon be the only officer on the designated frequency working the stolen vehicle call.

Without warning, their stolen car stopped abruptly in the middle of the road. The two teens got out of their car and ran in opposite directions. I quickly stopped behind the stolen car and made ready our foot chase after them. Bill got out, chasing the passenger suspect who ran south on the street. After hurriedly ejecting the car radio to get my portable radio, taking precious seconds, I chased after the driver going north. Already having a considerable lead on me, the driver ran toward a large college campus. Just as my luck would have it, this college (now, Grand Canyon University) was hosting an outside circus, complete with rows upon rows of animal cages. The suspect could not only blend in, but there was no way I could search every cage.

It is a common tactic for criminal partners to run in opposite directions to divide the cops and their resources, later rendezvousing at an agreed-upon location. Though Bill later regretted chasing after the passenger and wished we had both chased the driver, he kept rubbing it in how he caught *his* suspect in short order. Bill unknowingly had been broadcasting his foot chase of the passenger over our routine precinct radio frequency, but that was fortuitous since it was being monitored by the precinct's three squads of police officers.

Ten patrol officers quickly mobilized to assist Bill with his foot chase, apprehending the passenger within minutes. The 17-year-old passenger was a documented gang member with a long criminal rap sheet. Bill and the other patrol officers returned the teen to their patrol cars and the suspect's stolen vehicle.

While I was still searching around the animal cages for the driver, Bill and the other officers found a large amount of stolen assault rifles and handguns in the trunk of the stolen car. Earlier in the week, the guns had been burglarized from a gun store with a prior stolen car, which they felt would be too hot to keep storing the guns.

The suspects stole the car tonight to provide new storage for their illegal gun-trade. The back-alley sales of these stolen guns would bring big money to their street gang. This street gang was a criminal enterprise, dangerously operated by armed juvenile criminals.

I, too, called out my foot chase, but on the separate emergency channel working the 911 stolen vehicle call, but since I was the only officer on that radio frequency, no one was listening, let along going to respond to my location. I was alone.

Bill learned from the passenger that the driver had an Uzi automatic rifle. By the time he learned this, I had chased the driver well into the college grounds. I didn't realize it at the time, but I chased a better-armed gangster into a dark campus with lots of places to hide. I searched for the driver among the rows of animal cages covered with heavy tarps, as unidentifiable roars, snorts, and pacing sounds added to my anxiety.

The driver could have been hiding behind the cages, or under one of the cages as the animal containers were perched on large wooden platforms. Precisely at the time I was looking under a cage with my flashlight in a push-up position, Bill came over my radio channel, having switched over to warn me that my suspect was armed with an Uzi automatic assault rifle.

The shock of hearing the news of a gangbanging, gun-running, car thief who could be pointing an assault rifle at me while down on the ground forced me to re-think my current push-up positioned tactics. I sprung to my feet, removed the gun from my holster and took cover behind an animal cage, requesting additional officers to help set up a perimeter to lock-down the well-armed suspect.

After releasing the talk button on my radio and receiving no response, I realized I was on my own; no officers could respond to my location. Without a perimeter to surround the suspect hiding in the large circus area, this gangbanger ultimately got away.

I was not accustomed to losing a foot chase, and having failed to catch my suspect and with my defeated tail between my legs, I left the circus animals behind, returning to join Bill and the other cops. Bill had moved our patrol car to the college parking lot, and started the booking paperwork for the passenger suspect, arresting him with a single charge of trespass.

Since we could only place him as a passenger, he couldn't be charged with possession of a stolen vehicle or any of the stolen guns in the trunk. The passenger gangster simply lied, saying the guns were already in the trunk when he got picked up on the side of the road. The unproveable lie would make charging him with any crime other than trespassing impossible, unless the crime lab found his fingerprints on one of the guns. Additionally, any lawyer could get the trespassing charge dismissed with little effort. Most times, the passengers in stolen cars are never charged with a crime.

I asked Bill if he had read the passenger his Miranda rights, wanting to interrogate him for the driver's identity. Bill advised the passenger of his constitutional rights, ending with a standard question, "do you understand your rights?" The suspect only replied "Yes, fuck you," laying backdown on the seat. That ambiguous, if not colorful statement only acknowledged his rights, not invoking them. His insulting response, "Yes, fuck you!" made him fair game to be questioned, as he didn't ask for an attorney. As a gangbanger, he would not snitch on his partner in crime, but he could be tricked into giving up such information.

Using the patrol car radio, I pretended to be talking to the radio dispatcher, surreptitiously turning off the radio before talking. I told the imaginary dispatcher we needed medical paramedics to treat an imaginary dog bite. Bill played along perfectly, asking "What happened?", loud enough for the backseat suspect to hear. I explained, for the prisoner's benefit, that the driver got mauled by our canine (K-9) dogs, with an elaborate and detailed tale of my search with canine support, culminating with the combative suspect receiving severe dog bites to the "meaty portion" of his leg.

I am not sure what inspired me to use this ruse, or why I used the words *meaty portion*, but it worked like gangbusters. The passenger suspect asked about his partner's injury but I ignored him, continuing to tell Bill about the driver's grisly injury. I described the intense pain, how he screamed in agony when the dog caught him.

The passenger more forcefully implored about his injured buddy, "Jose" and the severity of his dog bite wounds.

I continued ignoring the passenger's questions, only giving simple "yes" or "no" responses to him. He kept biting at the ruse, like a big mouth bass hitting at the lure, repeatedly wanting more information about Jose's injury. I allowed for a long, uneasy quiet to hang in the air, not responding, waiting for the passenger to break the silence, demanding to know more about his buddy Jose. The silence tactic, also used many times during my sex crime and homicide interrogations, creates an uneasy atmosphere, making a person want to break the awkward silence by saying something, something they might not otherwise speak out and only think.

The passenger asked if Jose would be going to the hospital, and again I simply said, "yes." The teen looked around at the multitude of police officers inventorying the guns, searching the stolen car, talking on the radio, and all around looking busy, which laid a foundation of a hectic and chaotic scene, adding believability to my ruse. I then pulled in the hook, telling Bill the hospital staff needed the parent's information to treat the dog bite wounds, explaining the driver's pain was too great for him to speak, and without the parents' consent the doctors couldn't treat the massive dog wounds. The passenger fell for my false story, hook line and sinker by blurting out Jose's full name, his parents' names, and their complete home address and telephone number.

When the passenger was booked for trespass at the juvenile detention center, I informed him of the good news, the bad news, and the dog bite ruse. The good news was his friend wasn't bitten by a dog; the bad news was he gave up his friend's information. His mouth opened wide, but said nothing as shock spread over his face. We left the speechless passenger with the detention crew, and went to arrest Jose at his parents' home.

Twist

The reason none of the police officers could leave the stolen vehicle scene to help me was because they were dealing with a huge mess. Bill and I had no idea, but the stolen vehicle never stopped at all;

it only slowed down. While chasing after our respective suspects, the stolen car continued traveling forward. The driverless stolen car rolled a short distance, striking an unsuspecting Arizona State University patrol car. The university cop happened to be straying outside of his jurisdiction near this other college. Upon impact, the stolen car changed direction, driving off the roadway and rolling into the campus. The stolen car rolled over various landscaping, finally stopping after striking and knocking over a historical tree. Amazing how much damage bad teens in a stolen car can cause, but luckily no one was killed or hurt.

Within a few hours, the teens were released to their parents' custody to await future court proceedings. Ultimately, the passenger's trespassing charge was scratched by the prosecutor, as we feared. The driver was charged with the car theft, possession of the stolen guns, and burglary of the gun store. And he was only sentenced to six months in juvenile detention, as the law requires him to be released upon his 18th birthday. Without appropriate consequences, juvenile delinquents often become dangerous adult criminals.

CHAPTER 17

The Woman Who Screams at Cars

AN "unknown trouble" radio call can be about most anything, as this type of call gives a limited amount of information, and we discover what the trouble is once we are immersed in the call. I have blindly responded to many of these calls throughout my career, and this next twisted tale began with my response to a large amount of 911 calls describing only that "a crazy woman was screaming at parked cars."

Numerous neighbors called police stating the woman was screaming and throwing things at parked cars along the street. What concerned me about these calls, is that this neighborhood was a high-crime area. The same street where the woman was screaming is notorious for prostitution, drug deals and other vice activity. Most residents, being desensitized to most acts of violence, don't think to call 911, so for them to call about a woman screaming at cars was very ominous.

This den of prostitution and drugs was surrounded by good communities, inhabited with caring citizens, many of which formed great block watch groups, trying to keep their community safe from the criminal elements thriving on a street known as "Crack Alley." If a few criminals live in the neighborhood, more like-minded individuals tend to move in. You can compare it to seeing a cockroach in your house; you are likely to see more later.

I requested a backup officer, but on this hectic night no officers could break away to help. Driving in the area, I immediately recognized drug dealers and pimps, who were usually averse to my presence, now strangely happy to see me. The salutations from pimps and thugs must be a warning sign, or perhaps their thriving drug and prostitution trade is in jeopardy from the antics of a single woman.

It didn't take long to find the woman screaming at the top of her lungs. Her unintelligible shrieking indeed targeted parked cars, rather than people, at least not until my arrival.

Many of the drug dealers or bystanders gathered down the street a safe distance away, watching the spectacle. A couple dozen men and women looked on as the woman appeared unaffected by her audience. Some took cover behind non-targeted parked cars, concealing themselves from this deranged car-yeller. The reasons for her auto aversion was still a mystery, as her screams didn't provide a clue to the reason for her car and truck taunting. She was running amok, throwing mud at these innocent parked cars, never explaining what they did to upset her so.

Not wanting to telegraph my presence to the loud and volatile woman, I parked fifty-yards down the road. As I got out of my patrol car, my sense of smell kicked into high gear. She had not been throwing mud, but pitching poop. The stench carried well beyond her impressive pitching arm. With every step toward her, I felt betrayed by my lungs, trying desperately not to breathe. I fought my impulse to vomit due to the overpowering smell of excrement as I walked on.

The last thing I wanted was to get into a physical altercation with the feces-throwing female to rescue drug dealers' "pimp mobiles" from damage. To "serve and protect" had never been more literally and grossly applied. For now, no real damage had been done to any of the cars, her only culpable crime was disturbing the peace. And I really should have determined if anyone's peace was disturbed enough to agree to testify as a victim before confronting the screaming woman.

My enthusiasm to do the right thing motivated me to walk toward her, but the vomit inducing smell gave me pause to first try and get help, after all, no one was presently in danger from the crazy acting woman. I stopped advancing toward her, and asked the radio operator to send another patrol officer to assist. The "Queen of Feces" heard me talking and paused her poop-pitching, glaring at me with a major case of "stink eye." Few things are as intimidating as getting the attention of a large-framed, screaming woman covered in her own excrement—at least I assumed it was her own.

I was standing on the sidewalk more than ten yards away from her, and like a "Mexican standoff," we both stood staring at each other. I was happy for the standstill, it afforded me precious time to get additional officers to respond. She then began approaching, looking very unhappy about my presence. Her screams changed to growling sounds. With each step that she advanced, I stepped back, delaying a physical confrontation until I had help.

She suddenly stopped, turning away from me and focused her attention back at a parked car. I was relieved to avoid, or even prolong making physical contact with her. No longer content with screaming at cars, she began striking the car windows with her fists. To my displeasure, I would now have to intervene, preventing her from sustaining a self-inflicted injury from a broken window.

Without thinking, I sprayed her with mace, which was readily available on my pistol belt, but more importantly, a non-contact weapon. I hoped the pepper spray would protect her from seriously hurting herself, and allow me more time to avoid physical contact. In hindsight, I should have known a crazy woman covered in fecal matter would hardly be bothered by pepper.

The chemical spray hit her dead center, having no effect, other than literally cleaning shit off her face. She continued her assault on the parked car. I dropped the ineffective can of pepper spray, grabbed the growling woman's arms, and tried to stop her from breaking the car window. The fight was on. I held onto both her arms, but tried keeping her at arm's length. She came at me like a powerful locomotive. Trying to keep her away, I tried moving backwards but tripped, falling hard to the ground with her on top of me.

Once on the pavement, our momentum drove us into a roll. She tried to pull my hair, but luckily for me, her diarrhea-drenched hands couldn't get a firm hold. Much of her crap covered me from head to toe. My years as a high school wrestler kicked in and I locked her hands behind her back, gaining control. Soon, the "Queen of Feces" was in handcuffs, growling and laying harmless on the ground. However, my wrestling skills did nothing to prevent the inevitable transferal of sweat and feces.

My adrenaline rush from the fight slowed down, and now, I began feeling the adverse effect of my previous dispersal of pepper spray. My eyes were burning and tears flowed, but not enough to ease the pain. Other than the painful effects of a chemical agent, my main concern was not being able to see. Massive tears clouded my eyes, but I had to stop the instinctive urge to franticly wipe them, as rubbing them would only make the stinging worse. Completely exhausted, with the entire neighborhood of drug dealers, pimps, and whores standing there watching me with amusement, I felt intense disdain for everyone. I then heard a single soft voice at odds with the rest of the cruel environment.

A barely audible young boy was asking if he could help me. In response to his sweet offer, I yelled "get me a hose!" The young boy had difficulty understanding me at first due to my dry-heaving and interspersed vomiting, but translating the gurgling sounds, he understood my request for a water hose.

The boy quickly returned with a garden hose, and using the water to splash the muck from my eyes, within minutes, I could see again. With clarity of sight, I instructed the boy to spray me down from head to toe especially in my mouth. I did not even remove my gun belt, let alone any items of clothing for the soaking. The boy washed away large volumes of chemical agent and fecal matter from my clothes and skin.

The huddled criminal masses subsided upon the arrival of my fellow officers. The boy was escorted away by what I assumed was his father, vanishing along with the rest of the dispersing crowd. The arriving police officers ran to my side, taking over the hose-washing duties and washing the crazy screaming woman as well. She still had no reaction to the pepper spray, and just screamed for the sake of screaming.

I learned the arriving officers had responded to assist due to additional 911 calls from good citizens advising of my situation.

Apparently, some of the criminals in the crowd were overheard planning to attack me. I could not have been any more vulnerable having been blinded by feces mixed with pepper spray. Thanks to a small boy, a cavalry of cops, and good citizens, I no longer felt angry at the neighborhood, but felt a part of a good community.

Twist

The drive to the jail was horrible, as she still smelled like shit. She continued yelling at me and my patrol car during the entire drive. Once there, I had to fight to get her out of the backseat, as she kicked and lunged her wet feces soaked body at me the whole time. I got her into the jail and she was placed on a psychiatric hold; the medical staff needed to wait for the drugs in her system to fade before being able to determine if she also had a mental disorder.

After leaving the jail, I went to the precinct to clean up my car of the biological waste. The clean-up took hours, using a special cleaning formula and bagging everything for destruction per the hazardous waste policy. Once done, I could still smell a strong odor of urine. I finally realized, during my struggle to get her out of the car, it wasn't just water on her clothes, she also urinated all over herself. I just want to set the record straight, she both shit and pissed on me.

CHAPTER 18

Halloween Hellhound

I LOVE Halloween. I was obsessed with horror movies as a child, and Halloween was a great outlet for my imagination. Starting when I was in the Army, I used my dark ingenuity to create a series of large haunted tents for military families celebrating the holiday on base. The haunts would continue to grow in both size and complexity each coming year.

When I came home to Phoenix, every year, we renovated our home into the neighborhood's premiere haunted house. My son loved helping with the demented decorations, many times coming up with the best ideas himself, especially as he got older. One year, DJ wanted to be transformed into Freddy Krueger, the killer from the *Nightmare on Elm Street* film series for a Halloween party at school. Happy to comply, I turned my eight-year old angel into the hideously disfigured killer, mixing clear gelatin with red food coloring, painting his entire face. I added red and blue facial veins with colored string, running just below the gelatin-surface. I know it sounds a little over-the-top for a third-grade class costume party, but so worth it when he raced home to tell me he won first place.

The only down-side of that great father-and-son moment was peeling the home-made monster creation off his face later that night. DJ's ear-to-ear smile became a series of painful facial grimaces as

I tried removing the sticky mess. I carefully peeled the mask into one major piece, trying to minimize his discomfort. I still have the brittle and flaky mask sitting in a box in my closet; a memento of our Halloween magic from over thirty years ago.

Halloween was a special holiday for DJ and me, but really our mutual love of horror movies and all things scary, made our creepy-fun collaborations even more special. My wife, Coleen, and I had a daughter in 1991, and when she was older she too enjoyed helping with the haunted house decorations. Her Halloween costumes were less scary, more intellectual and sophisticated. When she was 24-years old, she made a costume displaying many large red flags, covering every inch from neckline to the bottom of her skirt. Each flag reflecting various character flaws, like "Addicted to quality crack", "Love lighting butterflies on fire", "Banned at all Walmarts", and "Naming my first-born Ebenezer, regardless of the gender." My children definitely inherited my dark sense of humor.

Today my entire home, including the front and back yards, garage, bathrooms, and even the roof, display dozens of homemade monsters on Halloween. My favorite is a six-foot tall man-eating plant named "Audrey 2" from the film *Little Shop of Horrors*. I also made a ten-foot hell-beast, shooting a fountain of blood from its neck. Suffice it to say, our entire garage and two storage sheds are dedicated to the storage of Halloween decorations, yet all our Christmas decorations are sufficiently stored under the bed.

Halloween is one big party week, and nobody knows that better than a cop. Having worked many Halloween nights, my most memorable involved, of all places, a doughnut shop. In late 1990, I responded to an audible alarm call. The anonymous caller couldn't pinpoint the exact location of the loud alarm, providing only a general area. The still-blaring siren sounded like it came from a business in a small strip-mall.

The lack of an address led the radio operator to hold the call for hours, since there were higher priority calls in need of service. I felt there would be no need for a backup officer, as no sane burglar would stick around for an hour inside with an alarm blaring.

I found the business easily, following the blaring alarm straight to the shattered front window of a bakery. The front parking lot was covered in broken glass, and debris blanketed the front walkway as well. I radioed back to dispatch that it was a valid burglary while lighting up the business with a high-powered spotlight from my car. I focused the bright beam on the obvious point of entry, lighting up a deep path inside the bakery. Most of the customer area was visible, but the employee area behind the counter remained pitch-black.

Suddenly, and to my surprise, animal sounds came from inside letting me know I was not alone. I could hear noises, as if an animal was eating. Using my regular flashlight, I walked toward the business to get a better look inside. The munching and slurping changed to snarling, like a human imitating a rabid dog. I yelled blindly inside the business for the suspect to raise his hands and walk out. The suspect just growled louder, which really freaked me out. The growling got closer, as the dog-man continued snarling with more intensity. Hearing the human-made dog sounds in the darkness seemed surreal, and as my anxiety rose, so did the animal-like beast sounds.

I immediately requested a backup officer. Trying to control the sound of my shaky voice, I described my encounter with a growling, burglary suspect. I wish I could have seen the look on the radio dispatcher's face when she calmly but confusingly asked, "Growling?" I told her the suspect would only grunt and bark, refusing to obey my commands to surrender. Several police officers answered up to help from a long way off, but soon, I would be alone, face-to-face, with my Halloween hellhound.

The growling got louder as "it" approached me. I continued flooding the store with light, adjusting my car spotlight and flashlight searching for its approach. The blinding lights finally illuminated an old man creeping out of the darkness. His wild bushy hair could be seen first as he crawled toward me, on all fours. What made this sight even grizzlier, bloody goo was foaming from his mouth and scraggly, gray beard. The suspect's dirty transient appearance made the visual even more disturbing.

The bakery intruder, acting like an alpha dog protecting his food source, growled as red slime fell from his chops, crawling out from the darkness in the back of the store toward me. The closer he came, details of his bloody face became clearer. Now, I could see that what I thought was blood, was actually jelly filling left on his face from devouring doughnuts.

The man-dog broke into the bakery shop, smashing the front window, then all the doughnut display cases, feasting on all the tasty treats. He had been gorging for over an hour, all the while the alarm rang out, and still gobbling cream and jelly-filled delights upon my arrival. He would have feasted all night, if I hadn't responded to the alarm call.

He crawled outside through the smashed front window, like a wild dog stalking its prey. Out of the blue, I pretended he was a real dog, dropping my confrontational tone for the happy greeting a dog would hear upon his master's homecoming. I kept patting my thigh, greeting him with, "Here, boy. Here, boy."

The suspect initially appeared puzzled. I half-expected to see his head tilt to one side. The confused "mutt-man" stopped in his tracks, his bewilderment quickly evolving into a happy dog. His four-legged approach, on hands and knees, becoming non-aggressive. I swear if he had a tail, it would be wagging.

I continued saying, "Good boy" as my backup officers arrived to witness my Dog Whisperer skills. He approached me, ready to lick my hand, but instead of scratching under his beard, I grabbed his red-goo covered wrists, placed his paws in handcuffs, and arrested him for commercial burglary and theft. Almost 100 partially eaten doughnuts were all the evidence I needed. As he quickly turned back into the rabid dog as he was placed in the backseat of my patrol car, I was a bit startled hearing a real dog barking behind me, but this time, it was a K-9 officer and his dog.

Twist

During the ride to the jail, the "mutt-man" sounded like he was imitating an Alice Cooper stage show. Now he was chanting curses upon me instead of barking. I often wonder if the curse worked, based on my crazy career as a cop and personal tragedies. Just a thought.

CHAPTER 19

The Shoot-Out

EVERY police officer swears an oath to protect the public; the community relies on us to keep people who want to harm others off the streets. No cop wants to take a life, but we are trained to use deadly force if the need arises. It's a moral contradiction—sometimes a law enforcement officer must take a life to save himself or others. My career as a police officer came down to one simple, maybe altruistic premise: I was dedicated to saving lives, but I also took one.

April 13,1995. I still remember every detail of when I faced a dangerous bank robber and had to make the tumultuous decision to kill him. Albeit it was justified self-preservation, but ask any cop who has done the same thing, it changes you. It should change you.

It was Thursday, and I had recently switched to daytime hours. There was no denying that sleeping normal hours and being on the same schedule as my wife was a welcomed change. Criminal activity during the day is very different, and working in daylight seemed less dangerous. But I was very wrong.

I had just finished my ten-hour work shift and was driving back to the precinct when an emergency call crackled over the radio— bank robbery in progress. The bank was far outside my beat, but catching a bank robber was something I could only dream about working nights, I eagerly responded to the call.

My patrol car was equipped with an electronic receiver designed to help locate bank robbery suspects fleeing with a transmitting triggered bait-bill. When the bank teller pulls the bait-bill from her cash drawer, it triggers a signal that is received by both dispatch and those patrol cars equipped with the special device. The alert signal happens instantaneously when a bank teller includes the bait-bill with the cash given to the bank robber, so as patrol officers, we are alerted to a bank robbery well before a bank employee calls 911 to report the crime. Since I was out of range, I responded to the 911 call, having not received the signal from pulled bait bill.

The bank, with its grand structure and marble columns, was in an upscale business district. Violent crimes are uncommon to most high-finance districts, but any bank, regardless of its location, is a target for robbers. Most bank robbers commit their crime in a subdued, almost silent manner. They try to blend in line, looking like any other customer, waiting their turn to be helped by the bank teller. Once it's their turn, they approach the teller and slip them a note, demanding the teller remain calm and put all the money from their till into a bag. The bank teller, usually, doesn't scream or make a scene, they follow the instructions because they don't want to upset or make the bank robber angry. The last thing any bank branch wants is a robber to fire a weapon, take hostages, or create an armed standoff with police. Most times, the teller calmly hands the bag (along with the bait bill and a dye-pack slipped into the bag) back to the robber and watches as they leave, making mental descriptive notes of the robbers' height, weight, what they wore, anything that will help the cops arrest the person. They then quietly tell their manager upon the robber's departure, so they can lockdown the bank and call the police.

That's the "typical" way bank robberies go down. But some bank robbers, like in the movies, come into the bank brandishing a weapon, yelling for the customers and employees to get down on the floor. These are called "takedown robbers." And then there are those criminals who take violence to a whole other level entirely–this was one such bank robber.

This prolific bank robber was already on our radar, having hit seven other banks with his own unique style. He always made grand chaotic entrances, yelling at all the patrons to lie on the floor while threatening them with a handgun. But his outrageous actions were matched only by his clothing, wearing disco-themed apparel like bell bottom pants with platform shoes. And if his outfits were outrageous, his arsenal was stone-cold sobering.

The 911 caller told police the bank robber was carrying a large military-style duffle-bag and armed with a bomb and a handgun. Not any ordinary gun, but a silver plated, eight-inch barrel, 357-caliber Magnum revolver, almost as big as the kind "Dirty Harry" used. This time he was dressed in a two-piece suit and rode up to the bank on a pink, girl's bicycle. The outlandish clothing and over-the-top weapons seemed more suited for a Hollywood movie than a simple bank robbery, which earned him the "Hollywood Bandit" moniker from the robbery detectives.

"Hollywood" arrived, leaning the bike against one of the marble columns closest to the banks' large etched-glass doors. Briskly walking into the bank, he immediately started screaming for everyone to get down on the floor, while pulling a handgun and grenade out of the duffle bag. "Hollywood" held the gun in his right hand, aiming at the tellers, while holding the grenade in his other hand. Quickly walking over to the closest tellers' window, he slammed the grenade on the counter and screamed, "I've got a bomb!" His self-described "bomb" was later identified as a military-grade smoke grenade. But to the shocked bank patrons and employees, that smoke grenade looked like a powerful bomb. Brazenly, he left the grenade sitting on the teller's counter as a threatening statement to his confidence, which freed his left hand to retrieve a small, white, plastic grocery bag from his pants pocket to collect his loot.

Swinging his outstretched right arm wildly, "Hollywood" surveyed the entire bank floor, making sure everyone saw his gun and had hit the floor. He then pointed his revolver at the young female teller, who flinched while putting her hands in the air as he demanded cash. "Hollywood" gave the white grocery bag to the teller, and she immediately started putting the money from her drawer in the bag.

Working from the highest to lowest denominations, she made sure to pull the bait-bill, stuffing it among the rest of the Andrew Jacksons and Benjamins. Triggering the silent alarm, the signal instantly reached police communications—which was the beginning of the end to "Hollywood's" violent heist, and also his life.

Retrieving the demand note and taking the white bag with all that teller's cash, he proceeded to walk down the line to every teller in the bank. One after the other, like a Halloween trick-or-treater, "Hollywood" shoved the white grocery bag in each teller's face. After collecting all the money from the tellers, he returned to the grenade still sitting on the counter next to the first teller's window. Looking around, ensuring he had everyone's attention, he yelled, "Look!" He paused, and dramatically pulled the arming-pin out of the grenade, catapulting the grenade's released handle wildly into the air. Then "Hollywood" tossed the live grenade to the floor among the panic-stricken patrons.

As soon as the grenade clanked onto the marble floor, smoke billowed out of the grenade canister, generating a thick, dark cloud. The screaming patrons sprang up from the floor, running in sheer terror out of the bank. "Hollywood" quietly disappeared in the shroud of smoke, leaving undetected among the crowd of patrons escaping out the doors. Lost in the mayhem was the bank robber and his pink bike. It was a well-planned heist and getaway.

Police officers arrived quickly, driving down small streets, crisscrossing the bank area and high-end shopping complex looking for the robber riding away on the bike. After searching for several minutes, a police officer radioed that none of the officers could spot the bank robber. The officers then began parking in spots around the entire grounds in hopes of seeing the bank robber trying to sneak out of the dragnet. I arrived just as the perimeter of approximately twenty-officers finished setting-up in positions along the small streets and parking lots and around the property.

The needle from the bait-bill receiver in my car began darting erratically all over the place, indicating the robber was in various directions, which means the bait-bill is surrounded by concrete or metal, causing the signal to bounce off the metal surfaces—like an underground parking garage.

I radioed dispatch and relayed my belief that "Hollywood" could still be in the bank's lower parking garage. Moments later, I could hear the police helicopter overhead, assisting us and tightening the dragnet over the site and bank's parking garage, ensuring the bank robber would not be able to slip away if he was still on bank property.

Within minutes of being on the scene, a man on a pink bicycle rode nonchalantly past one of the marked patrol cars on the west side of the bank property. The man riding the bike didn't match the bank robber's description, appearing much older, and both his appearance and ragged clothes looked more like a homeless person living on the streets.

In lieu of the glaring discrepancy with the suspect's description, the bike rider needed to be questioned by the police. Unfortunately, more than a few police officers had the same idea as a dozen patrol officers left their positions on the perimeter. The police helicopter also flew off to monitor the group of police officers chasing after the peddling transient several blocks west of the bank.

As I watched the helicopter chase patrol cars overhead, I thought about how "Hollywood" could have given his pink bike to a transient in the parking garage. That would create a sufficient diversion for the robber to simply walk out, undetected, wearing his new change of clothes that he brought with him in the duffle bag. Gaps in the perimeter would allow an easy escape for anyone not fitting the description of the bank robber in a two-piece suit.

I drove toward the east side of the bank, believing the robber would try escaping in the opposite direction, hoping to pin him down with my presence, until such time the many officers returned to their perimeter positions. Driving slowly east bound, I kept a watch on the bank grounds to ensure I did not drive past the robber. Driving a short distance, I spotted a man who looked out of place. Sticking out like a sore thumb in a business district, a man dressed in a blue mechanic's overalls with a military-style, green duffle-bag slung over his shoulder, walking quickly in a grassy area near the parking garage. My cop's intuition was telling me, "I found the bank robber!"

We immediately locked eyes and he stopped, confirming my intuition. Like a deer caught in the headlights, he froze on a walkway separating the grass courtyard from the bank complex. I parked in a tactical manner on the small street that extended past the walkway, positioning my car so I could stand behind it to confront the bank robber.

The bank robber pulled the .357 Magnum out of a pocket in his overalls once I stopped the patrol car. My excitement at apprehending a bank robber turned to cold seriousness, as my training kicked-in. I tried to tell the radio operator of my sighting, but couldn't get through due to the other officers' discussion about the homeless guy on the pink bike. Our police radios at that time didn't let an officer alert others to an emergency with a simple push of a button, instead I simply couldn't get on the radio when another officer was talking. Every time I tried talking on the radio a loud "bonking" noise would interrupt, preventing me from transmitting. I had no way to get on the radio, no way of telling anyone I found the actual bank robber.

The robber pointed his revolver down toward the ground with his eyes fixated on me. I remained surprisingly calm, utilizing years of scenario training. Maintaining a constant sight on him, I ejected my useless portable radio from the car's dashboard. I then parked my car at a strategic angle, providing the best cover possible when I get out to face the bank robber. I did all these things simultaneously, while removing my handgun from its holster, always keeping my eyes on the gunman.

I jumped out of my patrol car, yelling, "Police, drop the gun!", while pointing my gun at him. Despite my repeated orders to drop the gun, the robber didn't comply. My repeated commands degraded into pleas of "Don't do it! Please, don't!" With my right hand holding the gun, I fumbled with the police radio with my other hand trying to interject into the pink bike ploy chatter, getting the automatic "bonking" in response. The loud "*bonk*" continued to wail as I kept trying, as I kept my eyes on the robber, his gun still deliberately pointing down at the ground.

As our standoff persisted, I also thought about the innocent people around in the area in case of a shooting. I needed to ensure none of my shots could injure or possibly kill someone else. Running through every scenario, I kept my cool and just kept ordering "Hollywood" to drop his gun. I ensured no citizens, no matter how far way, were behind him and in danger of missed shots. The bank robber could shoot with complete reckless abandonment, but I would not shoot if innocent bystanders were down range.

We are trained in the academy, and during annual firearm certifications, when faced with a deadly situation like this, someone with a gun who won't drop it, the rules are clear for police officers: the decision to shoot or not shoot is completely predicated on the suspect's actions. If the suspect ignores my orders and raises his gun, I can lawfully shoot him. But it only takes a mere fraction of a second for him to squeeze the trigger at the same time, killing me, before I can even shoot back. It is virtually impossible for me to shoot first, if I am reacting to the raising and firing of his gun. Simply said, he can shoot me before I can react and shoot back.

By keeping the gun pointed down, he was in control, choosing the moment that best suited him to raise his gun and shoot me. With each slow stride on the sidewalk toward a small street, his gun never strayed away from his side as he deliberately kept the barrel downward, assuring he controlled the first shot.

The sidewalk and courtyards, once filled with citizens, now cleared out quickly upon my screams of "Drop the gun!" The gunman continued ignoring my commands, calmly walking west toward the other side of the small street. His path ran parallel to me as I stood partially protected from the waist down behind my patrol car. I had to keep adjusting my spot behind the car trying to minimize my exposure as "Hollywood" kept walking.

He looked all around, as if he was searching for an escape route or ensuring no police officers had arrived on the scene, coming to my assistance. His encroaching presence forced me to move away from my patrol car and behind a parked car along the west curb of the small street. He searched past me, turning his head 90 degrees, planning his escape route as his only obstacle was me. It was then that he discovered an alternate path to make his escape.

"Hollywood" fixated on a three-foot brick landscape wall at the far side of the small street. On the other side of the small wall was a parking lot at a much lower elevation, and completely out of my view. I knew this parking lot was for a typically bustling shopping area with restaurants and stores. Without knowing if the area was full of people, I couldn't allow him to jump over the wall to a potentially populated area, where he could take a hostage. His actions in the bank clearly demonstrated he would be capable of such violence, which made him an imminent threat to innocent citizens. I had to prevent him from jumping over the wall, so I shouted again, "Drop your gun or I will shoot you! I won't let you jump over that wall!"

He then immediately stopped and stood facing the wall. "Hollywood" stood still for a moment and then looked around, as if contemplating his next move. Keeping his gun pointed down and by his leg, he turned and faced me in a precision turn, as if executing a command for a military left-face movement. He stood in a position for a shootout, glaring with intense concentration–sizing me up.

Outwardly, I was strangely calm and resolute for what I believed would be an inevitable gunfight based on his look alone. The extreme pounding of my heart was the only evidence of my fear. As my heartbeat raced, the robber quickly raised his gun and instantly shot twice. In response, I squeezed my trigger and heard the crack of my gun, feeling the recoil as the gun went up.

His two bullets struck the headlight and hood of the car that I was standing behind. Thankfully, he missed me, but I did not, striking him center mass in the upper torso. In that moment, everything slowed, coming into sharper focus. In slow motion, I saw my bullet impact his chest, seeing the actual impression the bullet made on his clothing.

"Hollywood" remained standing, appearing unfazed at being shot. Unlike the TV shows, he had no physical reaction to being shot. I was surprised he didn't fall to the ground, but neither of us hesitated, trading shots in rapid succession. He missed again, but his aim was closer. My shot struck center mass, yet again, he remained standing and fully engaged in the gunfight. I now felt terror, thinking for the first time, I'm going to die.

All my years of police training never prepared me for the surreal and horrid experience of shooting a person that wouldn't fall. My calm focus was now replaced with what I can only describe as mounting pressure swirling in my head. I was no longer seeing things in slow motion, but rapid-fire reality, as I was shooting him without any apparent effect.

A thought flashed through my mind—he had to be wearing a bulletproof vest, or so high on drugs that getting shot had no effect on him. I decided to stop aiming at his chest, opting for a more difficult target, his head. His last two shots were close, as both bullets missed my head. Shooting back, I struck his chest several more times with no effect. I had to call for help on my radio. I needed to let another police officer know where we were so "Hollywood" wouldn't get away, in the event he killed me.

Ducking completely behind the front engine compartment of the car, I tried calling on my radio again. But I was met with another "bonk!" I tried several times before giving up, realizing help wouldn't be coming, it was all up to me—I needed a new game plan.

I could not remain hidden behind the car, as my hero Officer Ken Collins was killed after being shot in the head after kneeling behind a car. My plan was to surprise him by moving to another spot behind the car, before standing back up to shoot him. He might be caught off- guard at my changed location, and his delayed reaction might give me the time needed for taking such a difficult head shot.

As I prepared to rise from my new spot behind the trunk of the car, I heard more gunshots in the distance, believing the bank robber had moved. My fear was he had ran-off and was now shooting at someone else, maybe having jumped over the wall. I jumped to my feet, only to be surprised to see the bank robber was still standing in the same exact location. He was still shooting at me from the same spot. I immediately took aim and fired at his head. His body collapsed instantly, falling limp to the ground—the bank robber was dead.

I was finally able to get on the radio and within seconds the scene of the fatal gunfight was packed with police officers.

Less than an hour later, the police department's Command Staff arrived, and I relinquished my handgun. I provided a brief account of my shooting to the Duty Commander, so police could search the surrounding area, ensuring no stray shots injured anyone. A union officer was permitted to cart me away to a diner in the area, so I could gather my thoughts as to the sequence of the shooting, knowing I had a long night of interviews with both Homicide and Internal affairs.

Hours later, homicide detectives arrived and interviewed me for several hours about the shooting. After that, Internal Affairs conducted their separate interview, also taking several hours to complete. I remained in shock during the 13-hour post-shooting interview process, not getting home until well after working 24 hours. The actual shooting lasted less than ten minutes, occurring at the end of my regular scheduled ten-hour work shift.

The following morning, the reality of the shooting started to sink in. While on the mandatory day off, I watched in a daze as my three-year-old daughter Robyn played in the backyard. My teenage son left to spend the night at his friend's house, being almost 13, he was a bit too self-absorbed to understand what I was going through. My wife kept asking me if I was ok, but how do you answer that? I replied, "fine" but she had never seen me so fragile. I was alone as life bustled around me, trying to process many emotions after killing a man.

Twist

I discovered at a debriefing four days later, a bizarre chain of events fell into place during my shooting. Other cops and detectives were present and involved in the shoot-out with the armed bank robber. The shots I heard while ducking to get on the radio did not come from the bank robber, but instead came from a motorcycle officer.

The motor officer heard the shots from behind a building and rode a short distance to see the shoot-out. As he turned the corner, he saw the back of the bank robber and me falling out of sight behind a car, as if I had been shot. Thinking the bank robber killed me, the motor officer accelerated and opened fire on the bank robber, emptying his entire pistol clip at the suspect. He resembled a World War II fighter pilot's scraping run, scattering shots down at the enemy below.

The motor officer's "scraping run" caused a lifesaving diversion for me, as the bank robber stopped shooting at me and turned around to redirect his attention at the motor officer. I never saw the motor officer, but upon hearing the shots, I got back into the gunfight. Standing up, I shot the suspect in the neck, killing him, or so I thought.

In the meantime, a plainclothes robbery detective was driving in the area looking for the suspect, and saw what he thought was me falling to my death. Never seeing the motor officer, the detective drove his unmarked car in the middle of the shoot-out, stopping a few feet behind the bank robber.

Without knowing it, he positioned himself in the line of fire between the bank robber and the motor officer. The detective bent down to retrieve his ankle-holstered gun at the same time the motor officer began shooting at the bank robber. The bullets passed over the bending detective, breaking through the car's windows. The robbery detective remained crouched down after hearing the massive gunfire from the motor officer. He received minor injuries from the shattered glass, having been shot out by the motor officer. All this also occurred at the same time I got back up from behind the car to shoot and kill the bank robber, but did I?

Unknown to me, the motor officer, and the robbery detective; another patrol officer and his partner heard the shooting. They, too, had already responded to the area to enclose the perimeter from the pink bike ruse and saw the shooting from behind me. They drove up from the main road, but never saw the robbery detective or the motor officer. The driver, Steve Ong, who later became a very good friend and my partner on the bike squad, parked his patrol car a short distance behind me and shot at the bank robber–at the same time I did.

So, who actually killed the bank robber? We will never know since Steve and I both fired at him simultaneously.

During our debriefing, we learned "Hollywood" committed the bank robberies to finance his drug addiction. A lengthy subsequent homicide investigation revealed that he was also stalking some of the female bank tellers, writing in a journal about his fantasies of raping them.

The bank robber's parents flew from New York to Phoenix to make funeral arrangements. His parents were very kind and compassionate, but alarmingly informed us they suspected their son had contracted AIDS from his drug activity. Since Steve and I were the officers who checked on their son after the shooting, we were covered in his blood. We had to endure a battery of tests to ensure we didn't contract the disease. Typically, police officers will wear plastic gloves when they know they will be dealing with a bloody subject, but the bank robber's bullet wounds were of such a life-threatening nature, we immediately tried stopping his bleeding without first donning the gloves. It was ultimately a moot point, as the shot that killed "Hollywood" struck his head, killing him instantly.

In this urgent event, all these police officers had no knowledge of the others' presence. They only saw me and each risked their lives to save mine. In my case, I risked my life to protect the community. I can never thank these officers enough for coming to my rescue. I am dedicating this chapter to all of them.

998 - 24 St. Camelback - 1512:44 - 1536:41
April 14, 1995
Page 1

1512:44	Radio	Hot tone 211 Ist Interstate Bank, 5050 N. 24 St.
1514:30	Radio	Hot tone 211T Tower Plaza area
1516:30	A18	Air 18 still getting 4 to 5 lights
1531:31	?	998
1531:36	Radio	998 5050 N. 24 St.
1531:51	?	22 St. North of Camelback roll Fire
1531:56	P72	Code 4 998 suspect down roll Fire
1532:28	P72	22 Place Camelback implement EDP
1533:46	P72	It is Code 4 subject is down. He's in custody it looks like at least 2 officers involved. Like I said before I really need a couple of supervisors out here to give me a hand.
1535:25	Command	I'm sorry to keep giving you so many things to do. Please roll Bomb Squad ASAP.

Radio Traffic

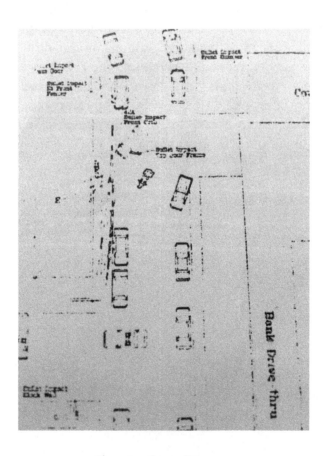

Shooting Scene Diagram

Photos by Michael Ging/The Arizona Republic

Police officials survey the area two blocks west of Biltmore Fashion Park where a bank-robbery suspect was shot and killed Thursday.

Shooting Scene

Photos by Michael Ging / The Arizona Republic

Police officials survey the area two blocks west of Biltmore Fashion Park where a bank-robbery suspect was shot and killed Thursday.

Police kill suspect in bank heist

Man fired 2 to 4 shots at officer after robbery, witnesses say

**By Susan Leonard
and Richard F. Casey**
The Arizona Republic

A bank-robbery suspect was shot and killed by police Thursday afternoon after he fired at then in a busy, upscale area of Phoenix two blocks west of Biltmore Fashion Park.

No officers or bystanders were seriously injured, but one officer was cut, apparently by flying glass from a window in his unmarked police car, which was hit by a bullet.

The exchange of gunfire also shattered a window of a car parked on 22nd Place just north of Camelback Road and some windows at a nearby office building.

The identity of the suspect was not immediately known.

Police said he robbed a First Interstate Bank at 24th Street and Camelback Road at about 3:10 p.m. and then fled west on Camelback on a girl's 10-speed bicycle.

The robber showed a grenade to a teller and said he would set it off if she did not give him money. The teller handed him some cash and tripped a silent alarm.

As the man left, he pulled the pin on the grenade, which later was found to be a smoke bomb.

Police refused to say how much money was taken.

Michael Ging / The Arizona Republic

A gun and canvas bag belonging to a suspected bank robber lay on the sidewalk next to the spot where he was shot by police. No one was hurt in the gunfire exchange, but one officer was cut, apparently by flying glass.

While walking on 22nd Place, just north of Camelback, the man opened fire on an officer who was looking for the robber.

"The cops did what they had to do, as far as I'm concerned," said one woman who saw the shooting while standing outside having a cigarette behind her office on Camelback Road.

"He shot first."

The woman, who asked not to be identified, said the man "ended up flying in the bushes

from the power of the shots fired at him."

Another witness, Al MacBeane, a computer programmer, said, "When a guy pulls a gun, he's asking to be killed."

The witnesses said the man fired two to four shots. Four officers — three in uniform and one in plainclothes — returned fire, striking the man in the chest.

A .38-caliber revolver and a small handgun

— See **BANK-ROBBERY**, page B2

Slain bank robber tied to 4 heists

Crime spree believed to be drug-related

By Pamela Manson
The Arizona Republic

A bank robber who was shot to death Thursday after firing at police has been linked to three other heists in Phoenix, a crime spree that might have supported his drug habit.

A search of the home of Andrew Henning Christensen in the 1700 block of West Missouri Avenue turned up drugs, including cocaine, and drug paraphernalia, police said Friday.

The previous holdups were at Bank of America branches, police said. Christensen died Thursday after robbing a First Interstate branch.

Christensen, 35, was killed in an exchange of gunfire with officers near 22nd Place and Camelback Road, two blocks west of Biltmore Fashion Park. Police said he had just held up the First Interstate branch at 24th Street north of Camelback and fled on a bicycle.

After abandoning the bike, he walked north on 22nd Place, opening fire on an officer looking for the bank robber.

Witnesses said Christensen fired two to four times. Four officers returned fire, striking him in the chest at least six times.

In Thursday's heist, the robber showed a grenade to a teller and threatened to set it off if she did not give him money. As the man left, he pulled the pin on the grenade, which later was found to be a smoke bomb.

Investigators think Christensen robbed these bank branches:
● Bank of America, 5755 N. 19th Ave., on Monday.
● Bank of America, 3334 N. 16th St., on March 19. A robber armed with a shotgun left a phony bomb that looked like sticks of dynamite attached to wires, a timer and a detonator.
● Bank of America, 6050 N. 16th St., on March 5.

Police have not revealed how much money was taken in the robberies.

Newspaper story about the shooting

Bike Squad

Steve Ong and Darren Burch on a Stakeout

Jake Bohi, Sam Farris and Darren Burch

DJ's Ride Along

Robyn and Jenny Burch's Ride Along

Allen and Darren Burch

Bill Schemers and Darren Burch celebrate retirement

CHAPTER 20

Bomb's Away

SHORTLY after the shooting, I joined Steve Ong on our precinct's newly formed Bike Squad. This concept is not new, but a familiar twist to the old walking beat patrol. Now, instead of slowly walking around, we could quickly ride in tough beats helping citizens in dangerous neighborhoods.

The daily activity of riding a bike is without a doubt the most fun I ever had during my entire law enforcement career. I experienced more rewarding jobs in advocacy and investigative assignments, but for sheer fun the bike squad takes first prize. Steve was already assigned to the squad when he assisted me at the shooting, but our subsequent partnership a month later seemed more like fate.

We never rode alone, always riding in two-person teams. When working particularly dangerous, high-crime areas, we rode in larger packs, sometimes with the entire six-person squad. The reason bike cops always ride with a partner is because we are vulnerable targets being fully exposed on a bike. We were especially at-risk riding through back alleys and dark parking lots, but the advantage was that bikes could ride through these areas much more quickly and unnoticed, unlike in a patrol car.

Riding stealthily in the bad neighborhoods was and still is a very effective crime-fighting tool. There are no other modes of police transportation that allow police officers to silently confront criminals during the commission of a crime. Steve and I, rode into the middle of many crimes in progress, such as drug deals, burglaries, car thefts, and even bank robberies—all on our bicycles.

Steve and I arrested seven separate car thieves in a single week, even catching three separate bank robbers in that same month. These arrests earned us *Officers of the Month honors*. Saturating small-crime areas in our precinct, we concentrated our efforts, devised a proactive plan, and made an immediate impact in those crime-ridden neighborhoods. Crime rates went down while quality of life vastly improved for these residents.

As much as it is an effective crime-fighting tool, we also had a lot of fun playing practical jokes on one another. The inflicting of practical jokes is not exclusive to just bike cops, it seems to be a right-of-passage for most police officers. As a rookie cop, I watched my training officer place a bag of eggs under the driver seat of his buddy's assigned patrol car while he was away on summer vacation. Upon the buddy's return from vacation, he was stuck driving around on his first work shift with the overwhelming stench of rotten eggs baked into his patrol car. As a seasoned cop, my practical joke of choice was placing a small, undetectable amount of black finger-print powder on my partner's steering wheel. By end of shift, invariably there would be incriminating "nose-picking" evidence in the way of black stains surrounding his nostrils.

Steve and I loved playing jokes on our fellow bike officers, but Steve loved it even more and had a natural knack for it. He is one of the best tactical police officers I've ever had the pleasure to work with, but his true calling is as a master trickster. His uncanny ability of picking a prank to play on the right person, perfectly (and hilariously) targeting their weakness or sensitive issue.

After the shooting, we both developed symptoms that would be diagnosed today as Post Traumatic Stress Disorder or PTSD. For me, it was forgetfulness. I would routinely leave sunglasses, notepads, my police radio or numerous other sundry items at report calls or crime scenes. Steve became hyper-sensitive to loud, sudden sounds—

he would physically jump after a sudden or unexpected noise like firecrackers or the backfire from a car.

In today's world, these symptoms would be diagnosed and treated. Since we didn't know about PTSD back then, we thought it was funny to use these PTSD-symptoms or triggers lovingly and hilariously against each other.

Steve routinely picked up my glasses or radio that I placed on a table at the home of a radio call, knowing I would surely forget about it. Later, realizing I left said item at a home or business he would let me drive all the way back before handing me a ransom note for the item. The ransom notes would provide cryptic clues to the forgotten item's whereabouts. My pranks were just simple opportunities—making the loudest noise at the most inopportune time (for him).

For example, I was waiting for him to finish using the restroom one day, when I decided to throw the metal trash can across the floor, smashing against his stall door. There is nothing funnier than hearing your partner literally jump off his toilet seat after throwing a large, heavy, metal trash can against his restroom stall door. Today I recognize it was a shitty move by a partner, but then funny trumped everything. Having a laugh, even at each other's psychologically-damaged or traumatized expense was how we coped back when I was on the force. But it also made us realize that we had to confront our fears (even if it was in the most childish ways). I doubt if this type of behavior would be acceptable between partners today, and I don't think any mental health professional would endorse our "group therapy" exercises. But this is what we did to provide a much-needed comic relief from our long, hard day, because most days were stressful and busy enough making arrest after arrest.

Hardly a day went by that Steve and I didn't pull a practical joke on each other or on another bike squad officer. Our best pranks were achieved when we worked together against other squad officers. We worked with an officer who was a perfectionist. We would completely reorganize her workstation and by re-organize, I mean it looked completely different, as if it belonged to someone else. The look of confusion on her face was priceless, as she tried to find the simplest of items. We also replaced photos of her family in picture frames on her desk with pictures of strangers that we cut from magazines and newspapers.

We pranked a time-compulsive officer by incorrectly resetting every clock in his work area, office, car, and pager to the wrong time, as little as five-minutes or as much as ten-hours. My favorite trick was tweaking the fingerprint powder prank, smearing the black powder on the handle bars of an officer who was a clean-freak. By the end of the day he looked like Rudolph the Black Nose Rider.

Two of our more testosterone-driven bike officers, Sam and Jake were worthy rivals, as they liked to mess with us. On one occasion, they used a syringe to inject cold water into the foam of our bike seats. In the beginning of our shift when we jumped on our bikes to ride, the water-infused seats would soak the bottom of our bike shorts. Jake served as a Marine and his partner, Sam, had a quick wit and was super competitive. Their "manly" attributes made them a great target for feminine-themed jokes. Using a word processor, I created a five-foot-long banner "Just Married" in a sweet, squiggly font, and attached it to the back of their patrol car. They finally figured out they were the butt of a joke when citizens on sidewalks were blowing them kisses.

Steve and I may have been arguably the most prolific pranksters, and the entire squad participated. But the best prank came from a complete outsider, a dirty-bird that executed a hefty prank against all us bike officers at the same time. It occurred on a day our bike squad was assisting on a multi-jurisdictional search warrant. Numerous raids were planned at a series of homes city-wide that were involved in robberies and drug dealing activities. Other tactical police squads assisted in the large operation, such as our SWAT officers, K-9 squad officers with their dogs, and a host of patrol officers.

The morning of the operation, our entire squad met at our bike squad office located at a business park, where all our bicycles and gear were stored. After mounting our bikes on the back of our patrol cars and gathering the tactical equipment needed for the raid, we met in the parking lot and inspected each other's uniforms and gear. We were excited to be part of such a large raid, wanting to show off our tactical skills. We looked formidable wearing our special tactical vests, SWAT-style uniforms, and specialized raid gear.

After the uniform inspection, the six of us gathered around the hood of one of the patrol cars, collectively discussing our roles in the operation, tying-up loose ends before we had to leave for the formal briefing for all the units involved in the raid.

As we were intensely going over tactics using the hood as our war room table, we never saw an uninvited pigeon fly over our heads. It had to be the largest pigeon in the history of birds because he dropped the biggest payload and hit his target with pin-point accuracy.

The bird shit right in the middle of the hood, splattering a "Big Gulp" sized crap all over us—The color and consistency was like a Cookies and Cream milkshake, striking the hood with such intensity, the aerial assault evenly distributed bird poop on all our uniforms, faces, and hair. Shell-shocked and gawking at each other in our bird-poop laden uniforms, we stood speechless, after first blurting out reactive expletives at the winged prankster flying by.

We had no time to clean up, as it was time to leave for the formal briefing, minutes away from the tightly-timed execution of the multiple raids. There wasn't even enough time to wipe the bird dung from our clothes. On the drive, we quickly wiped off our faces with anything we could find in the car, old napkins and the like. The smearing of the muck only exacerbated the problem. We arrived in bird-shit-spattered police apparel and hair gel.

Twist

As the designated arrest team, our squad was tasked with arresting and escorting those arrested from their homes to the "Paddy-Wagon." Handcuffing the suspects, we held them tight against our horrid clothes as we walked them to the transportation team. Typically, subjects arrested will say the same things; "I want an attorney!", "You have to read me my rights, I'm innocent," etc. However, our prisoners all pleaded, "Please don't touch me." We were more of a toxic hazard than their meth labs busted in the raids.

CHAPTER 21

Hippo Hell

BIKE squads are an effective tool for crime fighting and also helping to build good community relationships with various proactive programs. Once the neighborhoods were safer with our arrest sweeps, we would go back to and participate in various community and charity events.

These events included Block Watch meetings, public safety events, and other community outreach programs. One education program involved elementary school children by organizing bicycle rodeos, teaching kids to ride safely. We loved working bicycle-themed programs when assisting with these community events.

At one particular event, Steve Ong and I assisted the NBA Phoenix Suns basketball team and rock legend Alice Cooper at a Christmas charity event. The Suns donated 100 bicycles and helmets to needy children in our neighborhood. Our bike squad officers not only ensured each individual child was given the appropriate-sized bicycle, but individually adjusted the new bike helmets for each child.

These community charity events gave me an invaluable opportunity to talk with some families who were in the most need for a kind gesture. One middle aged mother shared with me the recent death of her daughter. I hugged her, relaying my heartfelt sorrow for her nightmarish loss. Having been a single father myself, I couldn't imagine the unspeakable horror and sadness of losing a child.

The mother explained that she had recently divorced her husband, and was raising two children on her own. As a working mom, she had to better organize her limited time caring for her 9-year-old daughter, and 7-year-old son. One helpful tip was preselecting her children's clothing the night before a school day, allowing her children to dress themselves after awakening. She would place each child's clothing on a hanger, hooking it on their bed. The kids could then dress themselves in the morning. Her daughter had never sleep-walked or fell out of bed, so mom never thought twice about leaving her daughter's hanger on the top railing of the bunk bed. Horrifically, one night the daughter fell out of bed, entangling her head into her clothes and hanged herself.

The horrified younger brother discovered the death upon waking up for school and started screaming. Mom woke up to the traumatized screams, and discovered her daughter's lifeless body. To make her nightmare worse, she missed work due to the funeral arrangements and lost her job. Even today, surviving parents are allowed only three bereavement days leave from work when their child dies. None of the other charity events hit me as hard as that woman telling me her story. What really struck me was how appreciative she was of a simple kind gesture, hugging me for ensuring her son's bike helmet fit properly and would keep him safe.

Because these wonderful events were filled with genuine acts of kindness and were so uplifting for people who really need it, I began volunteering at these community events on my own free time. For one of these events, I went to a Mardi Gras–themed charity. We wore animal costumes to celebrate with those attendees who donated money to a non-profit organization. Since I arrived late, I got stuck with the most undesirable costume: an oversized hippopotamus. Being rejected by every other volunteer, I was unaware why no one wanted to be a hippo until I put it on and realized it was a death trap. No one else would be stupid enough to wear a costume constructed in blatant disregard to every known OSHA law, but I did!

The outfit consisted of a top and bottom half, which were attached from the outside, making it necessary for someone to help me get in and out of the Iron Maiden of a costume. Metal zippers, clasps, and hooks designed to entrap its victim in the hippo-tomb weighed the costume down immensely, making movement difficult. The costume's size was designed for someone taller than six-foot. I stand at a towering 5'9", so my slender frame was dwarfed by the oversized Disney-reject hippo suit.

The hippo's screen-covered mouth provided practically no visibility, and even worse ventilation. This port allowing for sight and breathing was a foot over my head, making vision almost impossible. I had to pull down with both hooves, shoving the hippo head downward while standing on my tiptoes to even see the ceiling, and I needed to use the same procedure to fan air into the costume to breathe. After a few claustrophobic tries, I figured out that one hoof-hand could hold the head downward, while simultaneously using my other hoof-hand to fan air into the mouth-port. This oxygen-and-sight technique worked only marginally, inflating my fears of heat stroke, asphyxiation, claustrophobic seizures, and tripping over who knows what, because I could not see down or ahead–only up.

One of the other volunteers entrapped me into my hellish hippo costume, and led me into the rehearsal meeting. Unable to sit, I stood as the rest of the volunteers sat listening to an activity director explain the various roles in the event. He talked in a rapid and energized manner, sounding very much what I envisioned a Broadway choreographer would sound like. Those of us in animal costumes, to include myself, were to dance with "high energy" with the donors in a conga line. The court-jesters would dance wildly controlling the conga line, and we were told that after thirty-minutes, the jesters, who had actual hands, would shoot off confetti-filled "poppers," signaling the end of the show.

We were listening to the activity director for only ten-minutes and I was already dripping with sweat in the sauna-suit. I was exhibiting early signs of heat stroke and the Mardi Gras-like charity event hadn't even started. Without even being able to see the activity director, I hated him based on his stupid high voice, instructing everyone to dance with "high energy," and I was already tapped-out.

Showtime couldn't come quick enough, as we were led out into the ballroom, where festive music played during our entrance. I must have looked like an angry hippo with a toothache, constantly yanking my jaw downward while waving my hooves into my big hippo mouth. Out of nowhere, because I couldn't see, a woman grabbed my flailing hoof-hand and dragged me into the conga line. She placed both of my hoof-hands around her thin waist, and she proceeded to strut and bounce to the sound of the beat, with me in tow. Without the use of my hooves, I couldn't see and wasn't getting adequate air. Waiting patiently for the blast of graffiti poppers to signal the end, I held a tight grip on her hips, as much as you can with a hoof, and tried dancing with high energy.

After what seemed like an eternity of conga-line dancing in my hippo sauna, I heard the fire cracking sound of the "poppers," which marked the end to my hippo hell. Some smoke from the "poppers" must have filled the room, as a little smoke began to funnel into my costume. I assumed the smoke was from the pyro-poppers, so I tried to ignore it until the sudden screams from my dance partner clued me that something was very wrong, as the smoke continued to billow into my costume.

Pushing me away, she screeched, "The hippo is on fire!" Choking in the smoke-filled hippo-sarcophagus, I stomped, shouting some expletives, (not my finest hour), while running wildly and screaming for someone to get me out of the hippo suit. This may have looked like the high-energy dancing that the activity director was wanting, but I remembered what we learned as kids in elementary school— Stop, Drop and Roll. I fell to the ground with a thud but couldn't roll, instead the bottom of the suit just collapsed flat on the ground. I looked like a beached hippo-whale having seizures, and still on fire, of course.

Someone grabbed a fire extinguisher and sprayed me down, but that only made my predicament worse. A quick science lesson: a fire extinguisher works by propelling a chemical agent to extinguish the fire's oxygen supply. I had just one air hole in the hippo costume and now that hole was being pumped with suffocating foam. I couldn't even scream for help, as the suffocating foam made it impossible. Choking or burning to death in a hippo suit wasn't the heroic way

I envisioned my cop-life would end, saving lives running into a fire maybe, but this was just embarrassing.

At last, I could feel someone fumbling with my hippo belly zipper, but they were clearly having difficulty getting it open, as it was possibly damaged by the hard fall to the floor. I was close to death's door, when someone finally used a pocket knife and cut the costume enough for me to squeeze out.

Twist

My delayed extraction from the hippo suit was ugly, not to mention scary. Not just for me, but for the innocent, young children watching among the party goers. The fire extinguisher foam, infused with my sweat, created a slimy ooze that covered my entire body. Gasping for breath, I squeezed out of the cut section along the hippo's crotch and I crowned from the hippo's smoldering pelvis. I emerged from my birth-like extraction to a shocked six-year-old boy looking on with terror. The party came to a screeching halt, and undoubtedly many parents later needed to explain the birds, the bees, and the Hippo-cesarean.

CHAPTER 22

Liquid Person Bursting at the Seams

A DECOMPOSING body is certainly not pretty, so if you're hoping this story of a "Liquid Person Bursting at the Seams" is about liquid magically transforming into a pretty and well-endowed female seamstress, forget it. To the contrary, I will go into painstaking detail describing an actual liquid person; a real-life horror story involving nature's dead body rotting process. For those willing to continue down this twisted but true path, you may want to forgo eating while doing so.

On a summer day in 1996, Steve Ong and I responded to a "welfare–check" call at a residence. It was brutally hot on this day, which is saying a lot when you're talking about a Phoenix summer. The temperatures can soar as high as 120 degrees. Traffic crawls at a snail's pace along the melting streets, everything moves slower, but things decompose faster. During our investigation, we learned the person lived alone for many years. He didn't have any friends and no family visited on a regular basis. No one reported him missing, as he wasn't missed.

It was the foul odor from his house that prompted neighbors to call police to check on his welfare. As soon as we got to the house and stepped out of the air-conditioned, comfortable squad car, we were hit by two things immediately: the oppressive heat (which you can anticipate but never really get used to) and a foul and pungent odor. If the details of the call from dispatch didn't clue us in, the stench certainly did. We were dealing with a decomposing body, well before we even found it.

The neighborhood was predominantly occupied by senior citizens, with homes from an outdated construction period in the 1950's. The home in question was the same color of the dirt lot it sat on. We walked up to the small, run-down house, stepping gingerly on the wooden porch that was falling apart from years of neglect.

Steve knocked on the weather-beaten door, receiving no response from inside. I peeked into the home through a front window, and saw nothing moving in the darkness. After a reasonable waiting period, we had a duty to forcibly enter and check the resident's welfare. Like a haunted house in a horror movie, everyone knows only bad things would happen to uninvited guests going inside.

I entered the house through an unlocked front window. Crawling into the home, I pushed away cob webs while feeling my way through the darkness to the front door. Sunlight entered through the front window, making my initial walk into the dark home less difficult. The scorching heat from the outside, coupled with the disconnected electricity and lack of air-conditioning rendered the home into a dark, smelly, sauna. After opening the door for Steve, we retrieved our flashlights from the car. With flashlights in hand, we proceeded to search through the home for the resident.

The home had been stuffed with a lifetime collection of newspapers. Thousands of newspapers were tightly stacked in rows, forming a make-shift maze throughout the residence. We followed narrow paper-constricted paths, leading from room to room. Walking down one corridor, we could hear rustling all around. As our eyes adjusted to the darkness, we could see feline silhouettes peering down at us. A cadre of starving cats scurried along the top of the newspaper walls and around our feet. These emaciated creatures were intently watching our every move with their glowing eyes, as we continued through the dark paper-lined halls.

We were following the same worn and narrow path that the resident must have repeatedly walked. Dry rot from repetitive trips over the same path wore away portions of the wood flooring, creating football–sized holes pitted along the way. The virtual mine-field of holes made for a treacherous walk, forcing us to move cautiously. With our every step, creaking sounds from the dilapidated wood floors announced our presence to the cockroaches. Already miserable from the heat, we disgustedly slapped off cockroaches as they sporadically appeared and disappeared through the cracks along the paper corridors.

We reached a fork in the maze, but the intensity of the noxious odor made it clear where to go. To the left: the strong smell of decaying flesh. To the right: the stale aroma of rotten food. We turned left down a short hall, making our way to the bedroom. On the bed was the nude body of a dead man. He was lying face up, his face frozen in a grizzly grimace with his eyes and mouth both wide open, signaling a painful death. He lay spread-eagle with his arms and legs reaching their respective bed corners. The twin sized bed was inadequately small for such a large man, appearing to be more than 200-pounds. The small house, with its narrow corridor, along with the bed, seemed at odds for a man his size.

We couldn't determine his race because his decaying skin was blotched with varying shades of black, blue, and gray. Though Steve and I were good street cops, we weren't homicide detectives, so we didn't know about the different stages of a decomposing body. One of the more disgusting stages is referred to as the "bloating effect." In this bloating stage, the body begins to internally liquefy, creating gases. The body inflates due to the expanding gases, but eventually the outer-shell of the body breaks down, and the gas escapes. Unfortunately, we didn't know this.

Today, the medical examiner's office employs a staff trained to assist police departments with transporting dead bodies for such duties. However, during this period, we relied on a list of rotating mortuary businesses, who took turns in collecting dead bodies for transport to the medical examiner's office. The mortuary sent two teenagers, both brand-new to the undertaker job, so they knew even less than we did about bloated bodies. Why else would they foolishly accept my plan for lifting the bloated body off the bed?

My plan was simple: the four of us would each grab a limb, and simultaneously lift the body on the count of three, and carry him onto an opened body bag that the teens laid on the floor. The dead man's size made us think we needed to use an exorbitant amount of strength to lift his heavy body, not realizing he was actually thin before the bloating process. So, on my count, we lifted with all of our might, only to find us landing on our asses after falling backwards, as the man's limbs slid completely off their bones, exploding like biohazardous water balloons.

Twist

To my horror and distaste, my mouth was wide open when my limb, the dead man's left arm, popped off the body, bursting upon my face. The poorly planned dead body removal, literally left a bad taste in my mouth.

CHAPTER 23

Excuse Me, I Left My Wallet at the Crime Scene

I N December 1997, I reached my investigative career goal, investigating sexual assaults as a detective in the sex crimes detail. I spent close to eight years working on these difficult rape cases. That's not to say that all my sex crime investigations were difficult, as the story in this chapter will attest.

Regrettably, few rapists are as stupid as the idiot in this twisted tale. This door knob practically arrested himself due to a blunder and unbelievable gullibility. I've seen blatant mistakes made by many other suspects due to the consumption of alcohol, but this moron was stone cold sober. He did however use alcohol as a weapon to snare his victim.

Nightclubs and bars aren't always the best place to meet "Mr. Right." Many times, women end up meeting "Mr. Wrong," as these venues contain two key ingredients for sexual predators to carry out their rape plan: 1) a room full of strangers and 2) an unlimited supply of intoxicating liquor. Everyone understands the inherent danger of strangers lurking in the dark but for some reason, people let their guard down when talking to absolute strangers in dimly lit bars. Add to this the consumption of alcohol because liquor degrades the decision-making ability, allowing the talking to complete strangers to be less concerning. Many sexual predators go to bars for the sole purpose to select a victim under the pretense of an impromptu date when the bar is closing.

The term, "Date Rape" should never be used to describe these bar-trolling rapists. The unfortunate pairing of words incorrectly suggests that a regular date ended badly. Instead, sexual predators enter these bars for the sole purpose of looking for prospective victims. The rapist's pretense of having romantic interest ("date") is a ruse to help facilitate his sexual assault. The rapist's romantic role-playing provides three elements to help his crime succeed; 1) provides the victim with a false sense of intimacy, lowering her guard. 2) hoping to get the victim alone, making her vulnerable. And 3) mislead a potential witnesses pool in the event the rapist is eventually identified.

The victim was a 26-year-old, attractive, single female with a successful position in a corporate business. She and her friends met to celebrate her recent promotion at a well-known downtown restaurant, which also had a small nightclub style bar venue. While ordering a drink at the bar, the suspect flirtatiously introduced himself to the victim, initiating a conversation.

She initially described the suspect as an attractive, tall, 30-year-old male. But was unable to provide any clothing description and by the end of the interview admitted that her self-proclaimed beer-goggle impairment made her second-guess her "attractive" description. She could not recall his facial features, only that he had vivid blue eyes. When asked if she could pick him out of a line-up, she doubted any such likelihood.

The suspect bought her the drink that she ordered at the bar, and she invited him to join her and her friends at their table. He followed and remained sitting next to her at the table for the better part of an hour when "last call" was announced. She had been talking to him about her new job and didn't remember him talking about himself. They were flirting back and forth so much that she didn't even realize that all her friends had already went home.

She and "Mr. Wrong" continued talking past "last call" to the bar closing time. She invited him to her home for a nightcap. Based on the nature of their flirtatious conversation, she said there was an understanding that they would be having sex at her home. Since her home wasn't far from the nightclub, he followed in his car. She couldn't remember the make and model of his car, only that he parked across the street and met her at the front door.

They talked on her living room couch before kissing, then going to the bedroom to have sex. Once on the bed, he suddenly became inappropriately physical, hurting her wrists as he forcefully held her down. She immediately told him to stop, but ignoring her pleas, the rapist escalated his attack by choking her, squeezing her throat with both hands, telling her to "Shut up and enjoy it."

He punched her several times in the face, threatening to "hurt her worse" if she kept resisting. She began crying uncontrollably and stopped resisting. He pulled down his pants and sexually assaulted her for what she said, "seemed like an eternity."

After finishing, the rapist quickly pulled up his pants and left, not knowing his wallet was left behind. The suspect's pants fell loosely down by his ankles during the rape, which more than likely resulted in his wallet falling out of his back pocket, sliding unnoticed between the folds in the sheets. I later discovered, the rapist never noticed his missing wallet until the next day, not knowing if he left it at the bar or at the victim's home.

After the assault, the victim immediately called police. Patrol officers arrived to secure the scene for detectives, then the Night Detectives took over the investigation until the morning when I inherited the case. I practically did a "Happy Dance" when I read the report and learned the rapist left his wallet on the victim's bed.

After working so many difficult and complex rape investigations it was a great feeling to have a case in which the suspect left his calling card. Inside the wallet was a photo driver's license. I now had the suspect's identity, and a simple photographic line-up with the victim could positively confirm the suspect in the rape.

But my elation was short lived. I learned the night detective showed the driver's license photo to the victim at her home. This mistake completely prohibited the victim from ever identifying the suspect to police or in court. Legally speaking, law enforcement told her who the suspect was when showing her the photo from the suspect's wallet rather than her picking out the suspect's photo from a line-up of additional photographs with subjects that had similar facial features. In short, the night detective destroyed the value of the suspect inadvertently leaving his wallet at the crime scene, because without the victim identifying him in court, the suspect could testify his wallet had been stolen, preventing us from proving he was at the scene of the crime.

Without additional evidence, such as fibers, fingerprints, or DNA evidence, we wouldn't be able to prove he was the rapist. The suspect didn't ejaculate, so there wasn't any DNA evidence in the rape kit. The suspect left no fingerprints, appearing to the victim in hindsight that he intentionally didn't touch anything in the victim's home. I went to the bar and learned the video surveillance system wasn't working, so there was no visual evidence. I talked with the bar employees, and not surprisingly, they had no recollection of the victim or the suspect. None of her friends could pick the suspect out of a photo line-up because the two kept to themselves while dancing and talking during the night. Nothing from either the crime scene or the bar would help prove the suspect had committed the rape.

The case should have been a slam dunk, but the night detective's mistake could have irreparably hurt the investigation. With no DNA, no video, no fingerprints, no witness identification, and no victim statements to the suspect driver's license photo looking exactly like the suspect, the suspect could get away with the rape.

Even though the mistake was a major setback for me, I wasn't done. I had to come up with a way, a good ruse, to bring this rapist to justice. With some basic detective work, I found the suspect's telephone number and called him during work hours, hoping he wouldn't be home. Pretending to be a concerned citizen who found his wallet, I left a brief message on his telephone answering machine. I identified myself as a "good citizen," intentionally not leaving a telephone number, only saying I found his wallet outside a bar and dropped it off at the nearest police station.

I talked with the front desk officer at the police station closest to the bar, letting him know about my plan. The idea was for the suspect to eventually call the police station looking for his wallet, hoping that since a detective didn't contact him about the wallet at the victim's home he might take the bait. Before leaving the police station, I left my phone number, instructing anyone at the front desk to call me immediately if someone calls or shows up looking for their wallet.

I didn't have to wait long for a call from the front desk officer. The very next day, the rapist called the police station asking about his wallet. The front desk officer followed my instructions, telling the suspect that he would need some form of identification (just to help with the con) and would need to come down in person to sign for the property.

Eager to get his wallet back, the rapist came to the police station a few hours later, with his library card for identification. I had arrived at the police station only minutes before he did, but just in time to escort him to an interview room to talk about his wallet. I immediately dropped the bomb, telling him my standard "I got good news and bad news" line.

His face turned white as a ghost when I told him that there was no doubt about his guilt, and that my only confusion is if he intended to kill the victim. I then played with the truth, telling him that his DNA was all over the victim's neck from the brutal choking– which we didn't have after the victim washed her face while waiting for the police. He fell for my legally permitted fabrication, admitting quickly that he only wanted to rape the victim and never intended to kill her.

The suspect confessed to the entire rape, providing details that could only be known by the rapist and those working on the case. His detailed confession led to his plea to several counts of sexual assault.

Twist

I kept my word and made the wallet available for release back to the suspect. Since the plea deal voided the possibility of filing any appeals—the wallet was no longer needed as evidence. The suspect would need some form of identification and sign for it in person, once he was released from prison.

CHAPTER 24

That Sucks, Mr. Hoover!

AS a young man, I worked as a landscaper at an apartment complex. My worst injury on that job came after running over a chunk of concrete with a lawnmower, resulting in a genital injury. The injury, even worse than it sounds, is far too personal to describe without the consumption of a couple of stiff drinks. So, rather than telling you my own gonad-grating story, I will share a much grizzlier tale of genital disfigurement that I dealt with as a sex crime investigator.

During my long-career, I've investigated very few male rape cases, but this case stands out because the rape allegation involved an unusual, if not brutal cutting of the victim's penis.

By initial accounts, the penis-slicing occurred when a slew of unknown, masked men broke into the victim's apartment in the afternoon and attacked him. The young man sustained severe and numerous slicing wounds to his penis, leaving the mutilated member dangling by a thin piece of skin. His penis was truly hanging on by a thread.

The victim first disclosed a vague story to a nurse while being admitted in the emergency room. The victim's rape disclosure prompted the hospital staff to call the police. Dispatched patrol officers in turn called the sex crime detail to request a detective. I fielded their phone call and responded to the hospital, hoping to make sense of the extremely vague account. The victim's story left many unanswered questions; who were these men, why did they select this victim, what motive could there be for slicing the victim's penis?

The hospital surgeon showed me x-rays and pictures of the man's severely injured penis, repeatedly describing the tattered penis as a "*severe*" injury. I must have made countless involuntary grimaces every time I heard, "severe penis injury." Referring to the wound as a "severe penis injury" was a massive understatement, like describing a severed head as a "a bit of a decapitation." The sedated victim spoke to me in a surprisingly calm manner, having been brutalized with an attempted penis dismemberment.

Lying still in the hospital bed, he told me how four black guys broke into his home, and while holding him down, one of them carved-up his penis with a pocketknife. He couldn't give me a reason for why they violently attacked him, or why they targeted him—and his penis. Something occurred to cause the injury, but his story of four masked assailants randomly breaking into his home in broad daylight just didn't add up.

My suspicion increased each time he mumbled, "um" before responding vaguely to my questions; a common stalling method. People who are making up a story or lying will intentionally or involuntary utter some sound while trying to think of a response to the question.

Skeptical of his claim, I noticed he had no other injuries, not even a red mark anywhere else, on his body. The lack of injuries was inconsistent with four guys holding him down to cut off his penis. At least some bruising would be on his body from any struggle trying to prevent them from cutting his penis, and how could you NOT struggle!

On a side note, I'm really getting tired of writing the word, "*penis*" over and over, as I'm sure you are sick of reading it, therefore, from this point forward, I will use other words to describe his manhood that hopefully aren't too corny or cryptic.

The victim couldn't explain why after his junk was julienned he didn't call 911 for the police, or why he drove himself to the hospital instead of getting an ambulance. His only response for these and any other logical questions were, "I must have been in shock." He also had no reasonable excuse why he didn't immediately inform the hospital staff of the rape and mutilation. The hospital staff only learned of the attack and rape after repeated prodding about how the injury occurred; then the staff immediately called the police.

Not only did the details of the attack not make sense, the idea that the criminals' sole purpose would be to rob the victim of his manhood is ridiculous. The victim maintained his story, feigning fatigue when confronted with his unbelievably outlandish account. I agreed to postpone the interview until he regained his strength. I already had sufficient details and suspicion to help debunk his story.

When a detective is confronted with a false-sounding account, they need to look elsewhere to gather information to support or contradict the victim's story. The crime scene is a great place to learn the truth, as evidence doesn't lie. Cases can be proven or disproven based on the evidence analyzed at the scene of the crime.

In addition to the physical evidence telling detectives what happened in a crime, interviewing witnesses, family, friends, neighbors, and medical experts can also reinforce the truth. Medical experts in this case gave me their forensic opinion as to the mechanics of the "pee-pee" injury.

The medical staff unanimously said the victim's injury didn't appear to be self-inflicted, which surprised me because I was having a hard time believing someone else inflicted his injury. I knew from years of investigative work that self-inflicted injuries were typically committed in a slow and calculated manner due to the person's trepidation against the pain of hurting themselves. Most self-inflicted cuts that I saw were linear in pattern, easily reachable by the person, and typically not in a sensitive area—like the genitals. This attempted "dong-dismemberment" had none of those self-inflicted characteristics, as this was seemingly fast and chaotic, like throwing a hotdog down the garbage disposal. Though, his injury didn't look like a controlled, self-inflicted injury, it could have been a reckless act of self-mutilation or even accidental.

After leaving the hospital staff, I drove to the victim's residence to search for fresh clues at the scene of the crime. He lived in a large apartment complex, which consisted of hundreds of apartments. His apartment was on the second story with numerous neighbors on either side, above, and below him. There was also a court-yard with a grass area, picnic benches, horseshoe pits, and grills adjacent to his apartment building.

Upon my arrival, several of the tenants were outside playing horseshoes and grilling steaks. I talked with them, learning they were there setting up the grill and horseshoe pits at the time of the victim's reported attack. They didn't see or hear anything suspicious, but did hear a single scream from a second story apartment, but it didn't sound like an attack—more subdued, like someone being startled. A few of them knew the victim, and saw him walking quickly to his car a few minutes after hearing the shrill-sounding noise. Those folks believed he was the person who screamed, but he didn't look like he was in trouble as he walked past them to the parking lot.

Leaving the courtyard, I went to the victim's apartment building and spoke with the tenants on either side of the victim's residence. They too only heard one loud scream but nothing afterward. I also spoke to the other people that were home in the surrounding apartments. Not a single person in the entire apartment complex saw or heard anything remotely consistent with the victim's story of a brazen or brutal home-invasion.

Looking at the victim's apartment door, I saw no damage or evidence of a forced entry. The apartment manager used his master key to let me into the victim's apartment, where I found the place to be clean and well kept, which contradicted the reported struggle. The only mess was in the living room where I found a significant pooling of blood curiously next to a vacuum cleaner. The vacuum, a four-wheel canister model, seemed out of place sitting in the middle of the clean, living room floor.

This single piece of evidence provided the needed clarity to my investigation. I finally had a good idea of what might have occurred, the victim used the vacuum cleaner in an odd masturbatory manner and accidentally butchered his penis. This vacuum cleaner was the culprit that likely performed the "sausage slaying."

After examining the vacuum canister, my investigative theory was confirmed. I found a substantial amount of the victim's blood inside the canister and intake port. Upon further searching, I found pieces of the victim's "tool." That was all the probable cause I needed to take "Mr. Hoover" into custody.

I took the vacuum to the hospital, along with its various attachments, hoping the doctors could reattach the victim's "manhood." The medical team quickly retrieved the dirty pieces nestled among the dust and debris inside the vacuum.

The surgeon took one look at the victim's penis-pieces and quickly concluded he couldn't reassemble it. Unfortunately, the unsanitary conditions of this "shredded beef" prevented even trying such a surgery. The surgeon explained that an inevitable bacterial infection would exclude any re-attachment procedure.

Upon my return to the victim, he immediately admitted to the false rape allegation. He explained that he didn't intend to make a false police report, but went "in stupid mode" when confronted by the medical staff as to the cause of the penis injury. He was too embarrassed to tell the female nurses the truth about how he practically cut off his penis while masturbating with a vacuum cleaner, so when pressed for an answer, impromptu, he came up with what he thought would be a plausible alibi, as if there could be a good "dick-detachment" story.

I didn't charge him for the false reporting of a rape; it seemed cruel to add insult to the injury. But I did ask him the million-dollar question, "What were you thinking?"

He had read about a self-pleasuring method involving a vacuum cleaner in a pornographic magazine. The technique described that the rolling-style vacuum cleaner was best for achieving the desired happy ending. The key to success was placing his penis in the tube and far away from the intake port's fan blades. I asked why he decided to forego such a solid safety tip, shoving it directly in the intake port. In a completely serious manner, he replied, "I wanted more suction."

Twist

The victim imparted his flawed safety-testing procedure, which was meant to ensure the vacuum fan blade did not injure his penis. His failed safety-test consisted of him simply putting his index finger into the suction port to see if he could touch the fan blades. When he couldn't feel the fan blade, he felt confident that the safeguard measure would ensure his penis' safety. He never thought about the painful mistake of using his four-inch index finger to test for his six-inch "instrument," until after the damage was done and the fan blade shredded his penis. Less of a twist and more of a cautionary tale; vacuums are meant to clean floors, not for sexual gratification. Always use the right tool for the right job.

CHAPTER 25

Liar, Liar, Pants on Fire

ACCORDING to the Federal Bureau of Investigation (FBI), false rape allegations account for approximately 7% of all sexual assault investigations and, sadly, I covered a few in my law enforcement career. But what is more disturbing, the FBI found that 70% of rapists are never brought to justice. The vast majority of sexual assault accusations are valid, and of those infrequent false rape reports, they boil down to two components; incidents stemming from embarrassment or revenge.

In 1999, two patrol officers unexpectedly came into the Sex Crimes Bureau, asking for guidance on their handling of a kidnapping and rape call they received hours earlier. The patrol officers contacted the female victim at a convenience store after she called 911 about having been kidnapped while out in public and taken to a hotel where she was raped. After talking with the woman, the officers had a strong desire to immediately arrest the suspect, who was staying at a hotel. They relayed the victim's account to their sergeant, and their supervisor wanted them to first contact sex crimes detectives before proceeding to arrest the suspect.

The patrol officers were swayed by their emotions from the victim's account, and didn't catch the many holes in her questionable story. The 21-year-old woman said she had been kidnapped in broad daylight, after walking out of a busy convenience store. A man that she didn't know forced her into a car in the parking lot and blindfolded her before driving away to the hotel a short distance away. He then removes the blindfold and forced her inside the hotel to a room. Once inside the room, he rapes her for several hours and then releases her. She finds a nearby pay phone and called the police to report the kidnapping and rape, telling the 911 operator the name and address of the hotel, as well as amazingly providing the suspect's name and his room number.

As the patrol officers gave me the details, I heard many glaring inconsistencies with her story, starting with the location of the "crime." Police received a single call about this crime, from the victim. But the crime occurred mid-day at a busy store with many potential witnesses. When a violent crime happens at a busy and public location there are usually numerous calls to 911 from different people who witnessed it. Not this time and that alone concerned me.

Another discrepancy with her rape story was the suspect's actions: He blindfolded her and then took it off. That was a huge contradiction since, he placed the blindfold on her at a location that she already knew, which was the store. However, he then removed the blindfold after arriving at the hotel, allowing her to see something that was not known to her, where he lived. Kidnappers typically blindfold a person to prevent them from seeing where they are going so they can't report that information to the police, but apparently not her kidnapper.

And the woman told the cops that the man allowed her to simply walk away after the assault, knowing she could walk to the nearest payphone to call the police. Most perps are not that careless. And the most glaring problem with her story is that she told the cops the suspect's name, which I quickly verified was correct with a call to the hotel manager.

There were other red flags in her story, making me doubt the credibility of her rape allegation. Surprisingly, the patrol officers did not see all the red flags and unconditionally believed her story. Some inconsistencies are common with sexual assault accounts since the very nature of the horrifying event produces shock and rape victims will forget various details. Those types of discrepancies are completely understandable to police. However, when the entire story makes no sense, there is usually a reason; it's fabricated. Every facet of the alleged "crime" seemed more unbelievable than the next and those inconsistencies kept adding up.

Investigators are trained to gather many details of a crime from both the victim and witnesses. A police officer can't be prejudicial and should never doubt a rape victim's account at face value, but police are equally responsible to determine if a crime occurred or not. As sex crime detectives, we need to get minute and intimate details in respect to everything that happened, from beginning to end. Detectives will even ask questions in which we know the victim couldn't possibly know the answer, like asking them for the license plate of a car even though they saw it from a hundred feet away, if only to establish their honesty.

I took the investigation over from the patrol officers and needed to start from the beginning, establishing the suspect's identity from the registry. I easily found the suspect was registered under his real name, using his driver's license and car registration. I then used the information the woman gave us and verified his license plate, which she had written down after walking away from the hotel. I then ran a background check on the suspect, finding he had no criminal record. I also conducted a record check on the victim, discovering she had an out-of-state victim record, but the computer didn't provide the type of crime or the details of her victimization.

The next order of business, getting the video surveillance tapes from both the initial kidnapping location at the convenience store and from the hotel where the alleged sexual assault occurred. In a matter of hours, I had both the surveillance tapes. The store's interior camera captured the victim and suspect walking into the store together, completely in contradiction to her account of seeing him for the first time walking out of the store. But it wasn't just inconsistent, it was completely at odds with the kidnapping crime—they appeared to be a couple, laughing as he opened the door for her. They walked directly to the front sales counter where he purchased a pack of cigarettes, then handed the pack to her. They talked with the clerk for a moment, and the reported suspect turned away, walking to the door to leave. The victim stayed, and continued to laugh and talk with the store clerk while the suspect walked out of the store. After a few seconds, she left too. No coercion, no one forcing her to enter or leave the store and she was not acting like she was in fear of her alleged attacker.

The video camera aimed at the parking lot revealed her walking out of the store, and entering the passenger side of the suspect's vehicle on her own accord. She closed the car door and the car drove out of view toward the street. The victim never appeared to be under distress, never restrained or blindfolded. The video proved the kidnapping did not occur. Now, I wanted to talk to the clerk to learn what they were laughing about.

A few days later, I went to the store and talked to the clerk who served the suspect and victim, and not surprisingly I discovered even more evidence that her story wasn't holding up. The clerk vividly recalled the "couple" saying the lady flirted with both her male friend and him. She asked for a specific brand of cigarettes, but her "boyfriend" made the purchase and gave them to her. The clerk also confirmed she did not appear in need of help or acted like she was in trouble. To the contrary, the clerk said she was very flirtatious and jovial with the male customer. Having proved the kidnapping part of the allegation didn't happen, I then needed to try and prove or disprove the sexual assault allegation.

The hotel staff unfortunately couldn't assist me in the investigation, since none of the staff I spoke with could recall the registered guest or the victim. The hotel video also didn't assist the investigation, only showing a few seconds of the couple walking from the car in the parking lot to the hotel lobby door. At no time, did she appear in distress. None of the footage depicted images consistent with the victim's account of her kidnapping.

After two weeks of reviewing videos and conducting interviews, I learned a lot. But none more so than when I spoke to a Colorado detective about the victim's out of state victim record. I learned she also made a similar sexual assault allegation in Colorado, and that detective also reported that her story didn't add up. The Colorado report was closed, stating the victim refused to cooperate with the investigation after being caught making false statements.

Feeling prepared, I called the victim and asked for a follow-up interview. She agreed, and with a mountain of evidence to support a false kidnapping report, I could confront her and try to find out why. She arrived as scheduled, telling me of her eagerness to help find the rapist so I could arrest him. Letting her think I believed her entire account, I walked her into the interview room, consisting of two chairs and a table in a small enclosure. My gullible performance helped me gain her trust, allowing me to subtly turn the interview into an interrogation. Knowing the kidnapping didn't occur, I had a distinct advantage, but didn't want to tip her off.

I wanted to conduct the photographic line-up right away to determine her motive for making the false report. There are generally two motives to make false rape reports; revenge or embarrassment. If she identified him as the suspect, the motive is revenge, wanting to send this specific man to prison for some undetermined reason. If she didn't pick him out, the motive is embarrassment, only wanting the false report to explain away her sexual tryst to a possible boyfriend. In my experience, prosecutors are more likely to go to trial on someone charged with making a false police report if their motive is revenge, and were willing to send an innocent man to prison. Most prosecutors don't like trying a case in court where a woman made a false police report to avoid being beaten by a jealous husband or boyfriend.

Before I showed her a photographic line-up to confirm her motive, she politely conversed about the weather. I then handed her a single sheet of paper containing six photographs to include the photo of the hotel guest. Within seconds, she identified him as the rapist from within the group of six photographs of similar looking men. She was still insisting she'd never seen the suspect prior to him grabbing her outside the store, where he kidnapped her at gunpoint.

She pointed at the suspect's photograph, and began making crying sounds while wiping her eyes. However, I didn't see a single tear. I didn't confront her on her weak crying performance, wanting to first lock her into a detailed account of the kidnapping and assault, documenting all the lies, before I sprung all my evidence and confronted her.

Dispensing with the "victim" label for a more suitable title, I asked "Ms. Liar-Liar" to provide me with a complete account from beginning to end. I was making sure she couldn't later accuse the original reporting officers of getting her story wrong. As she recounted the kidnapping and rape allegations, she appeared to revel in my gullibility, thanking me for catching the rapist and looking forward to sending him to prison. Wickedly smiling, she told me that she would be happy to see him sentenced to more than 20-years in prison. Asking her to help me understand a part of the story, I set my trap, hitting her with one obvious contradiction at a time. As each question punctured holes in her hot-air-balloon of a story, I remained cool, acting like I still believed her allegations.

I then excused myself, leaving the interview room and returned with photographs from the store and hotel videos. Showing her more than 50 photographs, all contradicting her story, she slowly realized her story was crumbling. Again, she attempted another fake cry, making crying sounds but still no tears. Then, I dropped all auspices of believing her story and called her out on the bad performance, telling her, "I would get you a tissue, but you have no tears to wipe." She looked stunned and remained speechless for an awkward period, then she explained that her lack of tears was a medical condition. I immediately asked for the name of this no-tear "medical condition," invoking another long period of silence from her. I remained silent, just staring at her and letting her stew in her awkward silence, then she said, "I know it starts with the letter P." I laughed and replied, "That's all you could come up with in all that time."

Leaving the interview room again, but returning minutes later with a copy of a Colorado police report. Since she couldn't cry real tears, I thought she might after I confronted her with the report stating she made a false rape allegation. The Colorado report listed all her contradictions to the physical evidence. I confronted her with the similarities between the Colorado and Phoenix reports.

She showed no emotion and stared in silence, then finally admitted to making up the kidnapping story. She still lied, stating that she met him inside the store, even after she saw the pictures of them entering the store together. After confronting her again, she changed her story, saying they met while walking to the store. Again, another lie, as he drove her to and from the store. Looking exhausted, she tried correcting one lie after another with more lies. I stopped confronting her, realizing she wasn't going to simply tell the truth.

"Ms. Liar-Liar" explained the suspect offered to buy her cigarettes during their unplanned walk to the store. The suspect then asked her to join him at his hotel room to talk and she agreed. She admitted to the false blindfold yarn, agreeing to come to the hotel with him. Once inside his room, she agreed to engage in consensual sex, but asked him to stop before he finished. He continued to engage in sexual intercourse against her wishes, making it no longer consensual at that point. If true, this is a valid rape. It doesn't matter how it started, as once she says stop—he has to stop. The problem, she lied so much that nothing she said would probably be believed in court, she was a proven and documented liar.

I left the interview room again, returning with the suspect's file, advising her that I already talked with the suspect, getting his side of the story. He agreed to make himself available for a polygraph, wanting to cooperate to clear his name of the rape allegation. I then asked her to submit to a polygraph test first due to her numerous admitted lies, but she refused, eventually admitting she lied about the entire kidnapping and rape allegation.

The truth (maybe) was this: "Ms. Liar-Liar" engaged in consensual sex the entire time, but the suspect became "a jerk" afterwards, refusing to drive her home. His unwillingness to be a chauffeur, prompted the false rape report. I explained that her false allegations were criminal, and I would be submitting the case to the prosecutor's office. Since she admitted the truth after two hours of excruciating evidence explaining, I would forego arresting her today. It is just a ticket offense making a false rape allegation, which could have sent an innocent man to prison for twenty-plus years. For the first time, she seemed to have genuine remorse for lying and making the false rape allegation.

I walked out of the interview room to talk with the detective assigned to monitor and record the interview from a designated recording area. There were some things I wanted to check with Detective Renee before terminating the interview with "Ms. Liar-Liar." Upon walking into the monitor room, I saw Detective Renee laughing hysterically, telling me that "Ms. Liar- Liar" was flipping-me off every time I walked out of the interview room. Detective Renee isolated the video interview for each of the four separate occasions that "Ms. Liar-Liar" gave me a hearty middle finger salute, while my back was turned walking out of the interview room.

Returning to the interview room with this knowledge, I asked about her remorse for almost sending an innocent man to prison. She conveyed her deep sorrow, asking that I relay her heartfelt regret and apologies to him. I then turned to walk out the door, as a ruse to catch her in mid-birdy-act. I turned around to see the beginning stages of her middle finger salute, quickly putting her arm back down on the table, looking surprised.

Sitting back down to the table, I reiterated how store surveillance video ultimately proved this man's innocence from her false allegation. Further, stating my appreciation for the beneficial evidence of all surveillance video, telling her I didn't believe her apology. I told her that the jury would not believe her sincerity either, prompting another tearless-crying performance. She asked why I didn't believe her sorry excuse for an apology, and I explained there was a video recording of her as she repeatedly flipped me off seconds after acting apologetic. She finally told the truth, stating, "I hate stupid videos."

Twist

The city prosecutor's office wanted to take the false reporting case to trial, having everything a jury would need to convict. Routinely, false reporting cases are too difficult to prove, and since they are only misdemeanor crimes, it's too much work. The city prosecutor made an exception in this case, since "Ms. Liar-Liar" tried to put an innocent man in prison, and having tried it once before in another state. Unfortunately, "Ms. Liar-liar" fled the state before her trial. She is now living with complete impunity in another state, as the police can only extradite on felony crimes, not misdemeanors. What a crying shame!

CHAPTER 26

It Was Very Professional

MY son told me a funny story about his worst first (and only) date with this particular girl, saying they argued about everything. From the time he picked her up, to the time he literally ran out of the restaurant, leaving her sitting at the table alone yelling at him. I cried tears of laughter as he described the way they viewed everything differently, flabbergasted at how she could be so wrong about everything and not know it.

My son's twenty-year-old naiveté reminded me of a sex crimes report that reached incredulity in gullibility and hilarity. Like my son's bad date, I kept thinking aloud, "How could the lady in this report be so wrong about everything?", while sitting at my desk reading the report.

The sparse report made no allegation of a crime, leaving me baffled to the reason she made the report. I read and re-read the report a total of three times, but after the third pass, I was even more dumbfounded, thinking I must be missing something. It reminded me of a saying my brother used to jokingly tell his kids, "I hear you talking, but you aren't saying anything." My frustration led me to ask other detectives in the unit to read it. Maybe they could find the criminal allegation that was escaping me.

Several of my colleagues read the report and couldn't find any elements of a crime as well. The report said the "victim" wanted to prosecute a massage therapist after having consensual sex with him after a "particularly comprehensive" massage. The two-page report stated she made the private massage appointment, arranging for the therapist to come to her home after her husband left for work, and kids went off to school. After receiving the massage, she gave him a tip for his service and then called police to report a crime. In the report, she failed to describe any crime. There was nothing in the report about a rape or some sexual abuse, except for the report's title, *Sexual Assault*, which routed the report to my in-box for a follow-up investigation.

I decided to follow-up with a phone call, figuring my conversation with her would provide the missing criminal details of the alleged rape, which I assumed was accidentally omitted from the report. I called her in the middle of the workday to provide her with an atmosphere of privacy, knowing she was a stay-at-home mom and her husband and children would be out of the house. Hoping that if I spoke to her alone that she would speak candidly about the massage therapist, as that may have been the initial problem all along; she might have called police while her husband was home and was too embarrassed to tell the patrol officers the whole story.

I hooked-up an audio cassette tape recorder to my desk phone and called the woman at her home. She was very pleasant and thanked me for following up on her report. She had a soft, sweet sounding voice and spoke with a mild southern accent. Her vocabulary usage and conversational skills lead me to believe her to be an intelligent and educated woman, but after talking with her for an hour, to my profound amazement, I still had no clue about the crime.

The interview started with some clarifying questions about her family and their marriage. She stated they had been happily married for ten years, with two young children. Her description of the marriage was a union of heavenly bliss. The woman didn't strike me as wanting to cheat on her husband with a massage therapist. It's been my professional experience that some women have filed false rape reports after having had an extramarital affair, needing an alibi to explain away a sexually transmitted disease or pregnancy.

A neighbor friend told the woman about a great experience she had with this same massage therapist who made home visits. The friend gushed about the greatest massage she ever had, giving her the massage therapist's phone number. She called the very same day, asking if he was a licensed massage therapist. The master masseuse could have been lying, but told her he was a licensed massage therapist and would gladly schedule her for a visit. She never made an independent phone call to the state licensing board to verify his massage therapist credentials, feeling confident after talking with him that he was a professional.

On the day of the massage, her children boarded the school bus about the same time her husband left for work. She wanted to enjoy a professional massage at her home and didn't want her husband to know, thinking the guilt of spending money on such a luxury would ruin the gift to herself. The only way she could truly enjoy the massage was to be alone and her family unaware.

She described the masseuse as a black male, about 50-years-of-age. He had a receding hairline, with a thin build. I'm picturing "Mr. Jefferson" from the 70's sitcom. I truly believed her to be a happily-married housewife and the massage therapist didn't sound like the type of man who could tempt even a very unhappy housewife.

The suspect brought a portable table, towels, massage oils, and all the professional trappings expected in such a trade. I asked her if the massage therapist appeared as professional as he sounded on the phone. She told me that he was "very professional," describing the various massages he performed for her that early afternoon.

He promptly set up his massage table in the main living room, never making any inappropriate comments or gestures. She explained that he remained professional at each stage of the massage process, from his introduction to his departure. He handed her a large plain white towel, instructing her to undress in the bathroom and return covered in the towel. The oversize towel was more than adequate to completely cover her torso, and she returned from the bathroom as instructed.

I asked her if his instructions or the way he stated them were sexual in nature. She explained, "He was very professional," nothing sexual was implied during his towel covering instructions. He told her to lay face-down on the table, and lowered her towel to begin massaging her back, while explaining the various benefits to the specific muscles. Within a few minutes, he completed massaging her back and shoulders and explained the next massage to her lower back and buttocks. I thought to myself, "This is where we get to the bottom of the crime." Nope–she thought his actions were very professional, adding that he never said anything sexual or inappropriate.

He squeezed her buttocks, kneading her gluteus maximus muscles, or better said, he played with her "ass." The massage went well beyond her outer buttocks, his kneading treaded inside her rectum. I thought, "How could such an intrusive massage not make her feel violated?" He had touched her in a manner far beyond the scope of a massage therapist. But no, again, she explained, "He was very professional."

The massage therapist continued to explain the deep therapeutic values of such a deep sphincter-muscle massage, penetrating her anus with his circulating index finger. She explained the professional way he digitally diddled her butt, giving her the benefits of a thorough and deep anal-massage. After he finished massaging inside her anus, he began to massage elsewhere on her body.

I'm trying not to write this like some trashy romance novel, but this is what she was telling me; it just writes itself that way. The massage therapist then asked her to turn over so he could massage her front. She complied, rolling onto her back. Both her breasts and vaginal area now accessible from beneath her towel. The therapist massaged quickly past her face and shoulders, wanting to perform a therapeutic breast massage.

She described the breast massage in every detail, switching from one breast to the other, and then back again repeatedly. He firmly fondled both of her breasts, separately and simultaneously. She had my full attention when she described the way he squeezed her nipples, and pressed his index finger in circling patterns around her areolas. Yes, apparently, there is therapeutic value to nipple squeezing and areola circling. The massage therapist continued to tell her all the great therapeutic values of the massage.

I asked, in hindsight, if she believed the massaging of her breasts to be inappropriate or an actual criminal act. She explained that both his demeanor and actions were completely professional, and she felt the therapeutic value in it. She maintained that no crime had occurred, or at least not at this juncture of the massage session. He then stopped massaging her breasts and explained the wonderful benefits of a lower pelvic-region massage. I bet he did!

I asked if she gave him permission to massage her pelvic region, and she did, consenting to a very comprehensive massage to her groin and, like a broken record, marveled at his professionalism. He massaged her vagina, to include her labia and the outer surface of her vagina. As she described the vaginal massage, probing his fingers against both her clitoris and deep into her vagina, she still didn't relay any criminal concerns regarding the massage.

I thought that recounting her story of the massage would eventually lead her to believe she had been sexually violated, if only in retrospect, but no. She had no problem with the professional manner he massaged her anus, breasts, and vagina, either at the time of the massage, or reflecting upon it now.

The massage therapist explained to her in detail the therapeutic benefits of each massage of her vagina, anus and breasts prior to asking permission to perform each respective massage. She agreed to each massage before he proceeded, and was impressed with his professionalism throughout every massage.

What became shockingly apparent to me was she didn't have a problem with any of the sexual massages, which begs the question: Why did she make a sex-related crime report? I had become so fixated with that very question, I failed to realize all the detectives from adjacent cubicles had gathered around, listening in astonishment to my telephone interview. My constant description of her sexual body parts, asking questions like, "So he massaged the inside of your anus. How did that make you feel?", and then after hearing her response, I would repeat aloud, "Professional, got it." This back-and-forth aroused the attention of both male and female detectives, enticing them to gather around my desk in dumbfounded solidarity.

I briefly recapped all the intimate professional massages she received, specifically the way he probed her anus, manipulated her breasts, and penetrated her vagina. She consented to each massage prior to him touching that area of her body, never telling him to stop or wanting him to stop. He was professional, and from his first touch to his last she never felt violated. She vehemently confirmed my understanding, and then advised she wanted to prosecute.

Completely dumbfounded, I exasperatedly blurted, "Charge him with what?" She didn't know, but felt experiencing an orgasm, having never experienced that with her husband, had to be a crime.

Twist

Upon termination of my interview, I explained to her that the prosecutor's office could not successfully prosecute the massage therapist on sexual assault charges, explaining that she had consented to every sex act. He also didn't mislead her to the types of sex acts that he requested to perform, and he never strayed from doing exactly what he had first described.

She asked, "Well, is there any other crime, if not a sex crime, that you could make an arrest?" I told her, "The only elements of a crime present could be for prostitution." She gasped, "What?" Comforting her that I had no intention to either make an arrest or pursue such an investigation, I then explained, "You paid him money to touch you in a sexual manner, over-and-over, so basically, you paid for sex! (with an apparent satisfaction guaranteed)" Her soft, sweet sounding voice became raspy, raising a whole octave, replying, "Oh, my! I never thought of it that way, but it does kind of sound like that."

I assured her the report would simply be unfounded since the elements of a rape were not present, and that I wouldn't be forwarding the report to the VICE detail. She was very happy and thanked me—for my professionalism.

CHAPTER 27

No More Mr. Nice Guy

GOOD parents instill the importance of having a "sense of community" to their children; helping one's neighbor elevates us from the cruel savagery of the jungle to that of polite society. I truly embrace the "love thy neighbor" philosophy, but I wouldn't have gone to the extreme lengths that a Good Samaritan neighbor performed in this next twisted story. He went well beyond the call of duty helping his neighbor, and in the end, he paid dearly for it.

Sex crimes detectives routinely respond to hospital emergency rooms for interviews, as many sexual assault victims need immediate medical care. Seldom do they go to the hospitals to interview both an injured victim and a suspect in the same case. On a late Saturday evening in December, I was awakened by my sergeant and instructed to come down to a local hospital ER to interview the victim and suspect in a male-on-male sexual assault investigation.

The Good Samaritan, who I'll refer to as "Sam" from this point forward was by all accounts, an all-around great guy, as is the case with most Good Samaritans. His neighbors referred to him as always being in good spirits, giving a wave or friendly greeting to everyone in the neighborhood, and routinely lending a hand to anyone in need of help. It was this helpful spirit that placed Sam in harm's way during a very awkward incident.

Sam got a desperate phone call from his neighbor, and for reasons that will become apparent later in the story, I'll call him "Bud." Sam didn't immediately recognize the person who was panic-stricken and hysterical on the other end. After a few seconds, listening intently, he recognized the person's high-pitched and loud-voice was his neighbor who lived a few houses down the street.

He didn't know Bud very well besides the daily greetings when getting the mail, washing the car, and the other occasional curbside conversations. Sam knew he had a wife and several grown children, but not much else. Because of their infrequent and casual conversations, Bud's phone call came as a complete surprise. In fact, Sam wondered how Bud even knew his telephone number.

Bud began the phone call with, "Are you alone?" Sam wished he had lied about entertaining guests, but admitted he was alone. Sam responded, "Are you in trouble?" based on the panic evident in Bud's voice. Bud didn't go into detail, but said he was in pain and needed Sam's help, pleading for Sam to come over to his house right away. Sam suggested that he could call 911 to get paramedics but Bud implored him not to call. Bud explained that his family left him alone but his predicament was not life threatening and he wasn't in any real danger, assuring Sam that it would only take a few minutes, as he continued to plead for Sam to come over to his home.

Like a good neighbor, Sam relented and agreed to help with Bud's unexplained predicament. Bud advised that his front door was unlocked and for Sam to let himself in, and come into the garage. Sam walked over to the house, letting himself in and following Bud's loud pleas for help, which led him into the garage. Once in the garage, just past the doorway, Sam saw Bud leaning over a large wooden workbench.

Bud clearly looked distraught, but began crying tears of joy when he saw Sam, knowing that he'd come to help. Walking closer toward the large workbench, Sam made a startling discovery: Bud's pants and underwear were rolled all the way down to his ankles, and worse, a beer bottle was protruding out of Bud's ass.

Sam's initial impulse was to run as fast as he could out of the garage, but Bud appeared to be in such genuine distress, crying as he was leaning over the workbench. Gritting his teeth, Bud grunted, "It's stuck," as he looked to Sam for help. Sam noted Bud's wet and disheveled hair, a clue to his losing battle to dislodge the anal intruder. The open end of the beer bottle was concealed deep inside Bud's rectum, with the Budweiser label in prominent view. The image would have made for the perfect football game half-time commercial, if only Bud's buttocks was an ice chest.

With Bud's genuine plight in mind, Sam just stared in shock for several long seconds, before turning around to leave. Bud began crying uncontrollably and begged him not to go, pleading with Sam to remove the stuck beer bottle. Humiliated, Bud apologized for even asking for Sam's help, but explained that his family would be home soon and he didn't want them to see him like this, trusting Sam to not only help, but never discuss such an embarrassing situation with anyone. Sam turned back around, facing Bud and agreed to help his neighbor.

Sam reasonably proposed they discreetly go to the hospital, suggesting his family would never find out about the embarrassing incident. Bud decided against it, worried that an "inconspicuous" hospital visit would not go unnoticed by his family. He could be stuck in the ER when his family arrived home, or worse, his wife could wind-up seeing the medical release paperwork or billing statement for a medical "Rectal Beer Bottle Removal" procedure, and needing to explain just what that meant and why the hell it happened in the first place.

Sam relented, assuring Bud that he would stay but he too wanted to know how such a thing could happen in the first place. Bud explained his secret sexual fetish of looking at porn magazines while penetrating his own anus with a banana or other cylinder-shaped objects. Tonight, he was drinking a few beers while the family was out shopping and wondered what a beer bottle would feel like in his ass. He finished that beer and went into the garage to experience that feeling firsthand. He quickly learned a basic principle behind suction, as the open mouth of the empty beer bottle created a vacuum inside his anus.

For the last two hours, he tried removing the bottle with no success. The pain kept increasing with each tug, invoking an involuntary reflex that kept the bottle firmly stuck in his anus. Realizing he needed someone else who would keep pulling regardless of his pain, he thought of his good neighbor Sam.

Upon hearing Bud's formal, if not depraved explanation; Sam suggested someone else should try, declaring, "I really don't want to yank a beer bottle out of your ass." Bud retorted, "It will be quick, I promise. I already got it almost out." A disgusted Sam shot back, "Then keep trying, I'll go out and keep a lookout for your family." Accompanied with the sound of his crying, Bud implored, "I can't stand the fucking pain when I do it, it stops me right before I can pull it out. Please, I beg you before my family gets home." The actual complete dialogue consisted of many more excited expletives, sudden crying fits, and numerous exasperated pauses of disgust from both men.

Sam finally agreed, letting out a long sigh, he prepared himself to commit an act that went well beyond the parameters of a Good Samaritan. Like Androcles removing the thorn from the lion's paw, Sam was a slave to his compassion, willing to relieve Bud's pain by pulling a beer bottle from his butt. After an understandable amount of stalling, Sam finally gripped the empty beer bottle sticking out of his neighbor's ass and began to gently pull.

Since Bud spent two hours pulling and yanking before Sam got there, his rectum was already very sore. Adding to Sam's pressure of removing the bottle with the least amount of discomfort, Bud said his family was already overdue and could be home at any time, so time was of the essence.

Sam was straddled behind Bud, who was still bent over the workbench, with his two hands holding the beer bottle nestled deep inside Bud's rectum. Resembling a perverted gridiron scene, Sam as the quarterback appeared ready to take a hiked football from Bud as the center, but in this case, it was a beer bottle. Sam tried repeatedly to gently pull the bottle out with little success. Bud tried his best to stifle any cries of pain, knowing Sam would not pull harder, which Bud believed was needed to get the job done.

Camouflaging his cries of pain, Bud grunted words of encouragement like, "little harder, almost there." Sam may have started with gentle tugs, but quickly increased the force with each of Bud's cries of encouragement, each pull harder than the last. Sam began trying to yank it out in rhythmic pattern, erroneously thinking it might somehow help in the beer bottle removal. The pattern of harsh pulls was countered with a pattern of blurted squeals from Bud's attempt at not screaming.

Sam and Bud may not have been close before, but this event would most definitely bond them forever in an unusual way. Perhaps their new-found closeness was less about neighborly kindness and more a distorted version of Stockholm's Syndrome. Though, Sam was not being held against his will, his tendency to be "Mr. Nice Guy" placed him in a subservient role, committed to helping Bud, obeying each order to pull harder.

It might have been the intensity of the moment or just exhaustion that caused both Sam and Bud to be unaware of the sounds outside the garage. Then again, it could have been Bud's increasing loud howls of agony, and Sam's rhythmic and loud grunting noises that made them oblivious to the sound of the family car pulling up into the driveway. Whatever the cause, Sam remained hard at work straddled behind Bud, grunting and tugging on the beer bottle jammed in Bud's butt. The scantily dressed Bud was still bent over the work bench screaming at what could be mistaken as Sam sexually assaulting him with a beer bottle, as that is exactly what the family thought upon walking into the garage.

The family was already alerted to the (mistaken) rape of their husband and father by Sam's loud labored grunting sounds and the heartbreaking screaming coming from their father while parking in the driveway. Those alarming grunts and shrieks led the panicked family racing into the home, where a wife saw what she thought was a neighbor sodomizing her husband with a beer bottle, and a son and daughter saw a stranger with his hand up their daddy's ass.

This would be a traumatic and frightening sight, and understandably, anyone could jump to the wrong conclusions, thinking the worst. But the worst was yet to come. How could it possibly get any worse? Bud's eldest son was a hulking marine on shore-leave, visiting his family. This large-framed "Jar Head" instantly commenced to pummel Sam like a ragdoll, with Sam sustaining several facial fractures and broken ribs before Bud had a chance to physically stop his son from beating poor Sam to death.

Bud had little to no time to correct the family's mistaken beliefs, since numerous 911 phone calls had already flooded police dispatch about screams coming from inside the residence. Police arrived only moments after the family, hearing in the middle of the mayhem Bud's wife excitedly blurting out that her husband (with a beer bottle still inserted in his ass) was just raped. The officers also witnessed an out-of-breath rape victim trying to restrain his angry son, who beat the rapist into unconscious submission, thus unable to provide the innocent, albeit twisted, explanation.

Both the unconscious and badly beaten Sam, and the mistaken rape victim Bud, were taken to the same hospital. Bud's family remained at the scene, talking with the patrol officers as the only witnesses to the perceived sexual assault. This is when I was called to the hospital for the sexual assault investigation, ultimately interviewing an extremely injured Sam and a very embarrassed Bud. Before I spoke with both victims about the yet to be discovered misunderstanding, I talked with the medical professionals about their injuries.

The medical staff told me they asked Bud numerous questions, but because he was agonizing, with a beer bottle still imbedded in his torn rectum, he couldn't answer them. The medical team suspected something was amiss when the rapist arrived with worse injuries than the victim. The medical staff swiftly drilled a hole into the beer bottle, removing it easily from Bud's tender and sore anus. Had either Bud or Sam paid a little more attention in high school science they would have realized they just needed to break the end of the bottle to defuse the suction.

Bud and Sam were treated at opposite ends of the emergency ward, and the staff waited for my arrival to straighten out the mess. I interviewed Bud first, who candidly explained the entire incident, admitting that he should have initially tried harder to correct his families mistaken conclusion in the chaotic seconds that stemmed from his embarrassing discovery. Bud apologized for the nature of that false report, and felt terrible for the severe injuries his son inflicted on Sam. He asked that I convey his deepest apologies to Sam, whom he described as a "Good Samaritan."

Next, I talked with Sam, who didn't want to press criminal charges against Bud's son. Sam understood why the large marine acted the way he did, stating, "It must have looked bad."

Twist

Sam told me he will never again be so agreeable to helping a neighbor, describing himself as, "No More Mr. Nice Guy!" I suggested that he just draw a line at agreeing to pull a beer bottle out of anyone's ass.

CHAPTER 28

Bad Hair Day

I N 2004, I started a new career path, having been promoted to sergeant and assigned as a patrol supervisor to my old beat. Going back to work the streets was truly a thrilling experience, as that is where police can make life and death differences. Working as a detective is both rewarding and important, but it's completely different than working emergencies in progress as a street cop. As a detective, the crime has already occurred, your work is as an after-effect trying to bring the culprit to justice, but as a street cop you have an opportunity to prevent those very same crimes, stopping victims from being hurt in the first place.

I supervised a squad of ten young officers, working the graveyard shift with terrible, mid-week days off, always working weekends. I hadn't worked patrol in almost ten years, having been a case-carrying detective, and felt very rusty. For a decade, I worked plain clothes as a detective in burglary and sex crimes; I didn't even have a uniform that fit. I evolved into a good investigator in that time, but now I had to start over as a rookie supervisor for street cops.

The first nine years of my police career, including my time as a bicycle officer, was exciting. However, patrol is very much a young person's game with foot chases, combative prisoners, difficult citizens, and general daily craziness associated with patrolling the streets to keep citizens safe.

Early in my career, working patrol, I was injured on a regular basis, but always bounced back quickly. The harsh, physical, and combative conditions didn't faze me, but as a middle-aged man, it was harder and took longer to heal, and getting back up on my feet after fighting a suspect took forever. However, on the positive side of old age, I had almost twenty years of combined detective and patrol experience to draw on. I taught my eager, young street cops many advanced detective techniques that, investigative-wise, put them well ahead of their peers on other patrol squads. I enjoyed teaching my squad officers in a way that infused advanced investigative aspects, making them more well-rounded cops. I too needed training; there were countless things new to me in the role as a patrol supervisor.

I had the good fortune of being trained by one of the finest law enforcement professionals I had ever met. Sergeant Chris Moore's dedication and inspiration made my training as a supervisor both informative and invaluable. He also became a dear friend. Chris and I encountered many strange things working together for that relatively brief period.

On one sweltering summer day, Chris joined me to check on my patrol officers securing a homicide scene. As a patrol supervisor, I responded to various crime scenes, ensuring the officers followed proper protocols and rules of evidence and evaluated the need for detective assistance.

At this murder scene, patrol officers responded to a small, two-story apartment complex after a female resident inadvertently discovered a murder. The woman noticed some unknown liquid dripping from the ceiling and onto her head while she was vacuuming her apartment. She didn't notice the leak until the liquid dripped down her cheek. This prompted her to call the maintenance man, requesting he fix the leak.

The janitor, who had an uncanny resemblance to the janitor "Schneider" from the 1970's hit television show, "One Day at a Time," saw the spot on the woman's ceiling, where a steady drip of thick liquid pooled onto the carpet. The maintenance man went upstairs to the apartment above the woman to check on the problem.

After knocking on the second-story apartment, the door opened and the janitor was greeted by a middle-aged man who behaved strangely, staring intensely at him in the open doorway. The maintenance man noticed the strange man was wearing a heavy coat which was at odds with the hot weather.

The maintenance man explained he needed to look around to fix a leak that was discovered in the apartment directly below. The tenant continued his blank stare and then simply shook his head from side to side, indicating he would not let the maintenance man in. He then finally spoke and said it would disturb his roommate, and strangely, but politely, started closing the door. The maintenance man moved to block the closing door with his foot, explaining that the terms of his rental agreement allowed maintenance entry for emergency repairs.

The strange tenant said he would take care of the leak and asked the maintenance man to move his foot. Authoritatively explaining the tenant could be evicted for refusing him entry into the apartment, the tenant relented, allowing the maintenance man to enter. Immediately the maintenance man noticed a noxious odor and determined the exact location of the leak, which was a closet near the front entry way. He asked the tenant about the nauseating odor, initially laughing at the tenant's explanation, thinking he was joking when the tenant replied, "The odor is my roommate." He said it in a dead-pan tone, but didn't elaborate further, and just stood with the same blank stare on his face. It was after the long silence that the maintenance man became hesitant to open the closet door for fear the strange tenant wasn't joking about the roommate.

After a moment of awkward silence, the maintenance man opened the closet door, discovering the tenant indeed wasn't joking; his dead, rotting, roommate was the cause of the odor and the leak. The decomposing corpse had decayed partially into a large puddle of human-liquid, which seeped down through the carpet, into the floor boards, then dripped down from the ceiling in the lower apartment.

The tenant calmly explained he would clean up the mess and asked the maintenance man not to call the police. He also calmly confessed to how he killed his roommate, and then forgot he left him in the closet. He elaborated, saying his roommate had been dead for several weeks, but the intensely cold refrigeration helped slow the rotting flesh process, keeping the odor from permeating outside of the apartment. The shocked maintenance man ran out, and continued running straight to the office where he called 911, and then waited for the police.

To the surprise of the maintenance man and the police, the murderous tenant waited patiently for the arrival of the police. The tenant opened the door to the police, and politely let them into the apartment. He was immediately arrested upon verifying the maintenance man's bizarre account, remaining cooperative, and even apologetic for the murder and causing a messy stain in the closet.

Patrol officers transported the murderer to the main police station and notified homicide detectives of the murder. My patrol officers secured the main crime scene, the murderer's apartment, but failed to secure the second crime scene. I determined that the second crime scene was the first-floor apartment, where the problem was first reported. We also needed to secure the third crime scene, which was the young woman's wet hair, which contained evidence of the victim's liquefied body.

I contacted the young woman who was having a unique bad hair day, explaining the dead-liquid-roommate situation with the classic "good news, bad news" scenario. I told her the good news was that the cause of the leak was gone (to the morgue), and the bad news was the source of the leak was her dead neighbor. I also explained our need to process her hair for evidence, needing to take photographs, swabbing for the victim's liquid DNA, and vacuum as much of the victim as possible out of her hair.

Twist

The suspect gave a complete account of how he murdered his roommate to the detectives. The tenant struck his roommate with a ceramic ashtray while arguing over some forgotten sporting event they were watching on television. Mistakenly, he assumed the roommate had died, but he only sustained a brain swelling injury, rendering him unconscious. Thinking he killed the roommate, he dragged the limp body into the closet. The roommate eventually died in the closet without medical attention. The murderer turned on the air conditioning at full blast, using copious amounts of air freshener to mask the rotting-body odor. He planned to take the roommate out to the trash, but since he is a nut, he simply forgot all about the dead roommate rotting in the closet.

CHAPTER 29

The Ride-Along from HELL

A *RIDE-ALONG* is when a citizen rides with a patrol officer during the officer's work shift. This can include family members, friends, or police cadets (wanting to one day become a police officer) riding with a police officer known to them. One of the benefits of a ride-along for a family member is to give them an opportunity to witness a cop's job firsthand, gaining insight into what we do as law enforcement officers. The idea is that experiencing their loved one or friend handling the job will set their minds at ease, as the fear of not knowing is washed away with the reality of the job.

There is a common belief among patrol officers that there is a "ride-along curse," suggesting that when their shift involves taking a ride-along, it usually means the patrol shift will be mind-numbingly boring; a series of barking dog complaints, burglary reports, and the like. I only had one ride-along early in my patrol officer career and it was far from boring—the attorney who came along to see what I did on a typical patrol watched me wrestle with a knife-wielding, suicidal man, and that wasn't even the scariest thing I did that day. So, I concluded that I wasn't going to allow my wife to ride along with me since I didn't want her to worry.

But time changes a person's perspective. Twenty years later, I reconsidered my decision, taking my son and daughter on a separate ride-along because I was now a patrol supervisor with a better control of what calls we'd respond to. Additionally, twenty-plus years of experience made me better suited to handle most situations, regardless of the difficulties mustered by my dark cloud that continues to follow me.

For my daughter's sixteenth birthday, I took her, (Robyn) and her cousin (Jenny, who also turned 16) on a night time ride-along, giving them a unique experience riding around with a cop in a big city. It was also the coolest sweet-sixteen birthday present ever, or so they told me.

We went on a variety of exciting police calls, including an actual shooting in progress. I had them bunkered under the backseat of the patrol car, covered with two layers of bulletproof vests. We chased a vehicle, it was a short chase, but they were still excited. They even saw me lead an arrest team during a particularly violent domestic fight. All in all, the girls had a once-in-a-lifetime experience, which they will remember for the rest of their lives.

My son DJ was much older at 20, during his ride-along, but he was every bit as excited as his little sister was on her outing. He had an equally hair-raising ride-along with a shooting-in-progress scenario. This time, the suspect was running down streets and indiscriminately shooting things, targeting mostly parked cars and street signs. Later, DJ spotted a transient urinating in public, who we immediately stopped and placed under arrest. My son's eyes became huge with excitement, and thought it was so cool in helping arrest a peeing-drunk. I didn't have the heart to tell him transients take leaks in public every day. As a patrol supervisor, I usually looked the other way if the transient used a bush or other location away from the public. A common rule is not to arrest if the transient makes a solid effort to conceal their bodily function.

Both my son and daughter experienced unique and personal memories, while also seeing first-hand how police officers keep our community safe. I was so happy to finally share this wonderful experience with both my children, bestowing on them that same "sense of community," which motivated me every day as a cop.

Police departments also use the ride-along as a tool to help their community relations efforts, letting reporters or community leaders see the police department in action, hoping to solicit their support. That kind of reasoning was behind my early ride-along experience when I took the lawyer out on a patrol shift fighting the alcohol and drug-infused, suicidal man. Most cops I talk to swear the boring "curse" plagued them with their ride-along(s), but that has never been my experience, and as a new supervisor my squad officers saw my dark cloud firsthand with a ride-along from Hell.

On a Friday night, my lieutenant walked into the briefing room just as I was ending the squad briefing. The patrol officers were scurrying about, trying to avoid eye-contact with the Lieutenant, as they quickly walked past him toward the exit door. A lieutenant walking in on a Sergeant's briefing is a strong sign that there is going to be some unpleasant task needed, usually jobs worthy of avoiding like a ride-along.

Before my officers had a chance to sneak away, the lieutenant lowered the boom, telling me a city councilwoman would be riding with my squad tonight. I needed to assign the community leader to one of my officers, and they all heard it. No patrol officer in their right mind would want a city councilmember for a ride-along, as the thought of making a mistake in front of your ultimate bosses' boss is nerve racking. A simple, honest slip could be career-ending with such a high-ranking person on board.

The news of a city councilwoman ride-along sent the young officers stampeding toward the briefing room door. I quickly blocked the exit door, looking at the group of nervous young officers. I had to quickly make a choice. My most senior officer was a bit of a risk taker; the last person I wanted for such an important assignment. I also didn't want to assign the councilwoman to my most gung-ho officer, as he might get into a dangerous situation—the last thing I needed was for the councilmember to get hurt. The perfect pick would be an even-handed officer with a history of making good decisions, and would follow my instructions to avoid unnecessary trouble. I wanted to ensure the "ride-along boring-night-curse" would come to fruition.

I found just such an officer, Dave, standing in the middle of the pack. He kept his head down hoping I wouldn't notice him, but his facial grimaces confirmed he heard me select him for the ride-along assignment. I walked Dave back to my desk in the briefing room and instructed him to take routine paper calls; burglary reports, shoplifting, and any other non-dangerous radio call.

The officers were just filling gas in their patrol cars and ready to hit the streets, when an emergency radio call came out, describing an intruder in a homeowner's backyard. The shocked homeowner who called 9-1-1 said he and his wife were enjoying a nice dinner at their dining room table when they both looked out their window into their backyard, seeing a naked man, who was covered in blood, climbing over their wall. The caller also said the naked, bloody intruder was running wildly in circles, and shouting nonsense as he and his wife looked on in horror. This was not the call I wanted for the city councilwoman to be subjected to, so I cringed when Officer Dave immediately answer up for the radio call.

As a patrol supervisor, my responsibility was to go to these crazy-sounding, potentially dangerous, radio calls, so I followed suit and told the radio operator that I would be responding as well. I hated the idea that the councilwoman was going to a call where anything could go wrong, but I couldn't cancel my officer, as such an interference would be sending an even worse message to the councilwoman; I didn't trust my officer to handle such a call.

Ensuring we had more than enough officers needed, I instructed the radio operator to send another patrol officer to assist us. Within minutes, my two officers and I, along with the councilwoman, arrived.

She seemed a little rattled at just hearing the call's description on the police radio. This was probably not something she imagined seeing—a nude, bloody man running around screaming. As crazy as it might sound, patrol officers see this scenario, or slight variations of it, on a regular basis. Most of the time, the subject is on some form of illicit drug, which fosters an extreme paranoid state. The paranoia, coupled with physical delusions of intense heat, prompts the person to shed their clothes and run aimlessly in their neighborhood. I have never understood the attraction of these types of drugs. But then again, I hate the heat and don't look good naked.

The four of us, Officer Dave, Officer Mike, the councilwoman and I walked up to the caller's middle-class, single story home, which was in an otherwise quiet neighborhood. I knocked on the door and was quickly greeted by a white, forty-something married couple. The wife did most of the talking, welcoming us in their home, as the husband kept looking franticly in the direction of their backyard, concerned about their unwanted guest coming into the house.

The couple walked us to a large sliding glass door accessing the backyard, where we could see "Nude, Bloody Guy" running and screaming. In fact, we already heard the unwanted guest's loud, bloodcurdling screams when we parked and got out of our patrol cars. I couldn't make out the bulk of what he was saying from his mostly indistinguishable screams, but it sounded like he feared killers were hiding in the bushes.

"Nude, Bloody Guy" was running in continuous circles around an orange tree in the middle of the small, red gravel yard. He appeared to have been painted from head-to-toe with a blood-soaked brush, his eyes frantically darted around and he appeared to be in genuine torment. My officers and I tried calming him down, explaining that we were here to help. At first, he didn't react to our company in any manner, never slowing down to even acknowledge our presence. He just continued screaming and running in large circles around the tree.

For more than ten minutes we talked in calm tones, hoping he would calm down without needing to fight him. He finally looked at us with a blank, drug-induced stare. Those who work in the behavioral health field and street cops know this stare all too well, calling it the "thousand-yard stare," when they seem to look through you instead of at you. He didn't say anything, he just slowed his stride to a fast walk around the tree, but it was progress.

As a crew of firemen and paramedics walked into the backyard, "Naked, Bloody Guy" became anxious from their presence, resuming his pattern of running in circles. The firemen watched from the safety of the rear patio with smug, smiling faces (I say this with genuine respect and teasing fondness). Firemen are accustomed to watching the police, waiting for us to ensure any given situation is safe before they enter. Its protocol and they seem to thoroughly enjoy waiting for us to make these crazy situations safe and secure.

The homeowners were watching from the safe confines in the opening of the sliding glass-door, the councilwoman was standing on the back porch, and us cops were standing at the edge of the gravel trying to calmly communicate with "Naked, Bloody Guy." The firemen gathered around the councilwoman on the porch with their medical gear in hand, forming a semi-circle to get a better view of the upcoming show.

I devised a simple plan; on the count of three we three cops would grab onto the "Naked, Bloody Guy," forcing him to the ground, where we would handcuff him. We were standing only a few feet away from a part of his path, watching as he repeatedly ran laps in the small gravel yard. I waited for him to slowly fatigue himself from all his senseless running. After about ten minutes I whispered the countdown to my two officers. My execution was perfect, starting with the count of "one" as he rounded the far corner, and ending with the count of "three" just as he took the path toward us. We all lunged toward him, grabbing whatever part of his blood-soaked body that we could hold on to, as my plan didn't account for the slipperiness of his body.

From the back patio, a fireman commented loud enough for all of us to hear, "It looks like a wild turkey hunt!" as the three of us chased after "Naked, Bloody Guy" for several minutes before finally getting him corralled in the corner of the yard. Struggling with him, we forced him to the ground, slipping and sliding over his soaked body, eventually getting him in handcuffs.

Since he was totally naked, we didn't have to worry about concealed weapons, just blood-borne pathogens. We were now covered in this drugged-out idiot's blood. The firemen finally stopped laughing long enough to wash us off with a garden hose.

Next, the firemen started cleaning off "Naked, Bloody Guy's" body, so they could assess if he had any injuries. If he had at least one serious gash, cut or other serious health problem, the firemen would have to deal with that medical issue and transport him to the hospital—not us. The firemen sprayed all the blood off, looking him over, and we were all shocked to discover he had no real injury. His profuse sweating had mixed with countless superficial (bleeding) cuts all over his body, but not one major laceration. So, the firemen didn't have to do a medical-emergency transport—he was all ours. Ironically, before my police officers could take him to jail, they first had to get a medical release to give to jail intake, which meant taking "Naked, Bloody Guy" to the hospital for a doctor–provided clean bill of health.

The patrol officers and I were discussing the medical release process, secretly wishing we had chosen a career as firemen. The firemen were packing up their medical gear to return to the fire station, the councilwoman was watching the firemen, likely wishing she did a ride-along with them instead, and "Naked, Bloody Guy" was on the ground still looking for killers hiding in bushes. Everyone's attention was focused on their respective tasks, but an unforeseen trouble was brewing.

A drunk woman's bellowing telegraphed her impending arrival. Before she even stepped foot in the backyard, all of us turned toward the sound. The loud woman walked through the open backyard gate accompanied by a very large man. The woman in her 50s was dressed in a black outfit more suited for a nightclub than a backyard. In an opposing style, her 30ish male companion wore a colored t-shirt and jeans.

The obnoxious sounding, drunk woman nodded to the homeowners standing on the porch, as she walked into their backyard. Her heavy frame was dwarfed by her giant companion walking close at her side. The hulking friend stood approximately six-foot four-inches in height, and weighed more than 250 pounds, much of it muscle. He said nothing, just attentively watched the woman's every move, never straying more than a few feet from the boisterous woman's side.

Her intoxication was clearly revealed with her talking in a volume more suited to a crowded bar than a neighbor's yard, and barking orders at the departing firemen, angrily yelling for them to return. Then her anger quickly turned to my officers and me. I asked the homeowners if they knew who the woman was and they sheepishly replied in unison "she's our neighbor." I wanted them to ask her to leave, but they refused. The homeowners did not want to upset her, allowing her to remain in their backyard.

The drunken woman began yelling nonsensical profanities at me like, "Fuck the way you look somewhere else" from a relatively innocuous distance of twenty feet away. As her inebriated instructions for me to leave continued, she demanded that the firemen return. I tried my best to ignore the intoxicated woman. I couldn't arrest her for trespassing because the homeowners didn't give me authority to do so.

We were close to getting the prisoner on his feet and out of the yard, so I wanted to avoid any confrontation with the drunken woman. We disregarded her demands; as cops, we learn quickly that you can't argue with a drunk! I tried to appease the drunk woman, explaining we would soon be leaving as she demanded. I even apologized for any disturbance that she may have experienced, doing so with a straight face.

My attempt at appeasing her, only emboldened the woman as she demanded we release the screaming man so that he could go home with her. I stepped in front of her, blocking the screaming woman's approach toward my officers. This only enraged her. She screamed at me, in my face, hurling insults as quickly as her pickled brain could formulate the words.

Hoping that if I ignored her I could de-escalate her screams of anger, I turned my attention to the homeowners, trying to change their minds so I could arrest the banshee. The homeowners adamantly refused, saying they didn't want to incur her wrath. They believed the drunk neighbor would eventually walk away, assuring me she wouldn't "hurt a fly." The couple then looked at each other, and without saying another word walked back into their home. I couldn't believe how they didn't see the danger that this woman presented in their backyard—and then it hit me. They retreated into the safety of their house because they knew very well it was about to get a hell of a lot worse.

The mean-spirited drunk continued to loudly bark insults, trying to goad me into an argument, but I wasn't giving in, even as she ramped up her trash talking about hating police. Flailing her hands with her every insult, she was spraying beer from an open can, which kept splattering onto my uniform. I kept my composure and explained in a calm tone, that we were leaving with our arrested male trespasser.

When I mentioned "Naked, Bloody Guy," she was suddenly interested in his welfare. Watching after my officers with their blanketed prisoner, I warned her not to walk toward my officers, and for her to remain talking to me. The officers successfully got "Naked, Bloody Guy" to his feet, preparing to walk him out of the yard. The problem was that their path to the front gate would lead them past me and the drunk woman.

The loud, drunk woman added an addendum to her demands, stating that she wanted me to release "Naked, Bloody Guy" to her care. Her previous facial grimaces of disdain for me had turned to "last call" smiles at our escorted prisoner. She became almost not unpleasant, smiling at "Naked, Bloody Guy" and acting every bit of a woman wanting to make a love connection. She stared longingly at "Naked, Bloody Guy," while licking her lips as the officers walked him toward us.

Her tranquility quickly reverted to anger when I wouldn't release "Naked, Bloody Guy" to her loving care as she yelled to us "I want him!" Thankfully, the prisoner was completely oblivious to the drunk woman's budding romance. Disobeying her orders to leave the prisoner, I told her that we had no choice but to take him to jail. I did assure her that he would be well cared for, and insisted that she did not interfere with his removal from the yard.

She continued her boisterous demands for his release, all the while splashing more beer on me with each flailing motion of her beer-wielding hand. By this time, I had had enough. Her actions had already bordered on several criminal charges, such as; impeding a criminal investigation, assault (with beer) and a host of other disorderly statues, but I really didn't want to take her into custody because it would be a wasted (no pun intended) effort to book her for such small, inconsequential things. In other words, I was trying to give her an undeserved break. I also wanted to avoid another difficult booking for my already taxed police officers.

I just wanted to leave with my officers and "Naked, Bloody Guy" without another physical encounter with a drug-altered individual. That would not be the case. She shoved me aside, which is an assault on a police officer, and I grabbed her arm, preventing her from getting anywhere near my officers and their prisoner. She reacted by trying to strike me in the face with her beer can still gripped tightly in her fist. The only thing that hit me was more beer shooting from her open can, soaking my hair.

That was it—she needed to be restrained, so I arrested her on several charges. I grabbed the drunk woman, forcing her flailing arm behind her back in an arm-bar hold, stopping her from any further assault. As the patrol officers walked past, I followed behind them out of the backyard with the drunk woman in handcuffs.

Surprisingly, the large-framed young man who came with the screaming woman didn't say a word, calmly following, keeping a short distance behind. He never tried to stop me, or interfere in her arrest, but ignored my command to stop following. He seemed stoic, as he continued following too closely even as I kept telling him to stop following us. My primary concern was his massive size; he would be a handful to subdue and I was already exhausted from dealing with our two other prisoners.

The gaggle of five laughing firemen, three tired cops, two drugged-out prisoners, one wide-eyed councilwoman, and a large quiet man, all made our way into the front yard. As we walked past the home, I caught a glimpse of the homeowners peering out their front window. As we got closer to the patrol cars, the drunk woman became seething mad, trying to break free from my grip. All the while, I had to keep yelling at the big man to stop following us.

The two patrol officers placed the blanket-covered "Naked, Bloody Guy" in the backseat of a patrol car. Once he was locked away, they turned their attention to the bombastic woman I was escorting. They took her off my hands, so I could now focus my attention on the non-compliant large male. My patience had worn thin from dealing with the first screaming male idiot, and then dealing with the second screaming female idiot.

As the two officers placed the drunk woman in the backseat of another patrol car, the large-framed man then tried to approach my officers. I grabbed his arm, applying a pain compliance hold to stop him. Because of his size, I used a strong amount of force to ensure the hold worked. However, once he began crying, I quickly realized he wasn't a threat. I was perplexed that he still wasn't listening to my directions.

The man's cries prompted the homeowners to step out into the front yard, yelling, "Stop! He's deaf!" Horrified at my actions against a deaf person for not listening, I reactively released my hold on him. Now, as I thought to myself, "How could this possibly get any worse?"–the "Man-Child" took off running like a deer down the street.

I ran after him, but I was exhausted after dealing with two physically difficult arrests. I chased him to the end of the street, where he ran inside a home. He entered the home through a side carport door, leaving it wide open, so I followed him inside. My exhaustion caused me to miss the large "Beware of Dog" sign on the house. Having gone too far inside the home, after closing the door behind me, I couldn't make it back to that door when confronted by an aggressive Rottweiler. Quickly looking around, I jumped out an open window, narrowly escaping being mauled by the massive angry pet.

Busting through the window's outer screen, I fell, awkwardly landing on the concrete walk-way at the front of the home. The dog stopped short at the open window, as if a magic barrier prevented the attacking dog from leaving the home. I quickly closed the window and the protective pet trotted back to his sad master, who sat in the living room crying.

Keeping an eye on "Man-Child" and "Cujo," I radioed my two squad officers, instructing them to leave for the jail with their respective prisoners. My concern now, ensuring the welfare of the "Man-Child," after hauling away the woman, who I have now come to believe is a family member or care provider of some kind.

In hindsight, there were many clues to suggest something amiss about the "Man-Child" and his quiet need to be close to the drunk woman. It was not until I had asked the radio operator to call back the original homeowners of "Nude, Bloody Guy's" trespassing that I confirmed my suspicions. "Man-Child" is the drunk woman's little brother, with roughly the mental capacity of a ten-year-old boy; and was incapable of following my frantic demands.

We had taken away his drunken care-provider, and now he was sitting alone (with "Cujo" by his side) on the living room floor crying. Occasionally, the teary eyed "Man-Child" would glance over at me through the closed window. Yes, I felt terrible! Every time he looked over, I would smile ear-to-ear, hoping to calm his fears. In retrospect, I had to look frightening, appearing disheveled with blood and beer soaked hair and uniform, and sporting a creepy clown smile. How could "Man-Child" ever trust me, having manhandled his care-provider and chased him into his home? But I kept trying.

Fortunately, I knew some sign language and every time he looked over, I would sign a simple word with my hand. At first, I used words like, "*Hi*" and "*Sorry,*" and within a relatively short time he seemed happier when he looked over to the window at me. Using small words, I could sign quickly, explaining that his sister had too much beer, and was sleeping at a friend's house. Yes, I lied, but he seemed to completely understand, which made me think this was not his sister's first drunken tirade.

I asked him if there was a relative or neighbor who could stay with him, and if he would shut the dog in a room so I could come inside and sign with him. He eventually agreed, leading his dog into another room and shut the door. I went back to the carport door, and stood waiting for him to open the door for me. After all he had been through, I wanted him to open the door, giving him a feeling of empowerment since he must have felt terribly helpless watching his sister being arrested.

I was pleasantly surprised how quickly he appeared to forgive me. Seemingly comfortable with my presence, the "Man-Child" made himself cereal while I looked around the house for a family address book to locate a relative. Looking in the kitchen, attached to the refrigerator with a big red alphabet magnet was a list of emergency contact phone numbers.

Calling through the list, I located a sister living in the same city who agreed to drive out and take care of him until her drunk sister was sober and could return home. The sister arrived and apologized, explaining that her sister is normally a functioning alcoholic, but recently went through a bad breakup with her boyfriend. This may very well explain her sudden attraction to "Naked, Bloody Guy." I explained that I had no choice to arrest her when she began trying to hit me, but I would strongly request that prosecutors seek an alcohol intervention program instead of jail time.

It was the least I could do for my new giant friend.

Twist

So much happened that it's easy to forget about the councilwoman, and all the crazy things she witnessed that night on a single radio call. She talked nonstop to Officer Dave during the ride to the hospital and then to the jail with "Naked, Bloody Guy" about her exciting ride-along. Several weeks later, she even wrote a glowing letter of commendation... for the firemen.

CHAPTER 30

What a Wonderful World

IN August 2006, I left patrol work, accepting a supervisory assignment well outside my wheelhouse, as an Administrative Sergeant for an investigative bureau that supported two separate advocacy centers; one facility was dedicated to abused, neglected and molested children, and the other facility advocated for men and women victimized by sexual assault. These two advocacy centers housed doctors, lawyers, therapists and detectives, all working together on behalf of the victims.

My Administrative Sergeant duties consisted of overseeing the day-to-day operations of these two separate buildings, which at times also permitted me to supervise the investigative detectives when their regular assigned supervisor was sick or on vacation. Working with these detectives to bring sexual predators to justice was a welcome change from my administrative duties, making it obvious that I needed to look for another assignment better suited for my skill set.

By November 2006, I returned to investigations, accepting a position as the Night Detective Sergeant in the Homicide Unit. These detectives worked exclusively during graveyard shifts, investigating both natural deaths (heart attacks, old age, cancer) and homicidal deaths (murder, suicide, accidental death, industrial deaths, justifiable homicides and unknown deaths).

The difference between a Night Detective Squad (with three detectives) and daytime working Homicide Detective Squads (with ten detectives on four squads), is the difficulty of the death investigations themselves. Night Detectives with their limited manpower investigate what is referred to as non-complex homicide cases, such as suicides, accidental deaths and murders cases with known suspects. An exaggerated example of a non-complex murder investigation would be when the murderer is seen standing over the body with the smoking gun in his hand, admitting aloud, "I killed her" to a bar full of eye-witnesses.

In contrast, the four daytime Homicide Squads with a collective compliment of 40 detectives worked more difficult murder investigations in which the suspect was not readily known to the police. Those cases could take years to investigate. These more time-intensive murder cases occurred during both day and night of course, so since the night detectives were already working graveyard hours, we would go to the crime scene first and work the scene until the (day-shift) detectives could be awakened and rolled-out to assume the complex investigations.

The night detectives would ensure the area was appropriately secured, draft search warrants needed to enter buildings and homes, and complete other duties to make the hand-off smooth for the arriving (day-shift) homicide detectives.

It was common for my three night detectives and me to investigate four separate death investigations in a single night. During the holiday season, we average four suicides a week. The sheer volume of suicides and murder during the months of November and December take their toll on a detective's holiday cheer. Even as a supervisor, I would work death investigations to help reduce my detectives' heavy caseload.

Typically, each shift I liked to meet my detectives at police-friendly coffee shops in a high-crime section of the city. Even though I couldn't enjoy the greasy, carb-filled culinary delights because of my stomach issues, the restaurant and coffee shop owners appreciated our pro-active presence, prompting the riff-raff to quickly leave upon seeing us. And these meetings allowed me a venue to talk with them about their respective investigations and provide tips or resources as needed.

One night, in February 2007, I met my detectives for one of our midnight lunches after parking my unmarked detective car among the squad's other unmarked cars in the diner's parking lot. When I say "unmarked," we weren't fooling anyone with four cars, painted the same drab color, same make and model, all in a row. If someone mistook us for anything other than detective's vehicles, that was on them. Besides, most of the career criminals knew exactly the type of cars the police department provided for their plain clothes detectives. Unfortunately, the parking lot was located behind the restaurant and not visible from the main road or from us inside the restaurant.

I sat next to my three detectives, who were enjoying their greasy meals. One of the detectives, Jerry Hester, noticed an extremely intoxicated and flamboyant homosexual man at another table, focusing his attention on me. The none-too-subtle sexual advances culminated with a visit so he could loudly proclaim his affection for me. The well-groomed young man with tight-fitting, black, nightclub attire walked up to our table, looked me eye to eye and declared, "You are so hot." I politely thanked him for his "inappropriate" sexual advance, while sporting a friendly smile to downplay the spectacle.

The last thing I wanted to do was overreact, turning a silly, drunken come-on into a major disturbance. Trying to decline his sexually descriptive advances, I retorted, "Sorry, but I'm happily married." In his alcohol altered state, my polite rebuff made him even more interested in me, bragging, "I can make you forget her," while trying to sit next to me. It quickly appeared obvious to me, I was using the wrong approach, deciding a better strategy was to simply excuse myself from the table. With a roar of laughter from my detectives, I stood up and embarrassingly departed. The cop fanboy blew me a kiss and returned to his table. I left the restaurant amid the continued laughs of my detectives, which pleased me to no end. I relished their jovial break, a welcome stress reliever from their difficult death investigations.

I walked to the rear parking lot, and noticed a large volume of loose papers scattered on the pavement. The scant wind carried the loose papers between the sparse parked cars, the scene led me to believe one or more of the cars were burglarized. I've seen this type of scene all too often, thieves ransacking a car, removing numerous items from glove compartments, consoles and other areas within the car and with reckless abandonment discarding the unwanted contents outside on the ground. What I failed to immediately discern was the identity of the victim, which I quickly discovered upon picking up one of the papers. A sick feeling came over me as I saw the paper belonged to me.

Realizing I was the victim, I ran to my car at the far end of the parking-lot and saw my driver side window smashed out. My heavier personal items had been strewn about on the pavement next to my car. Thankfully, I keep my valuable items and police gear in the trunk. Most of the stolen items from my car were used solely for death investigations, like sterile gloves for collecting evidence, a large tape measurer used to obtain the distances of the body to some reference point in the crime scene, and many other unusual tools of the death investigative trade.

The thieves also stole my personal briefcase, where I stored notes and other personal documents. One of those personal items was the only copy of the eulogy I prepared for my brother's funeral a month earlier. My brother succumbed to the ravaging effects of pancreatic cancer, which he endured for three years. His medical case was not typical, most victims of the aggressive cancer survive only a few months after receiving the diagnosis, but there was nothing typical about my brother, he fought it for all those years.

Even as a young boy, he put a hundred percent into any sport he played, later earning basketball scholarships out of high school. As a child, I always envied his prowess and confidence, over my awkward speech impediment and poor grades. He seemed to excel in everything he did, to include fighting an aggressive cancer. He fought valiantly for those years, but in the end, he fell prey to the full demoralizing effects of the disease.

I searched frantically among the papers scattered across the parking lot for my brother's eulogy while recalling with vivid clarity the exact moment in time when I received the news of his diagnosis.

The phone call came while I was working a child abduction and rape case. I was canvassing the neighborhood with my partner, Detective Renee, when my mother called about my brother, Allen's sudden admittance into the hospital. After which, I watched helplessly as my only sibling suffered through radiation and chemotherapy, dwindling his body to half his normal weight. My cherished eulogy, a testament to his courage, was taken and surely later discarded like trash by thieves.

While still shocked at the discovery of my burglarized car, an emergency broadcast of a fatal shooting rang out. The shooting was the type of call that I would respond to the scene with my detectives. But I could not, my car was evidence in a crime–burglary from vehicle. I would have to remain with the car and get a patrol officer to take a report since as a victim I could not take my own police report.

I remained at the parking lot and instructed my detectives to respond without me, directing them at the scene by telephone and radio. By the end of the night, I ended up working three separate crime scenes, providing instructions to my detectives, all while still dealing with my vandalized detective car in the diner's parking lot. After working this job for a year, I became accustomed to working multiple death scenes at the same time. My mom once witnessed me working a total of five shootings and a suicide all at the same time while I was called upon during dinner. She marveled at how her D-average school boy had become capable of such an "amazing feat."

Within twenty-minutes of the first shooting call, a patrol officer arrived at the parking lot to take the burglary from vehicle report, and secure latent fingerprints and evidence. The car had to be towed to the main police shop due to the smashed windows and slashed tires. At one point, my cop fanboy walked out, joining me to watch my car get hooked-up for the tow. He smiled, then asked, "Can I give you a ride, honey?" Again, I thanked him for his kind "inappropriate" offer, but "I don't want that kind of ride… ever." He laughed and walked away. I ended up getting a ride back to police headquarters from the patrol officer.

I resumed my duties of a long night of dead body calls, a police officer involved shooting, and a very personal burglary from police vehicle. Everything stolen could be replaced, except for a simple piece of paper used to say good bye to my big brother.

Twist

The city mechanics who repaired the smashed and slashed car also decided to do routine maintenance. This resulted in a longer waiting period for the return of my office-on-wheels. What should have been a two-hour tire changing and window procedure turned into a month-long ordeal. I called about the excessive delay and the lead mechanic explained that an unusual incident occurred when they drove my car up onto a ramp. Intending to change the oil from below, the mechanic apparently forgot to put the car's transmission in park. The car rolled off the ramp and crashed into a brick wall, which caused major body damage. The damage made it necessary for the mechanics to have the car towed to a car dealership for repair. Once at the car dealership, someone stole the rest of my personal items from the trunk, including a favorite music CD titled, *What a Wonderful World.*

CHAPTER 31

New Year's Acid Trip

FOR most people, New Year's Eve is a time for deep reflection of the past year. Thinking of friends, family, accomplishments, opportunities both realized and missed, aspirations that lay ahead, and making resolutions for the New Year. These personal and professional reflections are a blueprint for self-growth or even a road map to rendezvous with one's destiny. Also, on New Year's Eve, people get drunk!

Some folks go further than just getting drunk, they get falling-down, stupid drunk. And of course, there is the time-honored tradition of fireworks, intoxicated individuals setting fire to handheld explosives and throwing them into the air. Every street cop has one or more stories about some New Year's Eve party gone wrong, or some party goer doing something stupid. New Year Eve's antics aren't just dangerous for police, as the next twisted story will attest.

On New Year's Day, 2007, I received a call from a patrol supervisor regarding a particularly ugly death investigation. After hearing the details, I assigned the case to Jerry Hester, having seen him deal with many horrific death scenes and felt he was more than capable of handling the grim task. Jerry and I met with the patrol officers that received the dead body call.

The patrol officer told us that a homeowner called police after she discovered a dead worker in her backyard pond. The worker was hired to clean the homeowner's backyard pond and arrived New Year's Day morning as agreed upon. The calling homeowner told police she could smell a strong odor of alcohol on the worker's breath, assuming it was from the previous night's New Year Eve celebration and hoping he was sober enough to handle the job.

The homeowner decided to allow the worker entry into the backyard, throwing aside her initial reservations that if intoxicated he could do a bad job. She told herself that the job wasn't brain surgery, it was just cleaning a fish pond—what's the worst thing that could happen cleaning a fish pond intoxicated?

She escorted the inebriated worker into the backyard, then left him to his work. The pond contained large Coy fish, so the worker began the process of removing the fish and placing them into a separate container. He then drained the pond of the algae-infested water and filled it with muriatic acid (a highly corrosive industrial cleaner), needing it to sit for several hours for the dissolving agent to clean the pond.

Several hours had elapsed when the homeowner looked out her kitchen window to check on the worker's progress. The worker appeared to be sleeping at the side of the pond, but his body was lying on the ground in an awkward manner. She understandably became concerned and started making loud noises to wake him up, but couldn't. At first, she felt he probably needed the rest after laboring in the heat. However, after several more hours passed, she finally went to wake him up. She found him dead, lying partially inside the pond.

Jerry and I discussed the death scene and the various possibilities; it's thinkable, though highly doubtful, that the inebriated worker fell asleep in the pond full of muriatic acid, thus drowning to death. It is conceivable that the overpowering poisonous fumes filled his lungs, killing him. The vapors could have rendered him unconscious and submerging into the toxic pond and dying from either scenario. It's feasible that he simply died of natural causes, like a heart attack, and fell dead into the pond. There was no way of knowing positively how the worker died without the findings of an autopsy performed by the Medical Examiner's Office.

I left the scene in Jerry's capable hands, with the mechanism of death still uncertain. There was no question in our minds to the cause of death: accidental. Now the medical examiner had to determine the mechanism of death.

A few days later, Jerry attended the Medical Examiner's postmortem examination (autopsy) and determined the victim died from ingesting toxic fluids into his lungs while asleep. The doctor found forensic evidence and scaring in the worker's throat that wasn't post-mortem, tending to indicate the worker's face was close enough to the muriatic acid to continuously ingest it in his sleep. The examination found no indication of muriatic acid in his lungs, but the Medical Examiner cautioned that determinations of death by drownings are only established in the absence of evidence to the contrary. All that gobbled-gook means is that there was no solid evidence to prove drowning by itself, the elements to determine drownings are established by the lack of evidence from any other evidence of death, along with additional information, such as, the body was found in a body of water or other form of liquid.

Twist

When we pulled him out of the pond, *he had no face!* His face had been completely dissolved away by the muriatic acid. A disturbing sight for even the most seasoned death investigator. The postmortem also documented that at the time of his death he had a blood alcohol content of 0.30. This can be lethal, even if you aren't sleeping in acid.

CHAPTER 32

Dog's Best Feast

OF the many homicides I've investigated, this next twisted tale ranks at the top of the most surreal and genuinely creepy in my entire career on the force. The case came during a particularly hectic week in the Fall of 2007, as my detectives and I each inherited our own domestic murder case. Plus, we also had divided dozens of suicides cases, as well as other less time-consuming accidental deaths cases. By the middle of our work week, we were exhausted from all that death. However, on the last day of our work week, our squad got bombarded with 3 additional death investigations, adding to an already long-list. I decided to work the last case alone, giving my "death squad" detectives a long overdue break.

Patrol officers responded to an "unknown trouble" call at a mansion-style home in a secluded mountain area. A neighbor heard bloodcurdling screams coming from a home with a five-acre wrecking yard business in the back. The wrecking yard was filled with junk cars and countless piles of scrap metal. Hearing the screams, the neighbor looked out and saw three teens jumping out of the wrecking yard over the eight-foot brick wall. The three teens were screaming as they ran to a parked car down the street, and sped off in a panic.

The neighbor called the police thinking it may have been a burglary, but it didn't make sense with the teens screaming as they ran away. The 911 caller told the operator that the only person living in the home was an older man. He owned both the home and wrecking yard business, running the entire operation himself. The business closed at sundown, so the neighbor felt it extremely odd that anyone would be in the wrecking yard during late-night hours.

After knocking at the front door of the large, old house many times, the patrol officers got no response. The officers walked to the brick wall of the rear wrecking yard and jumped over. Navigating through heaps of cars and twisted metal, illuminated only by moonlight and flashlights, the patrol officers worked their way through the hazardous maze to the back of the home. The officers knocked on the back door, but again no response. The officers then peeked into the home through a large window next to the back door. The inside of the home was brought to life by a few lights from deeper inside the house. The room on the other side of the glass appeared to be the living room, and the view out the window from inside that main room provided a panoramic view of the wrecking yard.

Their flashlights penetrated the darkness through the dirty glass, shining onto a body lying in the middle of the living room floor. The officers surmised he hadn't been dead long because the stench of decomposing flesh was absent. The body was partially hidden behind furniture, but the upper torso and head were in full view. Something seemed amiss, as the officers had difficulty making out the man's face. They could tell the adult male was lying face up, but his face wasn't there, only hair and patches of blood. It was then that the owner's dog reentered the living room to finish snacking on his owner's face. In death, the pet's owner went from being dog's best friend to dog's best feast.

When the patrol officers broke a window, entering the house, they were greeted by the friendly, tail-wagging black Labrador. They locked the late-night-snack eating canine in another room, preventing any further devouring of the crime scene. At that time, the police officers had no idea what caused the man's death and didn't suspect the dog of murder, just bad taste.

The patrol officers finished briefing me regarding their grisly discovery, and I entered the home to investigate the man's death; was there foul play, did he die of natural causes, or did a dog attack do him in? After processing the scene, and meticulously looking throughout the entire house, I determined foul play was not a factor in the man's death. The deceased pet owner appeared to have been dead for less than 48 hours, based on the appropriate amount of body decomposition, except for the absence of his face. A few patches of bloody flesh remained, otherwise his facial skin and muscle was licked clean and eaten to the bone. The creepy old house and the faceless corpse made for a surreal sight, especially with his eyes still resting in their sockets.

The crime scene revealed bloody paw prints coming and going over the living room carpet, reflecting his various meal breaks. No other blood impressions appeared on the carpeting, floors, walls, or any other surface. Crime scene photos depicted the lack of any disturbance inside the home other than the postmortem bloody paw prints. With the assistance of the medical examiner's office investigator, we rolled the body over to inspect for any sign of stab or bullet wounds, or any other trauma to suggest a murder; none were found.

Later, the autopsy confirmed my investigative findings: The eighty-year-old pet owner died of natural causes, having a long history of documented heart problems. The medical examiner's office conducted a thorough examination and concluded the victim died from a heart attack. The medical examination reflected the victim's chewed-off face, reporting that it was consistent with having been chewed away by the family pet.

The dog possibly went unfed for days and did what animals do to survive, ate some meat. As for the three suspicious teens seen screaming and running from the home; more than likely, they saw Fido eating his master's face during their preempted burglary attempt. Their screams may have been brought on after stumbling upon the dead man looking up with a bloody skull-face, glistening in the moonlight.

Twist

After completing the crime scene investigation, I needed to find foster care for the family dog. Looking around the house, I found a family address book lying next to an old-style 1960's landline, black dial phone sitting on the kitchen counter. After talking with an out-of-state niece, advising of her uncle's death, I learned about the deceased man's medical history and heart problems. She politely asked if I could tend to the arrangements for the dog's care, as she knew of no local friends or family, describing her uncle as a wealthy recluse with a once thriving business that rusted from years of neglect.

After calling numerous canine care agencies, I found someone willing to come out and take the dog, finding him a new home. I dealt with so many different tasks, other than just finding a home for the pet, that I never checked myself in a mirror. When the young woman arrived and picked up the dog, she appeared to be repulsed at seeing me, cluing me in on a problem with my face. Looking in the mirror, I saw that my face was covered with smears of blood and dog-drool. The dog had been licking my face, while I sat, trying to find him a home. I figured he gave me all the kisses for appreciation for finding him a loving home; maybe he was simply pre-tasting his next meal.

CHAPTER 33

Reginald

BACK in May 2005, two serial murderers joined forces in a massive shooting spree, and at the same time, an unrelated serial rapist killer was also terrorizing the greater Phoenix area. The "Serial Shooters" were randomly taking target practice at anyone they saw walking or standing outside as they drove around at night, while a completely unrelated homicidal rapist, which the press coined as "The Baseline Murderer," was also plaguing the streets of Phoenix; abducting, raping, and killing women for more than a year.

The "Serial Shooters," Dale Hausner and Sam Dieteman, combined with the "Baseline Murderer" Mark Godeau, committed no less than 17 murders, 15 rapes, and 29 non-lethal shootings. The three killers' infamous and prolific reign of terror only halted upon their arrests.

As a newly promoted patrol sergeant, I became involved in both investigations when my patrol commander, discovering my sex crimes expertise, assigned me to assist in the "Baseline Murderer" task force. As for the "Serial Shooters," I literally stumbled on that investigation after driving upon one of their first victims, before the police had even linked the murders together.

On an unusually slow night on May 24, 2005, I was driving aimlessly around my squad area just looking around to see if anyone needed help. Typically, I would follow my squad officers to one emergency radio call after another, but tonight I had the luxury of driving around in a proactive manner, seeing if I could help someone. And that is exactly what happened, I was waved down by a citizen while turning the corner of a major street.

A young, Hispanic man was waving his arms frantically, trying to get my attention as he stood next to a city bus stop. The transit structure was located directly across the street from a busy bar, which initially gave me pause, thinking he might be a drunk wanting a ride home after getting thrown out of the bar—Yes, I have been waved down like a taxi by drunks on more than one occasion.

I immediately drove into a shopping center located behind the bus stop, parking a relatively short distance away in the large parking lot. I wanted to provide some distance from the excited citizen in case he became a drunken-threat. It has been my experience that some intoxicated subjects like talking to cops, but will suddenly turn mean and violent when their demands, such as a taxi ride home, are not met.

The dark-green bus stop's design consisted of a heavy metal roof, providing much needed shade from the harsh Arizona sun, along with 10-foot tall metal walls at both sides, encasing a long bus stop bench, which was only visible from the front due to the surrounding metal structure.

My vantage point did not allow for a view inside the bus stop; I was only able to observe the animated actions of the man standing a few feet to its side. I asked him to walk to me since there didn't appear to be a need for me to walk into the dark area. Since I couldn't see into the bus stop, I didn't want to walk into a potential ambush. Upon instructing him to walk toward my location, the man excitedly yelled, "He is going to die!"

Hearing this, I immediately ran wantonly to his location at the bus stop. Looking into the structure, I observed a man lying face up on the bench. The injured man, later identified as Reginald Remillard, had a life-threatening gunshot wound to his neck. His head was close to me, and his feet were stretched to the other end of the bench. The wound on the left side of his neck rapidly gushed blood. A single gunshot had severed his carotid artery, spraying blood with a tremendous force, creating a bloody-cascade arching three-feet high. The life-draining fountain of blood splashed down on the sidewalk a foot away from the front of the bench.

I knew the shooting had just occurred since the pooling of blood was relatively small considering the large amount of blood jetting out of his neck. I instantly applied pressure to Reginald's wound, placing my left hand directly on the wound in his neck, while radioing for an immediate emergency medical response. With my back to the street, I applied pressure with my palm, hoping to stop the flow of blood from his neck. The once animated citizen was now looking on in horror, watching as I tried stopping Reginald's loss of blood.

While treating Reginald's grave injury, I simultaneously questioned the good citizen to what happened, wanting to retrieve suspect information. He had none, only describing a car that he saw at the time of the shooting as, "A gangster looking car." As I continued talking to the witness about the suspect's car, I kept my eyes peeled on Reginald. The look in his eyes seemed to start to fade.

His face paled, but his eyes remained focused on mine. I stopped talking to the witness and diverted my full attention to Reginald, trying to communicate with him. He didn't respond to my questions, wasn't nodding or blinking, and his eyes became increasingly distant as the blood continued gushing from his body. His skin color went from pale to gray in a matter of seconds. I knew that Reginald's life depended on two things: getting the bleeding to completely stop, and getting him into a hospital within minutes.

I got on the radio, explaining the dire need for a fast-responding medical team at the bus stop, but I was interrupted by a "Hot Tone." A loud, steady tone alerted me that an emergency broadcast would be following. The emergency broadcast was directly related to my shooting victim, as the radio operator announced an "excited witness" heard gun shots from across the street at a bar and saw a homeless man at a bus stop get shot.

The 911 caller explained he was waiting outside a bar for a cab when he saw a car drive by and heard gunshots directed at a homeless man sleeping at the bus stop. This was the witness that assumed I had arrived due to his 911 call; not realizing I hadn't a clue what was going on when he flagged me down.

After the radio allowed, I explained my presence already at the shooting scene to the emergency radio operator, and the need for paramedics in order to save Reginald's life. I was still having difficulty stopping the massive blood flow, unable to form a strong seal on Reginald's slippery neck. The more I tried to apply pressure to stop the bleeding, the more my hand would slide ever so slightly on the blood-soaked surface of his neck. The blood continuously seeped from beneath my fingertips, and if not corrected, Reginald would bleed to death.

Looking around desperately for something that might form a better seal, I observed the perfect item, a shoe. Reginald's bright-white, new looking sneakers were lying under the bus stop, appearing as if he took them off while preparing to go to sleep. The sneakers had rubber tips, which I thought would be an excellent surface to form a good seal. I instinctively grabbed one of the shoes and held the rubberized toe against the wound in Reginald's neck. The seal worked instantly as the bleeding stopped completely.

Within a few seconds, Reginald's facial skin tone returned to normal. He opened his eyes and looked at me, maintaining an almost life-pleading stare at me. He nodded ever so slightly to my repeated pleas, "stay with me, don't sleep." He then began nodding to my statements, appearing to truly understand the gravity of his condition. I continued to apply pressure with the tip of the shoe while simultaneously encouraging the victim to stay awake, and talking on the radio to expedite medical help.

I thanked the witness, learning his name was "James," telling him that he saved Reginald's life by flagging me down, but also by calling 911 and getting an ambulance rolling well before I requested one. I tried to get a better shooting suspect description from James, but he never saw the suspects inside the car. James said the suspect vehicle slowed down as it approached the bus stop, then he heard several loud gunshots from inside the vehicle. Immediately after the shots rang out, the suspect car accelerated past the bus stop, and continued driving west bound out of the area.

Since there were no other vehicles on the street and no one else outside, James feared the transient sleeping on the bus stop may have been the shooting target. He quickly called police on his cell phone and ran across the street to check on the homeless man who was indeed shot. Within seconds of calling 911, James saw me drive around the corner, and believed I responded to his 911 call.

After relaying the vague suspect vehicle description to the radio operator, I began the hectic supervisory-task of directing the responding patrol officers; instructing officers to look out for the suspect vehicle, locking-down the crime scene, locating potential witnesses, and many other jobs needed to secure the entire area and assist the investigation. Within minutes, more than ten patrol officers arrived, eager to help.

Now, my priority was instructing patrol officers driving in from the west to keep a look-out for the departing suspect vehicle, which minutes-ago drove away in that direction, telling them to stop any vehicle remotely matching the dark-colored suspect vehicle, but paying extra attention to any cars driving at a fast rate of speed. Because of my immediate arrival on scene, there was a good likelihood one of the responding officers would spot the suspect car driving away, but sadly, that wasn't the case. The suspect car went undetected.

The first patrol officer to arrive at the scene was Chris Barron, an energetic and highly dedicated police officer, and he had EMT training as well. Like a Boy Scout always being prepared, he arrived with an actual pressure bandage in hand. Running up to me, Chris gave me the specialized bandage, which I used on the gunshot wound, replacing the shoe. The pressure bandage remained on Reginald's neck upon the arrival of the ambulance a few minutes later. The medical team quickly got a lucid Reginald to the hospital in a matter of minutes. Oddly, it felt like a dear friend or family member left in the ambulance. I could not help but think of Reginald in such a manner, as I said aloud to myself, "They better save him," and they did.

The second officer, Tran, arrived, and with the help of other arriving officers quickly closed off the street from both directions in front of the bus stop. Additionally, I tasked other officers with securing a huge section of the shopping center parking lot behind the bus stop, wanting to prevent pedestrians from walking up on the crime scene. My hope was that a shell casing ejected from an automatic handgun or a rifle would be lying somewhere at the scene. Such critical evidence might lead detectives to the suspects.

I assigned a few officers to check the surrounding businesses, including the bar, looking for potential witnesses to the shooting. Some of the bar regulars might even know the transient, having camped out in the area, and aware if someone recently had an ugly altercation with him. At that time, we had no idea the shooting was actually random and the beginning of a serial shooting spree. The officers later returned, saying none of the bar patrons were outside at the time of the shooting, other than James, and none of them knew the homeless man.

Another dedicated and hard-working officer, Ryan, talked with the bar manager and took possession of the bar's video surveillance tape. The videotape footage didn't reveal any glimpse of the suspect vehicle, but it did show James walking outside and reacting to the sounds of the gunshots, which along with the original 911 call provided the investigation with the exact time of the shooting. Comparing the time of the shooting with the time that I was flagged down at the bus stop, I had missed the shooting by approximately 20 seconds.

I couldn't help but think that I missed stopping or interceding with the serial shooter's initial shooting rampage by mere seconds. Had my windows not been rolled up, I might have heard the gunshots. And such an immediate detection would have prompted me to accelerate faster into the area of the shooting, even by seconds, allowing me to possibly see the killers driving out of the area. Such a car chase may have led to an arrest, preventing the subsequent homicidal carnage. I could have stopped the killers at the very beginning of their two-year killing spree, saving so many lives.

The Homicide Unit's Night Detective Squad, the same squad that a year later I would be supervising, arrived to investigate the shooting. These detectives had no idea the shooting suspects were just getting started with a killing spree that would encompass shooting people and animals, which the killer Dale Hausner referred to at the time of his arrest as "Recreational" targets. This angered me to no end, calling Reginald a recreational target, simply at the wrong place at the wrong time.

The hospital staff initially listed Reginald in "stable but critical condition," and the surgeon successfully repaired his carotid artery. Reginald was promptly upgraded to a stable condition and a few days later was talking with his family at his bedside. I could not have been happier when I learned that Reginald was saved. Sadly, less than two weeks later, Reginald died.

We all saved Reginald's life that night: James, calling 911 for an immediate paramedic response, Chris with his prepared specialized pressure bandage, the well trained EMTs triage at the scene, the surgeon's skilled operation, and Reginald's shoe.

Admittedly, I was relieved when the doctor explained to me that his death had nothing to do with my unorthodox shoe seal. Reginald's demise was the result of complications relating to the large amount of blood loss, which adversely affected his already malfunctioning organs that went into complete organ failure. He lived long enough to reunite with his family. Reginald, rest in peace, my friend.

On August 3, 2006, Dale Hausner and Sam Dietman were arrested for a string of 42 separate shootings, claiming the lives of eight people, five dogs, and three horses, and hurting many others during their shooting spree across multiple cities.

CHAPTER 34

The Last Chapter

TWO years after the "Serial Shooter's" arrest, the Maricopa County Prosecutor's Office advised they needed me to testify about Reginald's murder during Dale Hausner's trial, which would start sometime during the following month. Dale's partner, Sam Dietman had already made a deal, pleading guilty to save himself from the death penalty.

Sam Dieteman turned state's witness, agreeing to testify against his murdering colleague. He told investigators there was no rhyme or reason in their victim selection; they opportunistically targeted innocent people walking or standing along the street when he and Dale Hausner took to the road.

The two murderers searched the streets late at night and in the early mornings with the sole intent to shoot at anybody they encountered, describing their killings as nothing more than satisfying a "recreational" desire. The random nature of their murderous actions made identifying the killers difficult, frustrating detectives and paralyzing the public. Detectives would need to work harder and longer to try and keep their community safe.

It's understandable that an incredible sense of excitement struck the detectives and patrol officers when the "Serial Shooter" murder trial was announced. These same frustrated cops who were unable to protect the public were now eagerly looking forward to the killers finally receiving justice for the pain they inflicted on the community.

That same community was also enthusiastic about the upcoming trial, trying to wrap their heads around why these two monsters would randomly search dark streets looking for someone to shoot. The "why" is never adequately explained, because there is never a reason that makes sense.

Once the trial started it played like a TV drama over the local media channels, garnering the tandem and prolific serial murderers much attention from the press. My testimony was not critical to the successful prosecution, so I was placed near the bottom of the witness docket.

The prosecutor finally set a preliminary date for my testimony, telling me I would be done after a single day, October 5, 2008. Prior to having been advised about the trial, I had arranged for a much-needed respite for me and my family to get out of the state. My family and I needed to escape the city in October, due to an unmeasurable loss almost a year earlier, the death of my son.

Over my son's 18th birthdate, while vacationing in Las Vegas, he suddenly exhibited signs of a grand mal seizure while asleep in the early morning hours. Thankfully, the entire family was staying in the same hotel room and we were all awakened by the horrific scene of my son convulsing wildly in his bed. I called 911 on the hotel room's phone while sitting with him on the bed, ensuring he didn't fall or hurt himself.

Though it only lasted a few minutes, he came out of it dazed and confused. The paramedics arrived quickly and DJ was rushed to a local hospital where he was ultimately found to be in good health. The hospital staff couldn't provide a reason for the seizure, prompting us to make a follow-up appointment for DJ with a neurologist upon our return home. This was his first seizure of many over the course of seven-years.

No medical reason was provided to explain DJ's sudden onslaught of sleep-time seizures. He was simply labeled with the catch-all diagnosis of Epilepsy, which the medical community provides when they are at a complete loss to explain the reasons for the seizures. All the doctors and specialists said the same thing; it just happens sometimes and it's not life threatening.

DJ died unexpectedly a few days before Christmas on December 20, 2007, from a cardiac episode resulting from a late-night seizure. The media-driven murder trial was set to begin over my son's first posthumous birthday, October 8th, the very date I pleaded for it not to be. DJ would have been twenty-six, and I didn't feel I could adequately testify on that date, knowing I was too grief stricken and emotionally compromised to hold-up against the ugly antics of a defense attorney.

It is the dubious job of the defense attorney to represent all those accused of a crime, guilty or not. Since the defense attorney can't attack the victim in a murder trial, they aim their venomous questions at the police officers sitting on the witness stand's "Hot Seat" to poison the jury against the police.

Defense attorneys will strategically attack the cops' investigation; insulting the report writing, their professionalism, discipline record, and anything else they can think of when there isn't a legitimate defense available to them. I venture to say, there is not a single cop that hasn't experienced a mean-spirited question or accusation from a defense attorney during their courtroom testimony.

I cried myself to sleep every day since DJ's death, so I had little doubt that I would fall apart on the witness stand on his birthday. With my black cloud smack overhead, I was set to testify at the trial on a day I needed an escape.

The reservations for my wife, mother, and daughter to join me at a mountain resort out of town on that day would have to wait, suspended until after the judge excused me from the witness box.

My family decided to support me at court, sitting patiently in the hard, wooden bench seats for me testify. Temporarily postponing our trip, with our packed suitcases lying in the trunk of my car, I sat waiting in a small, bland-looking witness holding room until instructed to enter the court and give my account of that sad day in Reginald's brief life.

My family sat riveted, listening to various police detectives and to the very same witness who flagged me down two years ago after seeing the killers drive by and shoot Reginald lying on the bus stop bench. My family listened to other critical testimonies about the investigation, which I believed made my account pale in comparison.

The wait was over, at approximately 2 pm, the bailiff walked into the witness room and instructed me to enter the courtroom. I walked into the packed courtroom and immediately spotted my wife and mother sitting white-faced in the middle of the faceless crowd. Wearing my best suit, walking past the judge, I stood before the court clerk, raising my right hand and swearing, "I do" upon my oath, "to tell the truth, the whole truth, and nothing but the truth, so help me God."

After a volley of questions from the prosecution and defense, I simply testified to a sad and frantic night dealing with a shooting victim and crime scene, and of my actions as poor Reginald almost bled to death. Recounting another life that I ultimately didn't save awakened similar memories from long ago, memories of trying in vain to save the life of the girl in a burning car and, worse, the son I did not even know was gravely ill.

My emotions ran high, detailing my failure to save Reginald's life to a courtroom filled mostly with strangers. My testimony was documented by a glut of reporters and video cameras, all capable of capturing my meltdown. I continued to answer questions pitted by both attorneys, talking directly to the jury and to Reginald's family, whom I failed.

My wife and mom had never attended a trial and certainly not a famous murder trial. They were mesmerized and fascinated, as the trial served as a diversion from their own problems. I too was glad they were there, needing that moral support in the audience to help me stay strong on the witness stand. My testimony was surprisingly competent and well received by the prosecutor, but more importantly, also by the jury.

Relieved that I did not have a meltdown, I quickly walked out of the courtroom after the judge excused me from the witness stand. My family awkwardly stood up amidst the crowd and hurriedly followed me out. They joined me in a large hall outside the courtroom doors. Several well-dressed women, in their late 30's, had followed my family out of the court just to talk to me. They were Reginald's surviving family members, to include his two sisters. They hugged and thanked me for giving their family a few more moments with Reginald. I really hope I conveyed my deep appreciation for their beautiful gesture, because it was an incredible act of love for them to even think of thanking someone during such a sad time in their lives.

After heartfelt hugs and well-wishes, Reginald's family returned to the courtroom. My family and I could now depart for our mountain getaway, but we were pleasantly interrupted by another person from the courtroom. However, this time, I immediately recognized the person as a local TV news reporter named Mike Watkiss. I had admired this reporter ever since he moved to the Valley after his celebrated nationally televised interview with the infamous serial killer, the Night Stalker in California. This distinguished reporter walked up to me, and in front of my family, shook my hand. He called me a hero and thanked me for my life-saving efforts. I was left speechless, stunned by his praise. After this classy act, the famous reporter returned to the courtroom to continue his coverage of the trial.

Released from my courtroom obligation, I drove my family to our retreat out of the city. On the drive, I thought about how much I had dreaded this day, fearing it would be a nightmare testifying on my late son's birthday. But it turned out to be a meaningful experience for my family, witnessing for the first time, not just any courtroom trial, but an infamous serial murder case that months earlier had terrified the Valley. My family heard my account of how I saved Reginald's life that night, and stood by my side as Reginald's family and a celebrated reporter thanked me for my life-saving efforts. On a day that we needed it most, we came away with a special birthday gift, helping my wife and I survive the loss of our beloved son, a great brother to Robyn, a loving grandson to my mom, and a wonderful person to all his friends.

(Or Is It Called a Eulogy?)

A YEAR later, in 2008, personal tragedy struck again. My mother was diagnosed with a horrific auto-immune disease called polymyositis, in conjunction with a stage-3 cancer diagnosis. With the death of my adult son in 2007 and the death of my brother in 2006 (my only sibling), I became my mother's sole caregiver.

It wasn't only a challenging time in my personal life, but also in my professional life. A month earlier, I left the Child Crimes unit to be the director of a Crime Stoppers Program called Silent Witness, where I worked daily with the media, soliciting anonymous tips from the community to help solve felony crimes.

One of the many media gigs included hosting a local radio show called "the 5-0 Info Show." On one show, I interviewed the "Serial Shooter" case agent, Detective Cliff Jewell, who coincidentally was my first training officer after graduating from the police academy. Cliff told me about a book titled *Sudden Shot* by author Camille Kimball, which chronicled the "Serial Shooter" case and my small involvement.

After the radio show, Cliff invited me to his *Sudden Shot* book-signing event at a local bookstore. I jumped at the chance to take my wheelchair-bound mother to the event, recalling her excitement at the related serial murder trial. Upon our arrival, Cliff let Camille know of my presence and to my surprise and delight, she invited me to join them on stage to autograph books. My mother not only experienced the excitement at the murder trial, witnessing people thanking me for my service to the community, but also watched me at an autographing session. She watched on proudly from her wheelchair as I autographed books for a large audience. That final twist of fate, meeting Camille, was the final gift my dying mom received before she died in 2010.

I was also a regular guest on a popular radio station's rock morning show. The KDKB radio station had me tell my "Twisted But True" tales in addition to soliciting tips for the various crimes of the week. However, it was my tales that became more popular than expected. I recall one night, hearing a KDKB commercial announce tomorrow's guests, "Gene Simmons of KISS and Silent Witness Sergeant Darren Burch" in the same breath!

After finishing one of my KDKB "Twisted But True" tale segments, I was approached by a fan waiting outside the station. Yes, I said *fan*–that still cracks me up today! The unidentified fan suggested I write a book with my funny "Twisted But True" tales. Excitedly, I thought his suggestion had merit as a fund-raising tool for the nonprofit Silent Witness program. I reached out to my new author friend, Camille Kimball, and she strongly encouraged me to write it. She had seen my various TV and radio segments and thought it would be a great project.

I would never have taken on a book-writing project if not for Camille's incredible encouragement. Again, the generosity of others is what keeps us going during our darkest hours and best of times. In the end, if the good outweighs the bad; you lived a fortunate life! I hope you too can laugh as you survive your own "twisted but true" tales.

DEDICATION

DJ, Mom and Allen - Rest In Peace

ACKNOWLEDGMENTS

(In order of importance…just joking)

Family and Friends:

Coleen- I couldn't have written this book without your love, support, and "corrrections!"

Robyn- My princess is the light of my life, a beacon to find my way when I'm lost and adrift!

Mac Watson- Thank you! Your expertise turned the manuscript into the novel I always dreamed it could be!

Camille Kimball- Thank you for helping me get started on the right track. Buy "Sudden Shot."

Kris Dugan- Thank you for your no-holds-barred critique, very much needed and appreciated; I only bled a little.

Police Partners:

Bill Schemers- Thank you for your lifelong partnership and dedicated service to our community.

Jerri Hubert- Thank you for being a great partner and for being so much prettier than Bill!

Steve Ong- Thank you for having my back, you are indeed the Master Jokester.

To all my police partners, and police officers everywhere- Stay Safe!

RETIRED Sergeant Darren Burch is a 28-year veteran with the Phoenix Police Department, having spent his last six years as the Crime Stoppers program director. His directorial duties included soliciting tips from the community to solve felony crimes through TV, radio, and newspaper outlets. He was a regular radio guest on a rock-and-roll morning show, imparting his professional experiences with a dark and humorous twist.

His investigative assignments included detective supervisor with the Crimes Against Children Unit, Night Detective Sergeant with the Homicide Unit, and detective with the Adult Sex Crimes Unit. With more than 3 decades of law enforcement experience, having also held positions with the Maricopa County Sheriff's Office and U.S. Army Military Intelligence, Darren received several medals to include the Medal of Lifesaving and Army Commendation Medal.

Darren was named Investigator of the Year by the Arizona Attorney General's Office and Detective of the Year by the Phoenix Police Department. He has over 100 commendations and has been the primary case agent in over 20 serial rape investigations. This includes involvement in the Baseline Murderer and Serial Shooters investigations, separate yet concurrent homicidal crime sprees receiving national media attention. After his retirement, Darren became a public safety expert for several local media outlets and hosts a radio talk show called, "5-0 Info."